THE LOVE OF DREAMS . . .

I went toward him. He drew me close, enfolded me, his breath hot and fanning my ear, his lips nibbling at my throat, then down to my breasts where he lingered, building my desire to a level with his own. Then he loosened his arms, held me a few inches away and stared piercingly into my eyes. I was totally aware of the power he had over me, of the rapid beating of my heart, of the persistent voice inside me telling me to give him all and everything he wanted. I forced myself not to listen.

As if reading my mind, his fingers suddenly squeezed my shoulders.

"I want you to know, my dear lady from the future, I care little for your reasons and procrastinations. We will love . . . and in the end, you *will* be mine!"

Other Avon Books by
Jo Ann Simon

LOVE ONCE IN PASSING

Jo Ann Simon

Hold Fast to Love

AVON
PUBLISHERS OF BARD, CAMELOT, DISCUS AND FLARE BOOKS

AVON BOOKS
A division of
The Hearst Corporation
959 Eighth Avenue
New York, New York 10019

First Avon Printing, November, 1982

With love to my children

KIMBERLY and KENNETH

*for their youthful patience
and understanding*

ONE

WE WERE APPROACHING Heathrow Airport. Below, the yellow lights shimmered, making golden snakes of the winding roadways. If it hadn't been for the deepening dusk, I might have seen buildings too, but their shapes were now only misty outlines blurred amid trees and grass. The lights of London were a brilliant bed of diamonds in the distance as I watched mesmerized through the window. Suddenly I was filled with excitement . . . anticipation. It had been so long since I'd had a vacation, and I needed one especially now. I'd reached a point in my life when I needed time to think—to reassess my life to date, to plan my future. The two weeks ahead seemed like the perfect opportunity.

The plane dipped, losing altitude. I swallowed hard for the benefit of my ears and reached to the empty seat beside me to find my overnight case. Checking its contents, I found the papers I'd be needing and transferred them to my purse on the floor by my feet. For some reason, security perhaps, I continued to grip the handle of the overnight case; I held it tightly as I resumed my study of the scene beyond the window. I expected to see the runway lights soon, twinkling blue and red, and beyond them the bright lights of the terminal buildings. I remembered it all clearly from my first trip to England, on vacation three years ago.

Yet, peering out for several minutes into the night sky, I saw nothing. The airplane jolted again, more sharply. Another drop in altitude, I guessed. Still there was only inky blackness beyond the window.

Then I saw lights, glowing yellow orbs, directly beyond. They seemed almost at eye level; I hadn't thought we were that close to landing. And the small window through which I'd been staring, my nose against the glass, seemed much larger now, and flatter, less distorting of the images beyond. I blinked, realizing as I did so that I could no longer hear the deafening roar of the jet engines or feel the rapid descent of the plane affecting my ears and stomach. Instead I felt a gentle rocking sensation; heard a muffled clopping noise. I studied the view from the window more closely. The softly glowing lights were some distance apart; not crouched on the ground in even parallel rows, but set up on poles of ornate metal design. Between them—now my eyes widened—there were trees; broad, leafy trees. I was on the ground—no longer airbound, but securely on the ground. Yet how? No plane landed *that* quickly. And no runway looked like what I was seeing outside the window.

I tore my gaze from the scene outside to look around me. My overnight case was still there, my knuckles white as I clutched its handle, but that was all that was familiar. No longer did I see the long aisle and rows of seats in the aircraft. I found instead a small, dark, upholstered interior with one seat stretching across its width, and one window to either side. In front of me was another smaller, sliding glass, but in the darkness I couldn't see beyond it.

Quickly I looked out the window again. Now I could see that I was traveling down a roadway, a narrow avenue bordered on either side by three-story stone buildings neatly aligned behind a brick sidewalk. The well-kept buildings each had clean white steps and lit entry lanterns; warmly illumined windows revealed the life within. The clopping noise I'd heard for the last few moments intensified, and I glanced to my right to see two horses and an elegant carriage flash by the opposite window. Were my eyes deceiving me? The steady swaying motion continued as, in disbelief, I was carried forward past the picturesque scenery: I too was in a horse-drawn carriage!

The vehicle I was in lurched to the right, throwing me against the seat. When I looked again, I wasn't on a quiet, unidentifiable street, but in a busy intersection. Now there were dozens of carriages and other horse-drawn conveyances around me . . . rushing past the windows, fighting for the right of way. Twinkling lights were all around; harsh calls; muffled laughter and voices. In the brighter light I could now see framed in the sliding glass before me the back of the driver of my own vehicle.

From the side windows I saw black-bodied and crimson-bodied and yellow-bodied carriages, some drab and faded, others glistening and bearing on their sides gilded letters and emblems that looked like coats of arms. I saw men in bright-buttoned coats seated on high seats, swinging long whips over the sweat-darkened hides of horses of every color and description. Unaccustomed smells assaulted my nostrils: the earthy scent of manure and turf and damp stone; the pleasant odor of leather and fresh paint; the less agreeable odors of human sweat not recently bathed away and, even worse, decaying garbage left too long in sunlight and in dampness. Where were the exhaust fumes; the smell of oil and diesel—the scents of a modern city?

My eyes raced from one window to the other, hurrying to catch glimpses of every unexpected sight before it passed away. Beyond the throng of carriages and horseflesh were sidewalks filled to overflowing with pedestrian traffic, just as the street was filled with four-wheeled carriages and four-legged animals. I saw ladies wearing long-skirted and high-waisted dresses, with capes and elegant little hats. Men sported long-tailed coats and top hats. I saw children in rags, and old, limping men leaning on canes. And in the side lanes, where the light of the street lamps barely penetrated, gaudily dressed women and furtive-looking men flitted in the shadows.

A child ran out from the side, off the sidewalk, through the tangled, moving wheels of traffic; a boy of no more than eleven or twelve, slight and ragged. He streaked almost beneath the hooves of one pair of horses, then barely between the wheels of a carriage. My heart rose in my throat at the prospect of his death in the heedless onrush. I heard the angry call of the driver, and a harsh curse; my own voice rose in the narrow confines of the carriage as I tried to call out. But then the boy was gone, through the traffic and onto the green verge that marked the center of the square. I saw him lift his hand in victory, and I breathed a sigh of relief.

Before I had a chance to see more, we moved out of the intersection onto another quiet road. On my left was a dark expanse of trees, a secluded wilderness; on my right, more buildings, set slightly back from the roadway and protected by fences. My carriage turned again to the right, onto a cobblestone lane, edged in on either side by more three- and four-story buildings. There was a street marker on the corner: Upper Brook Street. Where had I seen that name before? Of course—on a modern map of London. I'd even visited this particular section of Westminster, called Mayfair, walking through the charming, exclusive streets. But this looked so different from what I remembered. Where were the asphalt pavements and the brick-faced hotels lining Park Lane? And what was I doing here when Heathrow Airport was forty or fifty miles to the west? Until a few minutes before, I'd been on a plane making its descent. How—when—had I come to be in a horse-drawn carriage journeying across a city through streets that apparently hadn't witnessed the appearance of the automobile?

At least I knew where I was. I knew that Upper Brook Street bordered on Park Lane, which bordered on Hyde Park, which must have been the stretch of grass and leafiness I'd seen a few minutes before. Beyond that, my senses were in a whirlwind. If I hadn't been very sure I was awake—I was wide-eyed and breathing rapidly—I'd have been sure I was living out a vivid dream.

The neighborhood we were traveling through echoed wealth and elegance. I felt the carriage slowing down, and then we pulled up before one of the fine doorways. The elegant four-story Georgian town house was made of a light gray stone. From the four tall, many-paned windows on each of the three main floors, a golden light cast long rectangles onto the sidewalk. On either side of the wide marble stairs at the center of the house stretched a wrought iron fence of moderate proportions, meant more for decoration than protection; and at the top of the whitely gleaming steps, a set of grand double doors stood open.

Before I had time to realize what was happening, the driver had jumped down and was coming to my door, opening it with a sweeping gesture and lowering the two portable steps for me to descend. He extended his hand to help me. Too bedazzled and frightened to do much else, I accepted it, and stepped down. My overnight case bumped along behind; it slid off the step and landed against my thigh. The coachman quickly took it from me, then, standing back and bowing slightly, motioned me ahead of him up the stairs to the house.

At the top of the stairs to the side of the open doors stood a man in blue and gold livery, his expression impassive, immobile.

Walking as though in a dream, the objects around me having the quality of illusion rather than reality, I climbed the stairs, my calf-length skirt and trench coat brushing against my stockinged legs. I went hesitantly through the doorway and into the front hall. Another man in livery hurried forward to take my case from the coachman. The man who'd stood at the door—the butler, I presumed—stepped toward me and bowed impressively.

"Permit me to welcome you to Warringwood House, Baroness. We have been awaiting your arrival. I trust you had a safe journey."

My startled ears heard his words, and my eyes widened in disbelief. Somehow I managed to hide the depth of my confusion by nodding dumbly before I was led farther into the hall. The hall was large, marble floored, and decorated, though sparely, in elegant furnishings. Its double-height ceiling was graceful, and the room was lit by two sparkling crystal chandeliers. A wide, carpeted staircase rose at the far side and disappeared into a balcony at the head of its long flight of steps. The sight took my breath away, leaving me more dumbfounded than before.

My first reaction was to bolt and run, but where would that have left me but on a cold, empty street, knowing no more of what had happened than I knew at the moment? Stilling the tremor in the pit of my stomach, I walked with firm, slow steps into the center of the hall. The butler hesitated briefly and then resumed speaking. "A room has been prepared for you, Baroness. His Lordship, unfortunately, was called away this evening . . . ." He cleared his throat. "We were not, of course, sure of the exact time of your arrival. However, he will be back later this evening. In the meantime Mrs. Perkins, the housekeeper, will show you to your room."

A black-gowned, somewhat stout woman came bustling forward, the taffeta of her long skirts rustling as she walked. She spoke in even, natural tones, although her blue eyes were clearly inquisitive.

"If you will permit me, Baroness, I will show you upstairs. Your luggage arrived some time ago, and I took the liberty of having the maids unpack for you." Her eyes moved over me quickly, pausing at my hemline. She spoke again crisply, "Sad your maid was taken ill during the journey and could not remain with you, but His Lordship has seen to it that one of our maids will be available to assist you until you can employ another of your own."

With this she turned toward the stairs, and I followed uncertainly, listening with half an ear to her continuing comments. "You must be tired. Such a trek at this time of year . . . the roads still muddied from all the rain we've had. It's fortunate His Lordship had his chaise sent down last week in preparation for your arrival. You know these hired hacks can be most down-at-the-heels. Lady Caroline has had the blue room made up for you. She's resting at the moment, but would like you to join her for tea after you've freshened from your journey."

We were at the top of the staircase, turning to the left down a long hall. The housekeeper led me up a second set of stairs, and we approached a doorway. She turned the knob and swung the door wide. The room we entered was lovely—a warm combination of pale blue and rose colors, rich and softly feminine. Long dusky-blue drapes hung at the windows and about the canopied bed. A rose-and-cream patterned wool rug covered the wooden floor and cushioned my feet as I trod uneasily across it. A pale-blue velvet love seat and a dark-rose side chair of Chippendale design were ranged before a wide white marble fireplace, and between them was placed a fine-grained oval tea table. Along the wall stood a spacious wardrobe of deep mahogany that was twice the size of the closet in my New York apartment. Against the far wall, between the two long, multipaned windows, was a delicate lady's desk and a dressing table complete with a three-faceted mirror, tortoiseshell combs, and silver-handled brushes and crystal vials of perfumes that sparkled in the candlelight.

Mrs. Perkins gave me a moment to look around the room. "I hope you find everything to your satisfaction. You will want to wash up from your journey and rest a bit, I am sure. I shall send up a maid. And would you like some tea?"

"Yes . . . thank you."

"Good. We all hope your visit will be a pleasant one, Baroness, and if there is anything I can do for you during your stay, please call on me. Oh, yes, after you have finished your toilet, the maid will direct you to the Green Salon, where Her Ladyship will be waiting."

"Thank you."

She backed from the room and shut the door soundlessly behind her.

I was left to my own silent bemusement—astounded, wondering where in God's name I was and how I'd gotten there. Carefully I went over each detail in my mind: the plane descending, the sights and sounds I experienced as we were preparing to land, the slow realization that I was riding in a horse-drawn carriage, the unnerving street scene, my greeting at this remarkable house. Nowhere could I find a clue to my altered situation.

I'd been awake and alert—there weren't any fragments I was forgetting. But what was I, Monica Wagner, twenty-seven-year-old American tourist, doing in *this* London? Who was this baroness they had confused with me? How *could* I be mistaken for her? And where was she now, if I was taking her place? Why did everything around me suggest that I'd dropped back in time to the early nineteenth century?. . . No! That was absolutely impossible! People did not travel through time.

Was I dreaming, after all? Or was this all some fantastic charade?

I caught my reflection in the mirror above the dressing table. I looked tired, my features drawn in confusion. My dark eyes looked misty in the candlelight, distant and unreadable even to my own gaze. My hair and clothing were still neat enough, but so out of place in this elegant room.

In my distraction I let my eyes wander to the tabletop beneath the mirror. There I saw a small gold frame capable of closing like a book and holding two miniature portraits. I moved forward to study it. One portrait was of an attractive middle-aged man; the other, a young woman. Something about the woman was so familiar. I picked up the portrait. The high-cheekboned face stared back at me, dark eyes full of laughter. Red-brown hair was pulled high and framed the face in soft waves. The lips were full and seemed about to speak.

I gasped in shock. I could have been looking at myself in that small gold frame. Except for the style of dress, there was no mistaking the stunning similarity of our looks. A different person . . . yet me . . . the eyes, the nose, the mouth.

A knock sounded at the door. Startled, I laid the portrait face down on the dresser top, turned, and tried to force some composure to my face.

A small voice called through the door, "It's the maid, mum, come with your tea."

"Oh, yes, of course. Come in."

She was a tiny thing, seeming to have barely the strength to hold the heavy tea tray in her arms. I nearly rushed over to take it from her, but remembered just in time the role in which I had been cast so precipitously. *I* was a baroness.

The girl nimbly deposited her burden; apparently she was far less fragile than she appeared to be. "Shall I get hot water for you now, Baroness? Mrs. Perkins said you'd be wanting to wash up." For a moment her eyes flickered, wide as saucers, as she took in my unconventional clothing; but she quickly refocused them on a point somewhere between my nose and my chin.

"Fine," I told her, no more sure of myself or of what might be expected of me than she seemed to be. "I'll have my tea while I wait."

In a flash of awkward arms and legs, the girl was out the door. I waited only until I heard her footsteps retreating down the hall before hurrying to the wardrobe. Her curious stare had made me acutely aware that I'd better do something about the way I was dressed before questions were asked. I threw open the wardrobe doors to paw through the huge and varied collection of garments there, and found a full, dark-blue robe. Rapidly peeling off my own skirt and blouse, I stuffed them into the bottom of the closet and wrapped the robe around me. Now at least I looked less conspicuous. Still feeling dazed and shocked, I went to the couch and poured myself a cup of tea.

I chewed a fingernail and considered my dilemma. Only an hour before I'd been contemplating an entirely different experience, journeying to London to see an old friend, Robin Wade, a man I'd known well during my college years in Connecticut. Once we had been serious about each other, but happenings in each of our lives had drawn us apart. Though we'd kept in touch, we hadn't seen each other in five years. Then, unexpectedly, he'd written to me: Would I come abroad to visit him in London, where he was working for an American firm? The invitation seemed a godsend, following so close as it did upon the tragedy of my father's sudden heart attack and untimely death. My grief at the loss, combined with my disenchantment with my life in New York and my job in an investment brokerage firm, made the chance for escape to another country that much more appealing. I accepted the invitation, telling Robin I'd come to London in a few weeks, in June 1981. He planned on meeting me at the airport; I looked forward to the reunion. But his smiling face had not greeted me as I stepped off the plane; instead I'd found myself in the closed carriage—in another world, another time.

Sooner than I expected, the maid was back with a shining copper bucket, its contents steaming in the cool air of the room. She left the bucket by the washbasin, hurried from the room, and returned moments later with an armful of towels and a bar of soap.

"Will there be anything else, my lady? My name's Jane, by the way, and pleased to serve you."

"And I am pleased to meet you, Jane. Do you know what time the lady of the house expects me?"

"Mrs. Perkins said in about three quarters of an hour. Lady Caroline will be in the Green Salon. Would you like me to come back in a few minutes to help you dress?"

"Yes, fine."

She took that for a dismissal and, smiling shyly, left. My thoughts whirling, I sipped my tea for a minute. Then, filled with an irresistible curiosity, I rose to inspect the room more carefully. I didn't know where to begin to look, but knew the more clues I could find about the baroness, the closer I could come to unraveling the puzzle. The housekeeper had said the baroness's luggage had arrived and been unpacked; surely it included more than dresses, cloaks, and robes. Perhaps I'd find some helpful hints among her other belongings—something more personal.

I went to the dresser and glanced briefly into each of the drawers, finding layer upon layer of fine lawn and lace underwear and nightgowns. These didn't interest me, so I moved on to the desk and began checking its cubbyholes. In the top right-hand drawer I found a small clasped book bearing the initials *MvM* on its cover. I opened it to the first page, where there was an inscription: "Property of the Baroness Marlena von Mantz." Below that, in fine handwriting: "12 November 1807. To my beloved daughter on her sixteenth birthday with all wishes for her happiness. Papa."

The inscription was in German. I thanked my lucky stars that of the two languages I'd taken in school, German was one. As I flipped the pages, I saw the book was a diary. Fortunately the entries were in

English. They were infrequent, apparently made
only on the most important occasions in the girl's
life, and as I briefly scanned them, I noticed the tone
as well as the handwriting maturing with the girl
who held the pen. Toward the last of the entries I
paused to read more carefully. Several were made
about the same time—from April through June of
1815. The last was made on June 18, 1815.

We have had a rough crossing. Louise has been
so ill for most of the journey, I feel I have no choice
but to engage a physician and perhaps send her
home soon after we reach England. I feel her sick-
ness is as much of the heart as of the body, and so
my decision.

I miss New York already, and Aunt Eva and the
family. I knew it would be so. If I were on my way
to Germany and a reunion with my father, it
would be different. But he is gone now, and there is
no point in thinking of that.

I wonder yet why Papa's will provided that I
make this journey to England before the matters of
his estate could be settled. Are things in Germany
in such desperate straits, and were there none of
our countrymen he could trust? There is no telling
what my reception in London will be; how long it
will take; how many months will pass before I can
return to New York or continue on to Germany.

But, of course, it's been so many years since
Papa and I had a chance to be close—only that brief
visit of his to New York three years ago, and then
back to Germany to do what he could to protect my
inheritance from the armies of Napoleon. How
often I have wished he had not found it necessary
to send me to America. I know he was thinking of
my safety, but now, after ten years of being in New
York, it is difficult even to think of Germany as

home . . . to remember all the details of the mountains, of the great house and grounds. They seem so far away.

I find myself more and more unsettled about meeting this Lord Warringwood, Justin Pemberton, even though Papa assigned the man to be his executor. He is a relation of my mother's, but she died so many years ago, I know nothing of her family in England. What is he like? I have only those letters received from him after my father's death, but in their formality they give little indication of his character, only that he appears to be abiding strictly to Papa's wishes. I will stop now. I hear a commotion above.

There were no further entries. I closed the leather-bound pages and placed the diary on the desk. So this was the baroness for whom I'd been taken, whose room I was occupying, whose clothing I would soon be wearing, whose face in the miniature portrait was so frighteningly like my own. What had happened to her? Where was she now? At least I had a clue to where *I* was—in the home of Lord Warringwood, in London, in the year 1815. The last entry in the diary had been dated June 18, while she was still aboard a vessel approaching English soil. I'd left New York by plane on June 20. Unbelievable though it seemed, today must be June 20—1815!

Time was too short for daydreaming. Later on, when I was sure of being left to myself, I could dig into the diary. If only I could quiet the nervous clenchings in my stomach at the thought of what lay ahead! I still could not believe this was really happening. How was it possible? How was I to carry on in this strange world? My modern manners were sure to give me away. What was I to say to Lady Caroline? How should I behave? My closest exposure to the elite world I'd inadvertently entered had been through the pages of a novel, and I could hardly expect reality to follow the dictates of fiction, although at least that fiction had given me a clue to the formal manner of speech of the early nineteenth century aristocracy and I could try to pattern myself accordingly. I was thankful too that while I was growing up my father had always been such a stickler for good English, correcting the slang that had often popped into my speech, so that now my speech was well-formed.

I washed quickly in the cool room, adjusting a portable screen to catch the heat of the fire. Still, there was a draft drifting across the floor that raised goose bumps on my skin. After washing, I hid my modern underwear in the bottom corner of the wardrobe where I'd earlier stashed my skirt and blouse. I searched through the baroness's possessions for some substitutes and found a sliplike camisole, supportive enough to wear without embarrassment. There were underpants too—baggy, knee length, and lacy—and stockings that looked nothing like my discarded nylon pantyhose and were far less sheer. I wasn't certain how to hold these up, but found some garters and fiddled until the stockings were more or less secure. Now for a dress—or perhaps the maid would be a better judge of that. I donned the robe again and, taking certain items of my own modern makeup, went to the dressing table. With a careful hand I applied only small amounts, omitting lipstick altogether.

When I was finished, I hid the overnight case too in the wardrobe, and returned to the couch just in time to hear the maid's knock at the door.

After dropping a quick curtsy, she smiled. "Shall I get your gown, mum? Which would you like?"

"You choose one for me."

She fumbled within the wardrobe for a minute, then withdrew a green dress; it was long sleeved, low necked, and high waisted—elegant, yet of simple lines. "I like this one particular, my lady, if it pleases you."

"It certainly does."

She laid it on the bed, a matching pair of delicate satin slippers on the floor. I discarded my robe, and Jane carefully lifted the folds of the deep-green moiré gown over my head, smoothed it into place, and fastened the hooks up the back. In the candlelight the gown reflected the wavering hues of the deepest sea; the fabric felt silky against my skin. It was a pleasant surprise to find that the dress fit as though it had been made for me. I hadn't stopped to think beforehand what a fool I would have looked slipping into a dress of all the wrong proportions. But apparently the baroness and I were the same height and weight—another unsettling coincidence.

When I turned and caught my reflection in the long mirror at the side of the room, I could hardly believe the change in my appearance. I now looked the part of a woman of the past. The neckline of the gown was low, the material gathered just under my breasts to fall in graceful folds to the floor. I swirled several times before the mirror, delighted, feeling suddenly so much more elegant and feminine.

Jane was watching. "It's just lovely, Baroness. Would you want me to do your hair now? It's barely mussed. I'll just straighten a curl or two."

Here I was leery. My hair was long and hard to manage. I had swept it up and pinned it in a style that suited me perfectly. I was afraid that if she changed it too much, I wouldn't like it. Still, I wasn't confident enough to voice my doubts, and sat down at the dressing table.

She deftly took the brush, removed a few pins, and

smoothed up the loose ends, fastening them in high curls. Then she found a few stragglers, and brushed them one by one around her finger until they lay in soft curls against my cheeks. I was more than happy with the result.

She stood back, awaiting my opinion. When I smiled at her in the mirror and nodded my head, her face lit. "You'll be wanting some jewels, mum. Mrs. Perkins said to tell you she put your box in the bottom compartment here." She pointed to the dresser.

"Then get it, please."

When she brought out the square satin box and placed it in front of me, I had to force my jaw from dropping as I lifted the lid and saw the jewelry glinting back at me. "Well!" I said under my breath. Then louder, for her ears: "I think we should find a more secure place for these. Perhaps there's a safe in the house."

"Just as I thought myself, my lady. You never know . . ."

I lifted out a pair of emerald earrings and held them up to my face. An intensified hue of the gown that clothed my body, they complemented my skin and the dress perfectly, shimmering with green sparks in the candlelight. There was also a square-cut emerald ring in the box. I slipped it onto the fourth finger of my left hand with ease, flexing my fingers to send the sparkle radiating. A touch of perfume behind my ears and at my throat, from the bottle of my own special exotic scent I'd stashed on the dressing table, and I was ready.

Jane led as we left the room. We followed the hall to the staircase, where we went down one flight of stairs to another hallway. We stopped before a set of beautifully polished mahogany doors. She knocked quietly. A soft, lilting voice answered, and I waited as Jane opened the door and announced me. I steeled

myself for the encounter, praying my quick study of
the baroness's effects and my limited acting abilities
would be enough to fool the lady I was about to face.
When I touched my hands together, my fingers were
icy cold from nervousness, but I took a deep breath
and entered the room.

TWO

THE ROOM GLOWED SOFTLY with the light of several dozen candles burning in sparkling crystal chandeliers. Pale gold satin drapes adorned the tall windows, echoing the golds and greens of the interior. The thick Persian carpet under my feet bore a design of forest green on a beige and white background. The main grouping of furniture—two small couches, two wingbacked chairs, a richly glowing mahogany tea table—was before the pillared black marble fireplace, and a smaller grouping graced the opposite end of the rectangular room. There was a corner cabinet of curios, another of books; and on the tabletops rested gleaming brass bowls filled with arrangements of fragrant yellow roses. The gently dancing flames in the fireplace completed the picture of welcoming.

Lady Caroline wasn't what I'd expected, but then, I hadn't been sure what to expect. I'd made a few guesses, wondering if she was Lord Warringwood's mother, aunt, daughter, or wife. Now that I saw her, two possible identities could be canceled out.

She was young—about my own age—tall, willowy, and blond. Her fair hair was parted in the center and drawn into a twist at the back of her head. The smile on her pretty face held the warmth of sunshine; her movements seemed as unselfconsciously graceful as those of a leaf in the wind.

"Ah, Baroness, do come in." She extended one slender white hand. "Justin and I have been so anxious to meet you. We were worried when your arrival was delayed. I fear you have not had the pleasantest of journeys. Please accept our condolences. It is unfortunate that your father's death was the reason for this visit to us—would that it had come about under more pleasant circumstances. But just the same, welcome to our home."

I returned the light squeeze of her hand. "I'm happy to meet you, Lady Caroline."

"Not as delighted as I to meet you. Won't you please sit down. I shall have Williams bring in refreshments later; I thought perhaps we would wait a bit in the event Justin arrives. He has asked me to make his apologies to you. He was quite determined to be here to greet you personally, but at the last moment an urgent matter came up to call him away . . . something which, unfortunately, could not be put off."

"No apologies are necessary."

She gestured, indicating that I should take a seat on one of the green-and-gold striped satin couches. She sat opposite me on a wingbacked chair of matching fabric. "I am not one to stand upon ceremony, Baroness," she continued brightly, "and I am hoping we can dispense with formalities and become quite good friends. I think we should be Caroline and Marlena to each other. Do you agree?"

"Certainly. I would be more comfortable."

She frowned slightly, studying me. "You are quite like your portrait, you know. I noticed it when I inspected the bedroom before your arrival. The artist was excellent to have captured your likeness so well. My husband will be delighted. Though he would never admit to it, I think he feared we would be saddled with a dull, unattractive, and high-notioned heiress to pamper and cosset. I believe he is in for a pleasant surprise."

I smiled. She had just clarified another question. Lord Warringwood, Justin Pemberton, was her husband, and this news set my mind along new avenues.

"June is a delightful month to be in England," she continued, "and you will have time to catch the end of the London season. The Prince has made a late departure for Brighton this year, so there are a number of people still in town. . . . Ah, but with your recent bereavement, perhaps you wish to be out of society for a while?"

"My father always thought the living were meant to go on living, and told me many times before he died that the best respect I could show him would be to make the most of my own life using the values he had taught me." The words came automatically to me as I thought of my own father and his recent death.

"A wise man. It does no one good to sit and mope. I will ensure that you do not. We will introduce you and bring you round to some of the balls. And of course we must get you a voucher for Almacks." I'd read of Almacks—those London assembly rooms restricted to the most elite, whose admission was by voucher only at the sole discretion of a small group of society patronesses. "I shall speak to Sally Jersey," she continued. "If it were not for the fact that Justin needs you here in town, I might have been able to persuade him to let us go down to Brighton with the rest of the ton, though it is a bit late to find a respectable house to let. What date have you set for your return to New York?"

"I am not sure. I don't—I do not know exactly what has to be done."

"How like Justin to be so vague!" She laughed. "He always seems to think one can divine his intentions and understand his wishes without his voicing them."

"He has not told you a great deal?"

"Only that a room and entertainments should be prepared for you. Beyond that, not a great deal, but you will become used to his ways. You see, he can be somewhat aloof. I think it comes from his having inherited his title at a young age and being tied to the responsibilities of the estates when he should have been out about town with other young men. He lost his parents in a carriage accident when he was nineteen."

"I am sorry."

She smiled distractedly, as though her words brought other thoughts to mind. "Of course your own tragedy is a much more recent shock."

"My father's death was a shock, yes."

"Actually," Caroline mused, "it is through your mother's family that we are connected. I suppose you could say you and Justin are cousins—many, many times removed. Were you aware of it?"

"My father never mentioned the English relations."

"It was your mother's grandmother, your great-grandmother, who was a Delacourt and sister of Justin's great-grandfather's first wife. They had two daughters together before her death. Justin is the grandson of the eldest son of his second marriage."

"You are quite an authority."

"It is a hobby of mine, begun out of boredom and a need to do something besides worry over a piece of sewing. My mother instilled in me an interest in the

great ancient families, and I have carried it on . . .
more so now that I am married."

"Do you know why my father chose your husband
as executor of his will?"

"Justin mentioned it only briefly. Apparently his
father and yours were friends of long standing. Perhaps they met at the time of your parents' courtship?
Your father was in England during that period, I understand."

"I see."

"But I have not asked you what you thought of
New York. I have the greatest curiosity about foreign places, and Justin has one or two American acquaintances who have visited here and told me
about the States. I found them a pleasure, with their
easy manners and delightful way of speaking—
which I notice you also share, Marlena. Somehow I
expected a Germanic inflection in your speech."

"I have lived in New York for ten years."

"Yes, of course, and I imagine you were young
enough to quickly adjust to your new environment
. . . more quickly than an adult would. I have heard
so many fascinating stories of New York and have
always wanted to visit there. Unfortunately my
husband seems to feel I should be happiest close
at home, and he has too many commitments to
allow him to move about as the rest of our set do—
not that he is much for society. He would not hear
of my taking a jaunt farther than Brighton or
Bath, and then only in his company on the rarest
of occasions. Perhaps now you are here, it will be
different."

She kept the conversation going so naturally, I
barely thought of my earlier discomfort or wondered
what to say and how to phrase it.

About thirty minutes had passed when we heard

voices in the hall and then the sound of determined footsteps, and saw the door to the room flung open to frame a tall, finely built man on the threshold.

"Ah, Justin." Caroline rose from her chair. "You have made it in good time. I was hoping your business would not detain you overlong, and had Williams hold tea." She went to him and took his arm. "You must meet Marlena. We are such good friends already."

While she spoke, I studied him, barely having the power to pull my eyes away. He was imposing, with russet-gold hair, and a healthy color to his skin. His well-defined features were marked by a straight nose, a strong bone structure that would age well, and arresting eyes of a gray-green hue, the color of a stormy sea. There was a quality of cool, intelligent assessment in their depths, and a perceptiveness that made me wonder irrationally whether he was already seeing through my charade.

As he stood by the doorway, his head was turned, his eyes riveted on me even as he listened to Caroline's words. There was palpable curiosity, almost surprise, in his expression. With a straightening of his shoulders, he seemed to bring himself back to his surroundings; then he leaned forward to present his cheek for Caroline's light kiss.

"I am pleased you have seen so well to the baroness's comforts, Caro." As his deep and beautifully accented voice echoed in the room, he stepped forward with Caroline at his elbow.

"Marlena and I are already on famous terms," she continued, "and I have done her the service of warning her of your oftentimes forbidding and too serious manner."

"I hope the baroness is not acquiring an unfavorable impression of me."

"Not at all," I interrupted. "A pleasure to meet you, Lord Warringwood."

"The pleasure is mine." He stepped across to the couch to take my extended hand, and bent slightly over it. "Your servant, Baroness. I trust all your needs have been tended to and you find your room satisfactory?"

"Yes. I have received a very warm reception."

"And no doubt have had your ear filled to overflowing by my charmingly loquacious wife." He smiled for the first time, fleetingly.

"We have spent a pleasant hour discussing my trip and Caroline's plans for me while I am in London," I answered.

"Which, if I know Caroline, leaves you with a very full calendar. I hope you will spare me a few hours to tend to the business that brought you to England."

"Of course."

"But I daresay there will be time for everything." During our exchange, his eyes hadn't moved from my face in their level, unflinching gaze. "This is your first trip to England, is it not?" I nodded. "And how did you find New York? Quite a change from the home of your youth in Bavaria?"

"Yes, but it is an exciting city, full of growth, and the land is beautiful. Have you been to America?"

"No, perhaps someday. . . My carriage met you in good time at the coast, I see. Did you encounter any difficulties on your journey to town?"

"No."

"It was unfortunate your maid took ill. Caro has seen to a replacement, but should she not be suitable, you will no doubt be able to find a substitute here in London. My secretary would be happy to assist you in that regard."

"I like the girl—Jane."

He inclined his head and turned to his wife. "Will you ring for tea, Caro?"

"I have instructed Williams to bring the refreshments once you had arrived," she said, and then told him something further in an undertone. He frowned, answered her in a similarly hushed voice. I dropped my eyes from the two of them as my own thoughts captured me. Until Lord Warringwood had entered the room, the full impact of my situation hadn't struck me. I'd been too dazed to think that this was more than a dream; I'd assumed in the blinking of an eyelash, I'd be back where I'd started, in the seat of a plane headed toward Heathrow. Suddenly everything was altogether too real, and I knew I was involved in no light fantasy or easily explained case of mistaken identity. I needed time to think, to pull together the elements of a drama that was progressing too rapidly for me. Vanished was my earlier feeling of confidence during my chat alone with Caroline; now each passing minute was leaving me more confused and frightened. What if they should discover I wasn't the baroness? I could always tell them the truth of what had happened to me—that I was a stranger from another century—but who in their right mind would believe a story like that? I hardly believed it myself, though it was happening to me. No, they'd probably think I was a deliberate imposter; a contemporary of their own trying to gain the riches of a wealthy lady through impersonation. I didn't have any idea of the extent of the baroness's wealth; I knew only that it was sufficient to afford her expensive clothing and lavish jewels. And if I was found to be an imposter, innocent though I was, I knew it would mean a very unfriendly trip out the door to the street—and a future that made my blood run cold. This wasn't my world, or even my country.

I wouldn't know how to exist here on my own, and I had no friends . . . no one to call on for help. I knew this nineteenth century world was a harsh one of gross inequities—of poverty and strife on the one hand and extreme wealth and extravagance on the other.

I was startled when a shadow passed before my downcast eyes. I glanced up to see Lord Warringwood.

The look he gave me was so intense it made me uneasy. Yet I felt strangely drawn to him; sensed an underlying warmth that belied his cool exterior. "My wife tells me I am not being the best of hosts. Unintentional, I assure you, but I have had a trying day."

"Few people are at their best at the end of a busy day, myself included."

"I will not trouble you now about the business we have to settle between us—surely you have indeed had as tiring a day as I—but perhaps in the morning you would meet me in my study. Shall we say at eleven?"

I nodded my head. "I should be happy to."

He in turn nodded, and seemed about to say something more. Then, as if deciding against that impulse, he turned to sit on the couch as Williams entered with the tea tray, set it on the table before the couch and quietly exited the room. Caroline poured. She handed my cup to Justin, and he passed it on to me, the dainty Sevres looking like a toy in his hand. I accepted it, smiled, and tried to pull myself together.

Caroline took a sip from her cup. "Do you know if Sally Jersey has left town yet, Justin?"

"I have no idea. You know I take no interest in the activities of the ton."

"Except when it suits your political interests. It is just that I thought perhaps Sally could send a voucher to Almacks for Marlena."

"There are others you can approach if Sally is out of town."

"Yes, though I am not on as good terms with Lady Sefton or Princess Esterhazy."

Lord Warringwood had turned to me. "You are interested in visiting Almacks, Baroness?"

"Caroline suggested it as a place to see."

"I can imagine. And it would be, if you were contemplating placing yourself on the marriage mart . . . which I do not believe would be the wisest course for you at the moment."

"Oh?"

"When we have discussed the terms of your inheritance, I think you will understand me."

"What kind of ideas are you putting into her head, Justin?" Caroline burst in. "Pay him no regard, Marlena. As my husband himself admits, he rarely takes an interest in social goings-on. And Justin, you know that making an appearance at Almacks does not necessarily mean one is offering oneself up for a marriage proposal!"

"What I am trying to say, ladies, is that with the baroness's obvious physical and monetary attributes, it should not be necessary to advertise that she is an eligible party."

I was flushed when he turned to me. He stared for a moment. "Aside from which, it may help to hold the fortune hunters from the door if the baroness is more selective in the functions she attends."

"So that she can sit in this great house with her sewing as I have had to do these last years, since you have no inclination to go out or are too weary to do so and will not permit me to go out on my own! Such a beautiful house, but so empty when there is no one in it to talk to but oneself. Finally I am to have the companionship of a woman my own age to share my entertainments. I have no intention of letting the opportunity pass. Of course we will go to Almacks—London would not be complete without it."

"As you wish, Caro. I was only giving what I considered wise warning, though I trust between the two of you, you ladies will come up with enough good sense to behave circumspectly. Then too, perhaps I should begin to pay more attention to my responsibilities and escort you."

A quick look passed between husband and wife; on Caroline's part it was laced with amazement. I didn't know what to make of it, but didn't have the energy to puzzle about the matter. I only waited for a chance to excuse myself for my bedroom.

Before rising, I sat through a few more pleasant remarks from Caroline, during which time Lord Warringwood hadn't said a word—though his eyes were on me too often for comfort. I put my cup on the tray. "Caroline . . . my lord . . . I hope you will excuse me. It has been such a pleasure meeting you, but I am very tired."

Justin Pemberton stood. Caroline rose as well, but seemed distressed. "I am sorry. We have not chased you off with this conversation, I hope."

"No, of course not. But it has been a long day."

She smiled understandingly and extended her hand. "We will see you in the morning, then. I look forward to it."

"So do I." I slipped past her. Lord Warringwood came to take my elbow and walk with me to the door.

"I trust you will sleep well, Baroness."

"I'm sure I will. And you the same."

"Sleep always comes easily to me after a busy day. I will see you at eleven."

"At eleven promptly."

We'd reached the door, which he held open. "Shall I call a servant, or can you find your way?"

"I think I can at least find my room. Good night." I smiled quickly and, as he watched me, turned and slipped into the hall.

THREE

I LEFT the Green Salon no longer sure I was even moderately capable of handling the situation into which I'd been so mysteriously thrown—the elegant surroundings, the lovely Caroline, her handsome husband. If there'd been a choice for me, I would have blurted out the whole truth as I knew it. But I couldn't explain even to myself the extraordinary resemblance between the real baroness and myself, much less how I'd jumped back over a century in time. The fear of being cast out into the hostile streets stiffened my resolve to play out the charade at least a little longer. I had no alternative.

I pulled the tasseled bell rope near the head of the bed to call for Jane, and after she'd brought me hot water and helped me undress, I said good night and sat down at the desk with the baroness's diary in front of me. The only tools I'd have to work with would come from this source. Maybe in the morning I'd have time to go through her belongings more methodically for further information about her personality and life.

I heard the dainty clock on the mantel chime one o'clock before I laid down the diary, feeling both eyesore and chilled. At least I'd learned something about the twenty-four-year-old woman I was forced into impersonating—not enough to answer all my questions about her, but enough to fill in some of the blanks and let me carry on as her imposter with more assurance.

Baroness Marlena von Mantz had been sent to New York from her family home in Bavaria two years before the diary had been given to her for her sixteenth birthday. Whatever personal trials she'd experienced at being sent from her home to a foreign land were not described. She did mention her mother once or twice in passing, and from these references I learned that when the baroness was ten or eleven, the frail Englishwoman, relative to Lord Warringwood by marriage, had died of a respiratory ailment—consumption, I guessed. And here was another startling parallel between the baroness and me: I too had lost my mother in my youth. The baroness had never been very close to her mother; it was for her father that she felt the strongest ties, and she missed him dearly during the years of her forced exile in New York. Although they'd corresponded regularly, she'd seen her father only once since she was fourteen, he'd been able to arrange a brief trip to New York—made short by his need to return to Germany and do what he could to stop the encroachment of Napoleon. The only factor that had saved his ancestral home and lands seemed to be the isolation of these holdings in an out-of-the-way mountain valley not immediately essential to Napoleon and his victory plans.

The diary's pages were full of expressions of homesickness and anxiety for her far-away father, which faded only slightly as the years passed and she began thinking more as an adult, pondering her own future. Her upbringing must have been strict, because it was clear from her words that there was ingrained in Marlena a sense of duty to uphold and maintain the tradition of her family and her name by eventually returning to Germany to make a suitable marriage to a man of similar birth. The family lands and title would be hers on her father's death, since there were no male heirs. Perhaps that explained why, at the age of twenty-four, almost spinsterhood in her era, Marlena was unmarried.

She seemed to be a woman of intelligence and spirit, not afraid to flaunt convention in a mild way when she felt social strictures were too confining. Surprisingly, I didn't find any signs of a selfish streak I'd almost expected in someone of her background. In fact, I felt very much in sympathy with her and found that on matters of importance we thought alike.

Marlena's diary was cryptic about her trip to England and meeting with Lord Warringwood simply because she herself was in the dark about the details. She'd been heartbroken on learning of her father's death—news that had reached her via a letter from Lord Warringwood sent across the Atlantic by special clipper. After telling her the sad facts, Lord Warringwood had gone on to advise her that he'd been appointed executor to her father's estate, and that included in her father's last requests was the stipulation that she come to London for the reading of the will. Not only did Marlena feel shocked by her father's death; receiving such news from a stranger whose name her father had never mentioned was deeply distressing.

Marlena went to her father's attorney in New York, who'd also received a letter from Lord Warringwood, Justin Pemberton. The attorney confirmed everything Warringwood had said, verifying him to be who he claimed, although he couldn't shed any light on the baron's reasons for appointing the Englishman executor.

She was cordially invited—although in essence it was a command—to travel to London that spring. Lord Warringwood had booked passage for her on a vessel leaving New York in late April; would see to it that she was met on her arrival in England and brought safely to his home in London, where she would remain as his guest as long as was necessary for Marlena to settle the estate and take over the reins of her inheritance. He made no mention of her declining the invitation or of what she would do with her future once the details of the will had been taken care of. She presumed she would have no choice but to go on to Germany, at least temporarily.

Marlena had left for England not knowing what reception she'd receive from these strangers in a strange land, yet knowing her father must have had good reason for arranging things the way he had.

I closed the diary, and leaned back in my chair. The Baroness and I had each recently lost our fathers and not completely recovered from the loss. My own mother had died at an early age, when I was three, and my father had raised me, been my main support and staff of encouragement. He'd never remarried, once telling me that for a few brief years, he'd known a perfect love. For him to seek a duplicate of that would seem futile or, at the least, gluttonous . . . he had his memories. He'd smiled crookedly, tickled my chin. "And I have you, sweetheart, a little bit of your mother and me. What more can a man ask?"

I remember how I cried as I sorted his personal belongings after the funeral, only a few months before now—his favorite fishing reel, his wedding portrait, a worn wallet, the white handkerchiefs that had always been folded so neatly in his suit pocket when he left for his office in the mornings, a bottle of his favorite cologne, the spicy scent of which would always remind me of him . . .

But like the baroness, I was trying to put those sad memories behind me, to face the life that lay ahead.

I wondered where Marlena was now . . . what had happened to her when I had so capriciously taken over her identity. Was it possible we'd switched places in time? As ridiculous as it sounded, it seemed the only plausible possibility. Had she, a few hours before, found herself in a modern airport, seeing people and things that must have seemed unbelievable to her? And would my friend Robin have taken her for me, despite Marlena's nineteenth century clothing? What would he have thought?

For now, I had my own problems to face. If I was to continue impersonating the baroness with any skill at all, I needed a good night's sleep—yet I'd have to be up early if I was to search through the bureau and desk drawers before breakfast.

After laying another log on the fire and hoping it would keep the chill out of the room until morning, I climbed into the poster bed and, marking the position of the matches on the nightstand, extinguished the candle and pulled the covers over me.

I woke up to a sun-filled morning steeping through the curtains into my room. I sat up quickly and wondered for a frightening moment where I was. A glance at the clock on the mantelpiece told me it was eight-thirty. My mind began to clear. I was in the home of Lord Warringwood, in a strange city, in a different century, among people I didn't know. But it *was* morning, and things always seem more optimistic in the morning light than in the dark of evening.

I went to the washstand to splash some chilled water over my face and chase away the last vestiges

of sleep. As I picked up a linen towel to pat the mois-
ture off my skin, I suddenly missed the small bath-
room in my New York apartment, where I could
have luxuriated in a hot shower. I put the thought
from my mind and went to the wardrobe to dig out of
my overnight case my toothbrush and tube of
toothpaste—two more articles of twentieth century
hygiene I didn't think were in common use in this
nineteenth century world. I made a mental note to
conserve those modern items I'd brought with me
that would be difficult to replace should my stay in
this century go on for any length of time.

As I began my search for further clues to the baroness's background and personality, a chill of uncertainty again slithered down my spine. Despite my
befuddlement, it was slowly beginning to sink in
that this was no dream; not the hallucination of a
troubled spirit. I now existed in the reality of another century. But though I felt uncertain and
frightened, I also felt a pulsing excitement building
inside—a sense of awe at the truly extraordinary experience; of anticipation of the days ahead. I was
about to witness and be a part of a time I'd always
loved, and my natural curiosity made me anxious to
embark on the adventure.

I wondered, why me? Why had I been sent off on
this frightening adventure? What made me special?
Was it preordained, or just an accident? I shook my
head and shoulders to push the unanswerable questions away; went to the desk and began probing
through its compartments and drawers. I found only
a few tidbits of information—a few scraps of paper
listing spots the baroness should see while in England, a small address book with only a few entries
of friends and relatives in New York, among them
"Aunt Eva and Uncle Andreas, 10 Washington
Square." By nine-thirty I'd searched through every

drawer and cubbyhole in the room and discovered little more than I'd known after reading the diary. Defeated and conscious of the hour, I straightened the mess I'd made and rang for Jane.

She was there in a few minutes, smiling and anxious to please.

Using my overtiredness from my trip as an excuse for rising late, I asked if she wouldn't choose a dress for me and then bring some coffee.

"Coffee, mum?" she asked, surprised.

"We drink coffee in the mornings in New York," I said without thinking, then added, "Would it be too much trouble?"

"No, m'lady, I'm sure not. The cook prides herself on her kitchens, though it's not the habit of the house to take coffee in the mornings."

"Well, I have never been in England before . . ."

"I'll bring the coffee right up, m'lady."

While she was gone, I went to the bed to see the dress she'd chosen. It was a light muslin gown in a medium blue. I liked it. High waisted in the style of the period, it was chic and simple, as I was beginning to realize was characteristic of the baroness's clothing: there were no superfluous decorations to draw the eye to the dress and away from the woman who wore it.

Feeling much better after two cups of coffee, with Jane's help I put on the blue muslin gown, understanding the necessity of a lady's maid in that day; I could never have managed by myself all the small buttons up the back of the dress.

A few minutes later I went down to the front hall, but had no idea where to find Caroline. Indecisive, I wandered awhile before the butler walked up quietly behind me and, speaking in the voice of a well-trained and intelligent servant, told me that if I was seeking Her Ladyship, she could be found in the morning room. I followed him toward the back of the house, where he opened a door to an airy room, decorated in tones of cheery yellows, looking out onto the back gardens.

As I was used to modern cities with buildings crowded next to each other, the garden surprised me. Here, in the back of the house, was a fairly large plot of land covered by green grass, a few trees, and a formal flower bed, the whole surrounded by high walls. An apple tree, two shade trees, and various shrubs were placed so that the garden seemed much larger than it was.

Caroline was seated at a table before the window; her expression brightened as I entered. "Ah, Marlena, good morning. I hope you had a pleasant night's rest. I know how difficult it is to sleep in a strange bed."

"I did not hear a thing until this morning."

"I am delighted. Go fill your plate. There is enough to feed the King's Guard there on the sideboard."

"Your husband isn't joining us?"

"Justin? Heavens no! He was up hours ago, has already taken his morning ride in the park, and is now either out on an errand or closeted in his study, where he spends a good portion of his time."

"I am to meet him there at eleven."

"Ah—I had forgotten, and I had a morning shopping expedition planned for us. Well, there will be plenty of time another day. London has some of the best shops, you know, what with all the Parisian seamstresses rushing here after the Revolution." She cocked a scrutinizing brow in my direction. "Where do you get your gowns, by the way? From what I have seen thus far, you are quite in the mode."

"My aunt assisted me, actually," I improvised. "We have all the fashion books. I chose the styles and she the fabrics, and there are quite passable seamstresses in New York."

"My compliments, Marlena. There would certainly seem no need to rush off to Bond Street. By the way, for this afternoon I am trying to arrange an appointment with Lady Sefton. No point in wasting time—we must get you acquainted with London society. And since Lady Sefton is also one of the patronesses of Almacks, we can seize the occasion of our visit to obtain that voucher for you as well. I have no doubt my request to introduce you to her will be met with alacrity—she will want to be the first with the news. As secretive as my husband tends to be, rumor has gotten around about your arrival. Needless to say, there is a bit of mystery attached."

"I hope I have not put you in an awkward position."

"On the contrary," she laughed. "This is precisely what I needed to liven my days! Justin does his best, I suppose, but it is not in his nature to understand my yearnings for a gay social life. He is perfectly content as is, with regular trips down to Pemberton Hall in Sussex—the family estate—to break the monotony. But with you here, I will have all the excuse I need to go out as often as I desire. Life will be so much more entertaining!"

"Your husband did not strike me as a recluse when I met him last evening," I said thoughtfully.

"No, not in the true sense, but I think he has forgotten how to relax and find a few moments of pleasure. And then I was so young when we married . . . only seventeen . . . knowing so little. I did not understand him; I let him lead me. I had not experienced a London season. I thought after we were wed I would have an opportunity to enjoy all the excitement I had missed in my country life." She was silent for a moment, staring down at the food on her plate, though I

knew it was her private thoughts that preoccupied
her. "I love the city and shopping and fine clothes
and entertaining. He is more inclined toward politics
and his financial interests . . . the country . . ."

"Is he aware of your feelings?" I was so caught up
in her dialogue I didn't stop to think of the prying nature of my remark. She didn't seem to notice.

"Oh, he is aware . . . not that we have actually had
it out. Though I have suggested that on his next trip
to Pemberton, I remain in London, or perhaps go on
to Brighton with several of my friends. His reaction
has not encouraged me to push the issue further."

"How did you and your husband become acquainted?"

Her lips pursed; she touched her fingers to her
chin. Her eyes focused on the garden beyond the
windows and remained there. "As I have said, Justin
inherited his title very young. He was denied the
carousing, the year's tour to Europe of other young
men his age. His own seriousness kept him from the
gambling dens"—her eyes twinkled momentarily—"the cock pits, the fisting matches. I realize I am
supposed to know nothing of these masculine diver-
sions, but gossip does have a way of traveling. In any
case, from what I have since heard, the only diver-
sions Justin allowed himself were those of sport. He
was a member of the 'Four in Hand,' rode with the
Quorn, was a participant of every important foxhunt
in England—a true Corinthian. It was when he was
in his late twenties and knew it was time he thought
about getting married and begetting an heir that he
was attending a weekend hunt at a manor neighboring my childhood home. My father was at the hunt,
and he and Justin became acquainted. My father invited him back to our home to see some new horses
he had acquired.

"I was in the garden when they arrived, clipping

my mother's roses, and Justin saw me. I remember him looking over the stableyard fence, which was only a few yards from where I was working, staring at me, trying to listen to my father's conversation. I must have appeared a very shy and innocent thing—which is precisely what I was. I remember I was wearing an old straw bonnet to protect my complexion from the sun, and a dress I'd outgrown a year before—we were too poor to chance snagging the fabric of a new afternoon dress on the rosebush thorns. Though we were gentry, we lived below the average standards. My father was in possession of a title, but the assets that went with it had long since been dissipated. It wasn't Papa's doing, but his elder brother's, who was an inveterate gambler. When my uncle unexpectedly died in a boating accident and Papa succeeded him, there was barely enough left in the estate to pay off my uncle's debts. There was the manor house, of course, and its farms. They were prosperous, because my uncle had always left Papa in charge of their management. Still, there was not much left over for extravagance, and few prospects of my ever going to London for a season to be introduced.

"I did not even speak with Justin that day. I saw him from the distance and remember thinking he was a fine-looking man, but too old for my girlish interests. A few days later he had dinner with us. When Justin tried to draw me into conversation, I thought it was only politeness on his part. A week later my father came to me and told me Lord Warringwood had offered for my hand. I could not believe it! My parents were ecstatic, barely thinking to question me on my feelings before giving Justin their resounding approval. If I had been older and wiser and had time to consider, perhaps I would have put a stop to it until I could reflect. As it was, I was caught up by my parents' enthusiasm and the prospect of escaping my dreary country existence. And, I can assure you, Marlena, I was excited by the looks of the tall, handsome lord who was soon to be my husband. Our wedding was one month later.

"That was three years ago. Of course, we have gotten to know each other quite well in that time. I have a beautiful home, a house in London, a handsome husband who provides for me well; I exist amid the society of my girlhood dreams . . ." Her blue eyes gazed into the distance as her voice drifted off.

The clock chimed eleven. I was so caught up in her story I'd nearly forgotten the appointment I had with the man whose character was taking on new dimensions. Now I would have to hurry if I was not to keep him waiting.

I briefly took her hand. "Caroline, I must go to meet your husband. Shall we talk more later?"

She flushed self-consciously. "I have been letting my tongue run off. Forgive me . . . I suppose it comes from so seldom having a woman my own age with whom to chat. I shall see you when you are finished."

I found my way out of the room to the front hall and, with the butler's help, to Justin Pemberton's study. The butler announced me, rapping soundly on the door. "The Baroness von Mantz, my lord."

"Send her in." The double doors opened, and I walked into a paneled room of soft wood tones, and red and green leathers. A small fire burned in the grate. The walls were covered with shelves full of books; a desk stood before the windows, which shared the same view of the back gardens as the morning room. Lord Warringwood was seated not at his desk, as I'd expected, but in an armchair by the fireplace. His long legs, covered by tight beige pants and tall black leather boots, were stretched out before him. The sunlight streaming in through the

back windows glinted off his golden hair. His deep
brown cutaway coat accentuated the breadth of his
shoulders, the whiteness of the high, pointed collar
of his shirt, the elegance of the length of crisp cloth
tied intricately at his neck. A stack of papers covered
his lap. He didn't rise.

"Good morning, Baroness. I trust you slept well."

"I did, thank you."

"Good. Would you care for some tea? I was having
some myself."

I nodded.

He motioned to his man, who went to the tray, selected a cup, and poured for me. "Milk or lemon?"

"Milk, please; no sugar."

Holding the cup in my hand, I sipped the tea nervously while I waited for the butler to leave and Lord
Warringwood to begin. It was several seconds before
he did, and then only after he'd taken two more sips
from his own cup, set it down, and withdrawn a narrow cigar from his pocket. He lit it with the matches
on the table at his side.

"You do not mind if I smoke, do you, Baroness?
Most of my friends prefer snuff, but I find tobacco
superlative. An American weed. Do you find it the
habit of many men in the States to partake?"

He glanced in my direction as the end of the cigar
flared to glowing red. I was amazed that a man of his
era would smoke in front of a woman. "Yes, I know a
number of men who smoke, but generally not in the
presence of ladies."

"Oh? Do they usually withdraw to themselves?
The gentlemen? I thought perhaps in the company of
an American woman, more enlightened than her
English counterparts, my smoking would not be
minded."

"Do smoke, if you like; if it makes you comfortable."

He took a long puff and exhaled, and curls of aromatic smoke circled about his head and rose toward the high ceiling. "But you must be anxious to learn why I have brought you across the Atlantic. It would have been easier for both of us if I could have conveyed the whole in a long and legally phrased letter, but that, unfortunately, would have contradicted the terms of your father's will. At the time I admit to wishing, on discovering the responsibility was mine, that I could have washed my hands of everything. Now, after meeting you . . ." The gray-green eyes flickered. I wasn't sure if he was teasing me or being serious, and waited for him to continue. "But, of course, it would by necessity have been a long letter, which would probably have cost me as much effort as your visit here.

"Your father was an explicit man—he put many details into his will, in the foresight that nothing should go awry. I think he succeeded. That the responsibility for seeing his last will and testament carried out should fall on my shoulders, he did not foresee, and neither did I. Perhaps I should explain at this point, Baroness, that your father and mine were close friends. When he made his will, it was with the intention that my father should be executor. Unfortunately, my father died only a few months before your own—"

"I thought from something Caroline said last night," I interrupted, "that both your parents were killed in a carriage accident some time ago."

"That is what she believes, yes; as do the majority of people who knew my father. It seemed wisest at the time to let people think he was killed in the accident. My mother was, instantly—but my father survived, with severe brain injuries that left him incapacitated. For the last twelve years he has been in a private home for the care of the insane. Since he was considered legally incapable, the management of the estates ceded to me, and I took over the title. In truth I held out hope that my father's affliction was not incurable; that one day he would be well enough to take up the reins again."

I saw extreme pain and sadness in his eyes at that moment; a sadness I don't think he knew was evident, because the rest of his features were composed. "I never told your father the true state of affairs. When letters were received from him, they were answered by my solicitors. It was a foolish thing to do, perhaps, but at the time I saw no harm in it. Your father and mine had been such close friends at one time that to reveal the nature of my father's illness ran against the grain with me. I could have told him, as I told others, that my father had died, but since I was holding out hope for his recovery, I did not. It is all in the past now, anyway.

"But a few weeks before my father's death, my solicitors came to me with a disturbing piece of information. Outlined in the baron's last letter to my father was the request that he be executor to the estate. I do not know how much your father knew of his own state of health; perhaps he had an intuition all was not well. In any event, I immediately set out to put matters straight. Given the chaos attending the war in Europe, my letter may never have reached your father—or if it did, not in time. The next missive my solicitors received from Germany was the news of your father's death and the information that Lord Warringwood was indeed appointed executor and guardian to the Baron's daughter. Unfortunately, your father never specified *which* Lord Warringwood, my father—George Pemberton—or myself. So now, inasmuch as I am the current Lord Warringwood, it is I to whom the responsibility falls."

He paused, and lifted one of the papers he held in his lap. I thought he was going to go on into the dry business of the will, but he paused again. "There is one other thing. . . . With the rest of the documents, your father forwarded a sealed letter to you, held in safekeeping by his solicitors in this country until your arrival. I received one as well, and if yours reads anything like mine, I think you will find that matters have been complicated considerably. But I shall say no more until you have read."

He turned over a long ivory envelope in his fingers as though it held some unsettling truth, then handed it across the small distance that separated us.

There was a strange expression on his face . . . probing, almost angry. I hesitated, then finally broke the seal to four finely written sheets. The letter was set down mostly in English with a few sentences in German, as though the baroness's father had forgotten himself in the importance of what he had to say and reverted to his native tongue. It began with endearments and thoughts from the baron to his only child. I smiled, but soon the smile was wiped from my lips as the real message come through to me.

It has been many years, dearest daughter, since we have been together as we should. I sent you to America for your safety, and now I find that I wish I had not. It would have been selfishness to keep you here, but the selfishness of a man who has nothing else to love and cherish except a cold manse of stone and the gardens and grounds around it. I miss you dearly, but this you know, and there is no need to dwell on it now. Could I have it to do over, I would have you with me, but all men at one time or other in their lives wish to redo part of what they have wrought. However, what is done is done; we both must make the best of it. You will have to take these words as evidence of how much I have wished to have you with me these years, because, my daughter, I feel my time in this world is short. There will be no chance to look to the future. That is why I write this letter now. It contains my most cherished thoughts and wishes—ones I hope you will respect and try to carry out just as I know you would have tried to adhere to them had we ever been reunited and I had spoken them aloud to you.

I have been a sick man for some time. I have done my best to ignore the symptoms and, of course, have taken care not to reveal any of this to you. But now my physicians say there is not much time. I know it myself without their telling me. I grow weaker and more short of breath each day, and the pains come more often. My heart is failing, and anxiety I have suffered over the future of the estates—and over your future, with or without the estates—has not helped my health.

The estates, may we be blessed, have survived Napoleon and his warriors. All is intact for you—that which I could not smuggle out to England—the lands, the furnishings, all of the possessions of the barons von Mantz. It is not of these superficial things that I worry now. It would not be wise for you to return to Germany at this time, in any event. What I worry about is you—your happiness and your future well-being.

It is almost thirty years ago now that your mother and I first met in England. You may remember her telling you of it; I know I have seldom spoken of it myself—not for lack of feeling, but it did not seem my place to speak of such things to my daughter. Your mother was a beautiful woman, just as you are yourself. Once I had seen her, there was no forgetting . . . she was beautiful both within and without. Less than a year after we met, we were married; both our families were delighted. Your mother comes from a very fine one—the Delacourts, whom I hope you will one day be meeting. We were so happy I cannot describe to you the extent of it, and I am not an emotional man. But I digress. When I married your mother, I also became quite close with certain members of her family—one of her distant cousins, Lord Warringwood, in particular. He and I forged tight bonds of friendship, which have remained intact over the years. There is no blood relationship between him and your mother, although they are connected by marriage, and in him I felt I had found a protector for my family should anything ever happen to me. I have turned to him over the years in various matters, particularly in overseeing the trust fund set up for you by your mother, and more recently in depositing in safekeeping for me the assets I smuggled out of Germany. He is my closest friend and a man of utmost integrity. I have always felt it would be a wonderful thing . . . a sentiment he shared . . . if our friendship could be carried beyond a lifetime and our families joined more strongly than they are now, which is by the weakest ties of marriage two generations back.

With this in mind, Marlena, I will tell you our thoughts and personal wishes. Since the war began—about the time you were sent to America—George and I have not corresponded a great deal. It has been more expedient in these times of trouble to say as little as possible in a letter, but I know his thoughts could not have changed in this matter, any more than mine have.

George has a son, older than you by some eight

years. It has been our desire from the time you
were born that his son, Justin, and you be one day
joined in marriage. Before you cry out at this old
man's wish, hear me out. Justin is a fine young
man—I have checked through the sources I have,
and all say the same. He appears to be a man of integrity, intelligence, and good sense—and someone
who can provide you with the security and guidance I no longer can. You will be inheriting many
responsibilities—not that I am afraid you are not
capable of handling them—but you are a woman,
and a young and beautiful one, and I fear the obstacles the world will place in your path.

I cannot force you to marry Justin Pemberton,
any more than I could force him to marry you. Neither his father nor I would wish to use coercion,
but it *is* our sincerest desire that you marry.
Should my reports of his character represent anything less than the truth, of course, I would expect
you to seek instead a man of finer qualities; anything less than the finest I do not desire for you.

Before you make a decision, think over what I
have said. By this time you will be in London and
will have met George and his son. Judge for yourself that I have only your best interests in mind. I
have added a codicil to my will, held by my attorneys and to be read to you when you have visited
them in person. In it I have given you one year
from the date of my death to make your decision.
Until that time the great fortune you are inheriting will not come directly to your hands. I am
using this not as a threat, only as a protection for
you against unscrupulous people who would use
you for your wealth. You will be receiving a more
than ample allowance, of course, but until the end
of that year, the bulk of your inheritance will be
overseen by Lord Warringwood. You will be ac-

countable to him for all expenses you incur over and above your stipend for necessities, and he has the right to approve or disapprove any drawings beyond that point. If at the end of the year you do not find yourself close to an understanding with Justin Pemberton and cannot accept him as the man in whom you put your trust and wish to spend the rest of your life, then your fortune and all your inheritances will revert to you and be yours to do with as you please. Even if you find George's son totally ineligible from the start, I ask that this year's waiting period be adhered to. It is my way of giving you time in which to consider and understand the depth of your new responsibilities. I only hope that your final decision will be the one that would make my heart happy were I alive to receive the news in person.

George and I planned this many years ago. Since he has said nothing to me recently to put me off the course, I believe what I am doing is yet in line with his wishes. Justin will be advised of this by my attorneys. I have written him as well, but have given instructions that my letter not be turned over to him until after my death.

There is little else to say, daughter—or rather there is so much I would wish to say to you, it is impossible to find the words. Do not mourn for me. Rather I would have my passing invest you with all the joys and blessings that have so enriched my life—and may you know only enough of its sorrows to lend sweetness. I pray every day that you may be granted the strength to emerge victorious from whatever trials lie before you. I know in everything you do you will make me proud.

My undying love always,

Papa

It was several moments before I dared lift my eyes to Justin Pemberton. His expression was serious, discomfited; and I knew he'd been studying me all the time I read. I didn't know what to say, and it was he who broke the silence. "You see what I mean about complications," he said flatly.

"But you are already married! Surely he did not know that? And even if you were *not* . . ." I flushed.

"He presumed my father would have told him, and it never occurred to me to mention my marital state in the letters my solicitors wrote your father. At the time, it seemed of no consequence."

"I am very sorry, my lord."

"I think at this point we are intimate enough to address each other by our first names—and why should you be sorry? It was none of your doing."

"I feel somewhat responsible!"

"If there is any fault, it lies with me in not telling your father the true circumstances."

"There is to be a year's wait from the date of his death. . . . Did your letter say the same?"

"Yes. Mine was as explicit as yours. Since the baron died March third and it is now June twenty-first, by the terms your father set you have nine months left. I shall speak to your attorneys, however. Since I am already wed and very ineligible, it seems to me that fact should free you from having to observe the remainder of the waiting period."

"You will still be the executor?"

"That is entirely apart from this other. You have some objection?"

"No, no, of course not. Except that I feel I am an encumbrance."

"I cannot say I was delighted when I received the news; however, it shall be resolved shortly. When we advise your solicitors of the situation, I shall request to be absolved from my bonds, and you will then be free to take control of your newly acquired assets and future arrangements as you see fit. The settlement of the estate should not take much over a month, during which time, need I tell you, you will be a most welcome guest beneath my roof."

"You knew last night about the terms of this letter, did you not?"

He seemed startled, and after a moment inclined his head.

"That would explain why you looked at me so strangely."

"I did harbor a certain resentment, and a decided curiosity about the woman who had been preselected to become my wife. I do not enjoy being dictated to."

"No one does. But would you have adhered to your father's wishes?"

"Not out of hand. I see you are embarrassed."

"Yes."

"Were I not already a married man, the situation at this moment would be far more awkward," he said levelly.

"So it would."

There was a brief silence. As I studied the nervously laced fingers in my lap, I heard the clock tick rhythmically on the mantel, a carriage rumble by on the cobbles outside. I wondered how it was possible I was seated in this paneled library in 1815 London, opposite an attractive and intriguing man, a lord, his eyes intent upon me, listening to him discuss my future.

"Tell me, Marlena, why is it that a woman with your obvious attributes has not pressed for marriage before now?"

"There were men in New York," I answered, trying to think as the real baroness might have, "but I had a duty to my father, to my heritage."

"Now you know what your father actually had in

mind for you." He frowned, twisting the thin cigar between his fingers. "I wonder why he waited so long to make it known?"

"There was the war . . . he had many things on his mind . . ."

"Perhaps. I do not recall my own father giving me any hint; though I suppose, now that I think back, he did often speak of his great friend the baron and his beautiful daughter. However, comments such as those do not make too strong an impression upon a youth's mind. . . . Well! We have yet the will to go through, do we not? Though, actually, one of your father's attorneys should be present at the reading, due to the unusual circumstances they have given me permission to relay the details to you."

He took up the stack of papers at his elbow and began to leaf through them, continuing to speak as he did so. "Your father left you a very wealthy woman, Baroness. I am sure this comes as no real surprise to you. Although a number of your countrymen lost a great deal, your father was not among them. He appears to have been an intelligent man and one well versed in the arts of preserving and increasing one's assets in time of war. Aside from the estate in Germany, which you now inherit in full, the remainder of his cash and movable assets were either smuggled out of Germany or gotten out by legal means and now repose in a safe deposit box in a bank in this country to your benefit."

He found the paper he was seeking and drew it out from the rest. "Your father's last will and testament. I will relay to you only the substance. 'To my beloved daughter and only surviving heir I bequeath my ancestral home at Ehingen and all its lands and possessions. Unto her I also bequeath all funds, family jewels, and heirlooms which now lie in my name at the Bank of England and at the firm of Watkins and

Witt for her future use, with the exception that from
these funds I bequeath to the following members of
my staff and retainers of long service . . .'" He
paused in his reading. "I don't believe you are interested in that now. The figures are all nominal, and
well deserved, I assume."

I agreed, and he continued, skipping down a few
lines. " 'In addition to the above-noted items be-
queathed for my daughter's sole use, she is also to become possessor of trust funds established and maintained in England by both her mother and myself.
These trust funds and their dividends and income
are to remain in her sole possession and control until
the time of her death, not to be considered any part of
any marriage agreement which she may enter into,
and at the time of her death, any remains thereof
shall pass immediately unto her offspring to be di-
vided equally between them, and in the event there
are no offspring, shall revert directly back to the estate and holdings at Ehingen for their maintenance
and upkeep.'

"That is the gist of it," he concluded. "Of course,
these documents are at your disposal to read in full
at your convenience. All are perfectly legal and pro-
bated. Your father's solicitors have delivered to me
an accurate accounting of all this in pounds and shillings, aware that the mere reading of your father's
will hardly gives you clarification of your true holdings." He withdrew another group of parchment
sheets and began in a clerical voice: "Estates at
Ehingen with land and holdings—value indetermi-
nate in English currency but believed considerably
over £800,000; cash assets held in account Baron
Karl von Mantz at Bank of England—£500,000; family jewels and other deposited heirlooms—£250,000;
trust fund set up through Baroness Alisha von
Mantz, nee Lady Alisha Delacourt—annual income

£15,000; trust fund set up through Baron Karl von Mantz—annual income £30,000."

As he looked up at me, his eyes could hardly fail to see the confusion and incomprehension in my own at the staggering sums he was rattling off. In modern-day currency, each of the figures could be doubled to arrive at the equivalent in American dollars. I could only guess at their phenomenal buying power in an earlier, uninflated currency.

"Needless to say, Baroness, you are more than a wealthy lady. A princess to the throne of England could hardly be worth more. You see now why I remarked last evening that with your wealth, you would be sure to attract notice at Almacks. Every fortune hunter in England and on the Continent, were these facts revealed, would be at your feet looking for the blessings of your hand and your income." At the dismayed look on my face, he added, "Perhaps I am too direct, but these truths should be brought home to you, for your own protection."

There was nothing I could say. Imposter that I was, I hadn't any right to the inheritance in the first place; to comment on it would have been absurd.

Seeing that I had nothing to contribute beyond my wide-eyed look at him, he spoke again on a softer note. "There is more to it than this reading. There will be terms to be worked out, papers to be signed, and the disposition of your various assets to be determined before you can proceed either back to New York or on to Germany. Might I advise against the latter, by the way? Things are yet uncertain in Europe, and I feel for your safety it would be wiser to avoid traveling to Bavaria at the present time. I will see, of course, that all is looked after in your absence."

"How do you propose to do that?" I couldn't help inquiring.

"I have connections and men in my confidence who will be happy to oversee the estate and ensure that naught of your possessions comes to harm."

"I could not do that myself?" In the back of my mind I realized that I was going beyond the limits of playing a part; I was reacting as though I *was* the baroness and not her imposter. But I couldn't stop myself.

"You are a woman, Baroness," he replied in a dampening voice. "I think you will have to admit that in a troubled situation such as the present one you are not as able as a man to overcome unexpected difficulties."

"I believe I have the right to know precisely what is going on."

"And you shall."

But when such sums of money were involved, was it wise to trust anyone? Then again, this inheritance was really of no concern to me. It was only some ingrained sense of decency in me that made me want to safeguard the real baroness; we were sisters in this strange adventure.

"I have arranged an appointment for you with your father's solicitors," Justin continued, "for tomorrow afternoon. I will escort you, of course, and bring the necessary documents. I do not believe there is anything else we have to discuss this morning, except that I would repeat my admonition that you not go about London advertising the heiress you are. You do not know this tonnish world and will not be prepared for what you will encounter. Go with my wife and entertain yourself—but beware of ears and tongues, and guard what you say."

"I've been used to looking after myself to some extent in New York," I said airily.

He peered at me, lids dropping slightly over his observant eyes. "Might I remind you, Baroness . . .

behavior found acceptable in that wilderness of yours might not be deemed so in this civilized land. Women in this country have the sense to know their shortcomings in matters that can only be beyond their ability to handle. I trust you will see their wisdom and follow that example."

I stared at him, biting back the retort that sprang to my lips, as I remembered this wasn't my world; I wasn't dealing with a modern man indoctrinated in women's rights.

He was on his feet, towering over me, handsome and imposing, handing me the will and the accounting. "Read them at your leisure, but as they are the only copies I have, take care."

"You can be sure of that. I shall return them to you this afternoon."

For a moment his eyes remained glued to my face, probing. Then he inclined his head. "A pleasant afternoon, Marlena."

"And you."

As I left the room, I wondered what it was about the man that sparked the conflicting emotions within me—on the one hand a smoldering anger; on the other a strong magnetic attraction. I knew I should remain a distinterested bystander and not entangle myself in the lives of these people. But already it was growing difficult to remain uninvolved, particularly where Justin Pemberton was concerned.

I was back in my room only a few minutes, my thoughts whirling at the further complications to my plight, when there was a knock on the door and Jane entered carrying a small beaded bag. "Your reticule, Baroness. The groom found it while cleaning the carriage."

It was a small handbag, possibly left behind by the real baroness the evening before, just as I'd lost my own bag on the plane as I embarked on this journey through time. If so, then the baroness *had* been in the carriage. How odd that the driver seemed not to have noticed the difference in our appearance when he'd reached Warringwood House and a strangely dressed woman had emerged.

I took the bag from Jane's outstretched hand. "Thank you. With all the confusion last night, I did not even miss it."

"Is there anything you wish me to do, Baroness, now I'm here?"

"No. I was just thinking of going down to have lunch with Lady Caroline. Do you know if she has eaten yet?"

"It's her habit to take her meal half after noon."

"I have time then. I shall ring later if I need you, Jane."

The maid smiled, and dropped a curtsy. I went to the dressing table to straighten my hair, placing the reticule on the wood surface. Then, hoping it might contain something interesting, I loosened the drawstrings and searched within. My fingers touched on several feminine articles before they found some folded sheets of paper tied with string. I pulled them out and saw that the bundle contained the letter from Justin Pemberton the baroness had mentioned in her diary, and a letter from her attorney in New York. Justin's letter was what I'd expected; written in a forceful hand, the language abrupt and domineering. I stored them away in the desk drawer, then left again for the lower reaches of the house.

I found Lady Caroline in the morning room. A cold meal had been set out on the table before the windows. "So," she greeted me, "I see you are no worse for wear for your encounter with my husband. Did all go well?"

"We went over the important matters of the es-

tate, and there are some papers I have to read and return to him this afternoon. Can you spare me an
hour so I might put that task behind me, Caroline?"

"I do not see why not. We are not fixed to visit
Lady Sefton until three. Though surely there is no
reason for you to rush through your reading; Justin
could not object to your having these papers beyond
this afternoon."

"I told him I'd return them this afternoon, and I
like to keep my word."

"You are not letting him cow you?" she admon-
ished, laughing.

"Of course not."

"Nonetheless, I can see events around this otherwise dull house are about to become very interesting
and enlivening." She smiled. "But for now, let us get
down to luncheon. Wills are such tedious things, in
any event. I do not envy you all that dry business."

"Your husband and I are supposed to go to the solicitors' tomorrow afternoon." I slid a piece of cold
ham onto my plate. "I thought you should know in
case you had made some plans for us."

"We shall go out in the morning, and perhaps for a
jaunt in the park when you return. Do you ride?"

"Ride? Oh . . . yes, I do . . . though I haven't for
several years."

"I ask only out of curiosity. The fact that you are
an equestrienne may delight my husband, since he is
always fretting at me to accompany him, but I despise the sport . . . sitting there so high on a piece of
willful horseflesh with only a tiny bit of leather to
hold you on. No, thank you! I prefer the curricle—and
was thinking of that mode of transportation when I
suggested a jaunt. I am quite good at the reins, if I do
say so myself. We shall set out at five this afternoon.
I must say I look forward to it. It will be a pleasure to
have someone along with whom to chat other than

that immobile-faced groom who always rides behind."

"Your husband generally does not go with you?"

Caroline took a sip of tea and toyed with her food.
She wasn't a good eater, more often moving the food
nervously around her plate than putting it in her
mouth, which was probably the reason for her notable slenderness. "Not often," she replied. "As I have
told you, he does not care for the dalliances of the
monde and at that hour is usually busy elsewhere.
Ah, but I must tell him you ride. Perhaps you can
join him on his morning expeditions."

"I am not that skilled! It has been quite a few years
. . . I would need practice."

"All the better. He delights in instructing others
in the tasks at which he is accomplished." Pushing
her barely touched plate aside, she rose and went
restlessly to the windows. "I wonder if he was serious last evening about his plan to begin escorting us
out in the future."

"He seemed so."

"Yes. Well, we will see." Surprisingly, she didn't
appear very pleased with the prospect.

FOUR

CAROLINE AND I didn't see Justin Pemberton again until late that evening. We had gone to Lady Sefton's. My nervousness at meeting that august lady tied my tongue, but Caroline more than made up for any lack of conversation on my part. Lady Sefton had seemed favorably impressed, and was far more kindhearted and down-to-earth than I'd expected. Afterward Caro took me on an abbreviated tour through Westminster, past Carlton House, the residence of the Prince of Wales, down the Mall alongside St. James's Park to Buckingham Palace. I could recognize it all except for Carlton House, which by the twentieth century had been demolished. But how thrilling to see with my own eyes the London of 1815; to compare it to the old prints, the Cruikshank cartoons I remembered! Now a new life was injected into those old prints and drawings—a veracity, color, and depth.

Later Caroline and I had a quiet dinner by ourselves. Justin had already made plans to have dinner at one of his clubs with some old friends who were in London for only a few days. We were both surprised, therefore, about eight o'clock to look up from our places by the downstairs drawing-room fire and see Justin entering the room and crossing the carpet toward us.

He was elegant in his satin-jacketed evening dress, his dark-golden hair gleaming in the candlelight. So powerful an impression did he make on me, I must have stared. Thankfully, Justin didn't notice; he smiled and went toward his wife.

"Good evening, ladies. I see I find you in good spirits."

It was Caroline who answered, without preamble. "We have had a marvelous time today. And such success! I cannot recall ever having seen our dear Lady Sefton so taken off her stride as when I made Marlena known to her. One look at Marlena's face, and her jaw dropped near to the floor. So diverting! And then to hear her mutter under her breath before introductions had been properly made, 'Why she is quite *beautiful!*' What in heaven's name have you gone about town saying, Justin? That Marlena is a sheep-faced female, well up on the shelf but for her fortune?"

"You know I am not one to blubber such nonsense. I may have mentioned to one or two of my friends the baroness's situation and impending arrival, but I certainly made no comment on her physical appearance, since I myself had not yet met our guest."

"And in your odd comments you did not perhaps also hint that you were not delighted with your post as executor and temporary guardian, since, as she was well past the age of innocence, the baroness should be quite capable of managing her affairs herself?"

"I would not have put it so bluntly."

"You would have put it precisely that bluntly,"

she said mischievously, "for those were almost the exact words you uttered to me not two months ago in this very room!"

"Touché, Caro. The baroness gets an increasingly favorable impression of me with each syllable that escapes your lips."

"If I had known what havoc I was creating in your life," I broke in, addressing Justin, "I would have been more than happy to stay in New York and save myself as well a considerable inconvenience." The memory of our morning's meeting was still fresh in my mind.

"My wife exaggerates."

"Your wife speaks the truth."

"I will admit to being somewhat put out when I was informed I was executor, but this is not news to you, Baroness."

"Certainly not. Earlier you were quite explicit in discussing the matter with me."

"I believe we will both contrive to deal tolerably with the situation." He went to the rose satin wingbacked chair opposite us and sat down. "So it would appear you have both had a full day."

"Quite," said Caroline. "After visiting Lady Sefton, I took Marlena on a short drive to see Carlton House, St. James's, and the Palace. She expressed an interest."

His eyes swung toward me. "You were favorably impressed?"

"I was."

"Then you are not of a mind to board the next ship back to New York?"

"You should know as well as I that my hands are tied for now."

"Perhaps that will not much longer be the case."

"Why, she has only arrived," Caroline protested. "Whatever can you be thinking of! And I have such plans for the two of us. By the by, Justin, it appears Marlena is a horsewoman."

"Are you? Then you might enjoy accompanying me in the park one morning." I saw a spark of interest in his eyes.

"I'm afraid I would embarrass myself. I'm out of practice."

"Easily remedied. I pride myself on my stables and have several good quiet mounts until you have your seat back. Tomorrow morning, shall we say? I warn you that I rise quite early. Can you meet me at half past eight in the front hall?" His tone left no room for argument. He'd decided we would ride; and so it would be.

"Very well." I swallowed hard, but decided I'd face tomorrow morning when it came.

"Settled, then." Smoothing his pants over his thighs, though it was impossible to see where there were any wrinkles in the skintight cloth, he rose. "I will leave you ladies to your conversation. I have a few matters to take care of in my study. Good night to you both."

As promised, I was in the front hall to meet him at half past eight—earlier, in fact, because it was several minutes before I looked up to see his elegant form coming down the stairs.

"Ah, Marlena, well met. You are prompt to the point of making me appear late. The horses should be ready. Shall we go?"

He led me toward the back of the house, out a door that opened beyond the wall surrounding the garden, and into a narrow stableyard. A groom was standing holding the reins of two horses: one a huge chestnut stallion, uneasy and stamping; beside him a more petite gray mare, ears perked up at our approach.

"Come, I will give you a leg," he said, directing me toward the gray. The pangs of uncertainty I felt increased tenfold when I saw the saddle on the mare's back. How stupid of me not to have remembered I'd be expected to ride sidesaddle, a technique in which I had no experience. Not daring to let him see my fear, I let him hoist me in the air, and landed, amazingly, just as I was supposed to—my right leg gripped around the pommel, my left finding the stirrup. He vaulted onto his own mount and, without giving me a moment to catch my breath, headed off down the mews.

The narrow cobblestoned alley came out on Park Lane opposite the boundaries of Hyde Park. I was amazed to see how much larger the park was now than my last remembrance of it; and Park Lane too was different. It was no more than a small avenue bordering the green expanse—barely recognizable in comparison to the four-laned, grass-islanded highway it had become by the twentieth century. We walked our horses toward the park gate nearest Rotten Row.

Thankfully, since it meant fewer distractions, the park was sparsely populated at that hour of the morning, the air dewy fresh. Holding his prancing mount firmly in hand, Justin kept the pace slow, and as we followed one of the paths under the trees, he turned and gave me an assessing glance. "Let off on the reins a bit. She'll not bolt with you."

The mare moved up beside his stallion. "Better," he nodded. "Now I do not have to crane my neck round to speak with you. The company is pleasant for a change."

"I thought you enjoyed your solitude, my lord."

"Whatever gave you that impression?"

"Oh, I don't know . . . various things."

"You are rather hasty in your judgments. I *do* enjoy the company of others on occasion." His look was almost mocking. "But perhaps my wife has instilled in you this misconception? Since she does not wish to ride, she lets it be thought I never ask."

"She only mentioned her fear of horses."

"Which she makes no attempt to overcome." Though his words seemed harsh, his tone softened the impact.

"When you are that afraid of something, it is difficult to put the fear out of your mind. . . . She has told me she has interests you do not share."

The fair brows snapped down. "May I inquire what business it is of yours?"

"I'm sorry. I should not have spoken."

He made no response to this, but looked out stiffly into the distance and watched the mist rising off the grass. "So you like what you have seen thus far of London?"

"Very much. It is all quite fascinating, and the parks so beautiful."

Unadorned by the curly-brimmed top hat that I noticed was part of the costume worn by the few other horsemen we passed, his golden hair gleamed in the sunlight. The glimmer caught my eye and drew it down to the evenness of his tanned features—the strong chin; the determined mouth; the faint creases of worry in his cheeks, which hinted at a more vulnerable soul hidden by his shell of aloofness.

"View this one a few hours later in the day, and you will have cause to retract those words. There is such a throng of bodies, you cannot see the grass. Do you prefer the countryside?"

"As much as I enjoy the excitement of city life, after a while I feel closed in by all the buildings and the stone and the humanity."

"The very reason I have always chosen this ungodly hour to ride, when there is nothing but air and space about me. If you are with us for any length of time, I should like to show you Pemberton, my family's ancestral estate in Sussex. I think you would enjoy it—the rolling Sussex downs; the waters of the Channel in the distance, which change with the weather in mood and texture and color; the sea breezes; the miles of green parkland; the ripe fields. And the house itself, the home of my ancestors, is a sprawling Tudor masterpiece. As a boy I thought my life idyllic and saw no other future except that of continuing in my father's footsteps, living out my days on the land, perpetuating the tradition of centuries. Life, however, does not always go as one plans."

His eyes when he looked at me were too serious, too intent. I pulled my own away, conscious of a certain quickening of my pulse.

"Let us canter a bit," he said abruptly. "My stallion can endure this slow pace for only so long." He barely waited for me, heeling his horse forward, taking it for granted I was skilled enough to follow. Ten years before I would have been, but with my muscles out of condition, my seat unconfident in the unaccustomed sidesaddle, I had to concentrate hard just to stay aboard. My mare, in any case, had taken the decision out of my hands, as she bolted forward after the stallion.

I don't know exactly what happened then. I thought I saw a small animal dart out from the bushes; the next minute the mare was shying violently, rearing up in fear. I wasn't prepared. My foot slipped from the stirrup, and even the leg wrapped around the pommel wasn't enough to hold me. I felt myself falling backward, rushing through the air to hit the hard gravel path.

The breath was knocked from my lungs, and stars gathered in wild red array before my eyes. I couldn't move. I heard the thud of hoofbeats rushing away;

then hoofbeats approaching. I couldn't lift my head to see; I couldn't move out of the way. But the hoofbeats stopped abruptly. There were long legs beside me; strong arms gripping my shoulders; a voice telling me to lie still. The numbness was gone, but a terrible pain in my lower back replaced it. Hot tears rushed up behind my eyelids. I opened my eyes and saw Justin's face.

"Do not move," he ordered. "Stay still. Where is the pain?"

"My . . . back."

"Can you move your legs?"

I nodded, sending a tear down my cheek. "Let me try to sit."

His crouched form leaned closer; his hands held more firmly to my shoulders. "No, wait a bit. See if the pain subsides."

"Stupid of me."

"I saw nothing until your mare came tearing by at full gallop. What happened?"

"Some animal . . . came from the bushes."

"And she shied?"

"Yes." The pain was subsiding. He could read it in my expression.

"Could you not control her? I thought you were a horsewoman."

"I assure you, it is very easy to lose your skill when you have not been on the back of a horse for ten years!"

"You should have told me that when I proposed we set off at a canter."

"If you will recall, you gave me little opportunity! Could I sit now?"

"Lean on my arm," he said shortly, and began gradually lifting my shoulders.

There was nothing but cool irritation in our gazes as they locked, our faces almost level. But his body

was warm . . . ever so warm where he held me
pressed against his chest. I felt the heat; I felt his fingers tighten on my arm.

Just then there was a shout. An elegantly attired
gentleman approached on horseback, the reins of my
mare in hand. His hat was tipped rakishly on his
thick black hair; his manner was assured, self-
confident. His features were sharp but extremely
attractive—from the glittering dark eyes to the
strong chin and full-lipped mouth.

"Ho, there!" he called. "This your animal? Found
her around the bend with her reins dragging and
presumed there was some mishap."

As Justin looked up and set eyes on the stranger, I
was surprised to see his expression harden.

"Why, Warringwood," said the black-haired gentleman with a grin. "I did not recognize you at first. I
gather the lady took a fall."

"That she did." Justin's tone was curt. He immediately returned his attention to me as I tried to get to
my feet. It took me a few moments to straighten my
spine and square my shoulders, a sharp twinge in my
back accompanying each movement. I hid the pain
from Justin and smiled. "I should be all right now."

He helped me a few steps. I was far from steady.

"Is the lady fit enough to mount?" inquired the
black-haired gentleman, a gleam of bold interest in
his eyes as he surveyed my disheveled appearance.
His brows lifted, and his lips twisted in amusement.
"It does not appear to me she is."

"If you will allow me to escort her to that bench, I
will be happy to take the mare off your hands."

"I was not implying there was any hurry. I certainly have no urgent business calling me at this
hour of the morning."

By then Justin had desposited me on the bench
and was striding back to get the mare. I wondered at

his barely civil response to the other gentleman. Who was the stranger? He certainly appeared respectable enough, aside from that bold stare he'd given me, and he knew Justin by name.

I picked up a few terse words of their conversation as Justin collected the mare. "My thanks for your assistance, milord," he said, though there was nothing hospitable in his tone. "I trust we have not troubled you."

"Trouble? Not at all, Warringwood. Rather a diversion, I would say, from my usual morning's routine." Again the dark eyes gleamed in my direction.

Justin took the reins. "Good day, then."

The gentleman inclined his head briefly. "Do keep an eye on the lady. Too pretty a thing to be tossed in the dust." And with a carefree lift of his hat, he turned and cantered away, demonstrating his excellent seat and control of the stallion beneath him.

Justin returned quickly to my side. His lips were tight with irritation. "How are you?"

"Better. I shall survive, I think."

"Well enough to start back?"

I eyed the mare, and swallowed.

"The only remedy is to get back up and ride again immediately."

"I know *that*. Will you give me a leg?"

"It was only a freakish thing today," he said, suddenly mollifying in his manner

"I should have been prepared."

I let him lead me to the mare and help me up. He mounted in turn and started toward the park exit. I was intensely curious about the black-haired stranger and Justin's attitude; but Justin didn't seem of a mind to enlighten me as he sat silently frowning in the saddle. Finally I asked.

"Who was that man? You seemed awfully rude to him."

"No more than he deserves."

"Oh? I thought it was very kind of him to bring back the mare."

"I will thank you not to question my actions, Baroness!"

"I was not questioning your actions. It is just that he did appear to be a gentleman."

"On the contrary. The man is a rake and libertine—not the type with whom I would wish to have you associate. But if you must know, he is the marquis of Radford. We have not been on good terms for years—since the time his lecherous behavior toward the wife of one of my closest friends—and his own supposed close friend as well—nearly ruined her good name and destroyed what had been a happy marriage. Though it never became a full-fledged scandal, my friend learned of the affair and confided in me. When it blew apart, Radford beat a hasty retreat to the Continent. Yet, where another respectable man might have hung his head in shame for so betraying a friendship, on his return to England a year later, Radford showed not the slightest contrition, taking up his licentious habits with more fervor than before, flaunting his actions in their faces, rubbing in the hurt, so that his former friend felt he had no course but to remove himself and his wife to his country seat. No, I cannot like the marquis."

There was such a deep scowl between his brows, I didn't dare probe further. "I see."

We'd reached the mews behind the house when he turned to me unexpectedly. "We shall ride again tomorrow morning."

"We shall?"

"You require practice. Now I realize that, I am more than able to assist you."

"It might be decent of you to ask if I want your assistance."

"I am offering only because I feel you will benefit from the instruction," he retorted sharply.

"Well, as I have already requested, do not let me burden you. I can get along well enough in London without being an expert horsewoman."

"I do not accept burdens I do not wish to assume, Baroness." His voice was pure ice. "If I had not enjoyed your company, I would not have suggested a repeat engagement."

I smiled to myself, turning my head slightly so he couldn't see my response.

We were in the stableyard, and one of Justin's grooms had hurried out to the head of Justin's stallion; another to take my bridle.

Justin's voice rang out far more harshly than was necessary: "*I* will take care of the baroness. Wait inside until I call you."

After the two men scurried away, Justin turned on me. "Well, I *have* asked you. I am awaiting your answer!"

"I suppose I do need practice."

"Am I to take that as an affirmative?"

"You may."

"Then I will meet you in the hall at the usual time. And pray do not forget our appointment this afternoon." Dismounting, he came around to help me; then, his back rigid as an iron rod, he strode off with the horses, leaving me standing alone on the gravel.

What a difficult man he was—one moment quite open and almost warmly conversational; the next a proud, cold dictator. I shouldn't have let it matter to me one way or the other. What was I but a temporary trespasser in his life? But deep inside I knew it did matter, I wanted to learn more of this handsome, unpredictable Lord Warringwood.

FIVE

THE VISIT TO the attorneys' offices that afternoon brought us across town to a section of London I hadn't seen the day before with Caroline. We left behind the elegance and wealth of Westminster and entered the bustling city. I'd seen this section of London, of course, during my normal visit in the twentieth century, but this was so different. It was an indescribable experience to see firsthand a world that my own contemporaries had only been able to read about in history books. I wasn't prepared for the picturesque beauty of the old narrow streets bordered by narrow timber-and-stucco fronted buildings—the London that a few years later Dickens was to describe so vividly. Nor was I prepared for the hurly-burly of pedestrian and horse-drawn traffic: the street hawkers, the flower sellers, the pie men, the toothless old women crying out, "Fresh fish, fresh today, m'ladies and gents. Give 'em a look, will ye." I saw urchins in rags and bare feet, grimy faces begging coins at the carriage windows in a flippant and unhumble way. I smelled the odor of the open gutters and the refuse strewn out of view in the littered back alleys; heard the racket of carriage wheels on cobblestone, the lumbering of heavier dray wagons; the neighing of horses and the barking of stray, skinny dogs. I saw the varieties of clothing differentiating the poor underfed from the wealthier, modishly dressed businessmen and "Cits" going about their errands with little concern for the social contradictions surrounding them. What a blend it was—what a conglomeration of humanity and noises and smells to stimulate the emotions!

The law offices were located on a side lane so narrow it barely had the right to be termed a street. Ancient buildings rose on each side, blocking the light and giving the impression it was early evening rather than the sunny afternoon it was. The coachman dropped us at the door of a bow-windowed structure and then proceeded on up the lane. Justin had told him to return in an hour's time.

I'd already decided to be no more than the attentive observer during this legal session. I'd have to show some reaction to the proceedings, of course, if Justin's suspicions weren't to be aroused, but I was afraid of opening my mouth and saying the wrong thing, giving away my twentieth century sophistication about legal matters.

A clerk was perched on a high stool behind a desk. He merely looked up as we approached; but once Justin had told him who we were, he scurried off toward the back rooms, returning with a distinguished man I guessed to be fiftyish. The latter gentleman, Mr. Watkins, the senior partner of the firm, ushered us to his own domain in the back, where we were joined by a junior colleague of Watkins's and sat down to business.

The meeting took close to an hour. At its end I'd learned little more of the baroness's inheritance than I already knew. The solicitors read the will in full, confirmed the monetary value of the estate and other assets, and affirmed the validity of the codicil outlining the terms of the year's waiting period and the appointment of Lord Warringwood as guardian to the baroness. Here, of course, Justin interrupted, asking whether, since he was already married and obviously ineligible, this portion of the will could not be broken; the baron would assuredly not have put his daughter through such needless inconvenience and awkwardness had he known.

The legal brows flicked, the lips pursed, the fingers drummed together. No, they were afraid there was nothing to be done. Although the baron had hopes that my lord and the baroness would one day be joined in marriage, the year's wait did not hinge on this event alone. It remained a clause of the will regardless. Yes, it was unfortunate, and they understood the baroness's distress and the inconvenience to His Lordship, but there was nothing they could do. And, after all, a part of the year was already gone—only nine months were left—and surely the baroness could find many pleasures to amuse her in England during that time. . . .

Justin argued the point for several futile minutes. It took no great powers of observation to see he was furious. Did this mean, he asked, that he was tied to the role of guardian until the year's end? Guardian to a twenty-four-year-old woman well able to care for herself?

Yes; unfortunately, they were afraid, it was so.

But that was preposterous! Justin's fist slammed down on the desk; the color was high in his cheekbones. The two solicitors drew together for support, uttering their excuses with a simultaneous breath. There was nothing they could do, no way to break the will; but if there was any other matter in which they could assist His Lordship . . .

At these words, Justin grabbed my hand and fairly dragged me behind him in his furious haste to be out of their offices. His manner bearlike, he led me to the waiting carriage, climbed in behind me, and slammed the door shut with such force I thought he'd snapped the hinges.

"Home!" he yelled up to the driver, then withdrew to his corner of the seat to stare glumly out the window. The scowl on his brow was so deeply etched, I wouldn't have interrupted his thoughts if my life had depended on it.

Back at Upper Brook Street, we'd barely stepped into the hall before Caroline enthusiastically greeted us. A white envelope was clutched in her fingers.

"It has arrived, Marlena, already—your voucher from Lady Sefton. Even I did not expect it to come so soon. Oh, there is so much to do . . . not that we will plan our visit until a week is out. It would not do for you to appear too hasty in making your formal bow to the ton, but five days should be sufficient to flame their curiosity—and, of course, we will have to decide upon a gown . . . perhaps a new one from Madam Fere . . . or will there be time?" Her forehead crinkled briefly, then cleared. "My, I have not asked how your trip to the solicitors went."

"You will be delighted to know, Caro," her husband said, "that the baroness will be with us for some time yet—until early March, is it not?" The glance he gave me was almost lethal.

Confused by his tone, Caroline looked back and forth between the two of us, "Indeed? Until March? But that is marvelous! All the things we shall do! But first we must make plans for Almacks. Are you free? We shall go to your room to see which gowns you have that might be suitable. Justin, do you need us?"

"As a matter of fact, Caro, I should like a few words with Marlena in my study."

"Now? Well, if you must. Then I shall see you later, Marlena? Oh, and Justin, you have not forgotten this evening? We are all to dine at the Laughtons'. Only a small gathering of about twenty guests, but I thought it a perfect sort of affair to introduce Marlena. Lord and Lady Winthrop will be there, and the duke of Carlisle, with whom you are so friendly. You will escort us?"

"It would appear rather unseemly if I did not."

"We are to be there at eight."

"I will be ready." He turned toward me. "Marlena?" With a sweep of his hand in the direction of the study, he indicated that I should precede him.

Nothing was said until the study door was closed firmly behind us, but after pointing me toward a chair, which I took, he strode restlessly about the room, finally halting before me, legs braced and hands behind his back.

"I will not mince words, Marlena. This whole affair infuriates me, and unfortunately now there are a few additional details we will have to settle between us."

"I am no more pleased about it than you, but I do not know what you expect me to do."

"Have I asked you to do anything? I have brought you here only to discuss our obligations to each other under this guardianship—a discussion which would not have been necessary had the terms of the will been broken—as to any sound and logical mind they should have been."

"I am listening."

"And no pertness from you, miss!"

"Is it obligatory for you when you are angry to take it out on every individual around you?"

"My anger is my own concern!"

"Very well, then go tear that pillow to shreds—but do not talk to me this way, when I have done nothing to warrant it except to be thrown into this most unfortunate set of circumstances with you!"

"So we speak in plain terms. Good! At least we have our feelings out in the open and know precisely where we stand."

"You realize," I flashed back angrily, saying more than I intended, "that I am perfectly capable of visiting the solicitors and taking care of my financial matters myself, so you can rid yourself of that obligation."

"It would be unheard of. No woman has the understanding of such matters without guidance."

"Then I am like no woman you have met before! I am completely capable and will manage my affairs myself."

"Your father's intentions in the matter were clearly set out. I am to be responsible for you and all the dealings of the estate until the anniversary of your father's death, and although I am not delighted with the undertaking, I am a man who carries his responsibilities out to the letter."

"And I'm telling you I am removing that responsibility from your shoulders. That should make you happy. Since you want no part of me, you can give me a letter saying that I have your permission to act in my own behalf—"

"I will do no such thing!" he roared, his eyes wide with disbelief.

"For a man anxious to be rid of his burden, you certainly make a loud protest."

In the back of my mind, I knew I was reacting too strongly. I wasn't the baroness, and had no right to interfere. I should have kept my mouth shut and let him have his way, but his attitude infuriated me.

His face was dark with anger and frustration. He clenched his hands, and I thought for a moment he was going to find some inanimate object to smash against the wall. Instead he held himself firmly in check, setting his jaw that much more tightly. "Now to the subject of your allowance," he breathed harshly. "An ample one has been set aside for you out of the estate. A certain sum, adequate to your immediate needs, will be turned over to me each month, and I will place it at your disposal. The sum is two hundred pounds, which, considering you will be living under my roof and fed from my table, should be sufficient for any furbelows that might tempt you in the coming months."

"Suppose I should wish to make a more extensive expediture—such as a lease on my own house here in London?"

"What?" His eyes nearly popped from his head. "Your own house! Out of the question! You are an unattached female with respectable connections who are only too willing to accommodate you during your visit. How would it appear if you went out to set up your own household?"

"What you mean is how would *you* appear if I left your hospitably welcoming door! However, do not worry about it. I was only testing my restrictions. I do think, though, I might consider buying a nice saddle horse."

"After this morning's adventure," he snapped, "I wonder at your desire. However, my stables are amply stocked."

"But should I in the future find something more to my taste, will the money be at my disposal?"

"I suppose—but I reserve the right to last judgment in any purchase you make."

"Do you? Does that include the purchase of a new gown or a new hat?" I said innocently.

"You are impossible!"

"Are there any other restrictions I should be made aware of, my lord? I take it my social activities will be supervised as well?"

"I have no taste or inclination in that area. I am hoping you will behave with a certain decorum, and my wife is a good enough judge of what is socially acceptable."

"I cannot tell you how much that delights me, because I get along far better with her than with you!"

Rising then, I walked the few steps toward him with my hand extended.

"What is this?" he asked.

"I just thought now that we had settled all the points of our agreement, we should shake hands on it."

"You are overdoing it a bit, no?" Yet he brought his hand forward to take mine.

I returned his firm clasp. The warmth of his fingers as they held mine, and the pure, angry vibrancy in his eyes as he looked at me and we sealed our bargain, left a strange pulsing in my veins. I didn't understand him, but I knew that if my circumstances had been different, I would have been mightily attracted to this man. I shrugged the thought away, pushed it from my mind. Better to deal in realities.

SIX

DIFFICULT AS IT WAS at times during the next few exciting days, I was learning to adjust to my new environment. I was growing used to a life-style that could not always compare favorably with my previous existence: the new sounds and smells; the human imperfections that technology was not around to remedy, including teeth that were often far from flawlessly aligned and sometimes showed obvious signs of decay.

Clothing was made of natural fibers that wrinkled easily, stained quickly, and did not always fall in as smooth lines as synthetic material—but then again, the apparel was better cut and sewn.

Personal hygiene—or the lack of it—bothered me. People didn't place much importance on the daily bath or shower. They didn't have the facilities to do it, with indoor plumbing still a thing of the future, and they seemed to accept that certain body odors were native to man. Of course, among the upper classes cleanliness was more routinely practiced. Gradually I got used to the differences; almost forgot, after a while, that this wasn't what I'd lived

with before. During my first days in London, I asked
for and enjoyed a daily hot bath before the fire, but
the ordeal of the poor maid lugging pails of hot water
up three flights of stairs, and later carrying the same
number of pails of cold and dirty water down, pricked
my conscience. I wasn't a born-and-bred aristocrat
who could think of servants as a lower class of hu-
mans whose purpose in life was to wait on me; certainly I found it almost beyond my ability to affect
the superior attitude toward them that came so naturally to Caroline and Justin. I cut the bathing days
down to every other, and luxuriated in them as long
as the weather was fairly cool, settling for sponge
baths from the basin in between.

The chamber pot was something else again. From
the moment I found it under my bed, I pushed it into
the farthest corner of the room, hidden behind a
screen. But when I stopped to think that everyone
around me was subjected to the same discomfiture,
who was I to consider myself above it?

I still often felt like pinching myself to convince
myself I was awake, that what was happening
around me was real. As unsure as I was about my
abilities to continue the charade, no one seemed to
doubt that I was the real baroness. I practiced my
role studiously, mimicking speech patterns and
manners; rigorously drilling myself on the subjects I
should avoid if I wasn't inadvertently to let slip some
knowledge about my real past. I prided myself on
how well I was doing, yet was frightened to realize
how easy at times it was to lose sight of my own identity.

There were many things I didn't know. Nothing in
my background had prepared me for this world of nobility and wealth—the protocol, the proper form of
address and behavior to adopt in meeting people
from different levels of the aristocracy. Table man-

ners were different from what I had known: the handling of the silverware, the course after course of rich food, oftentimes served in combinations that made no sense to me. I'd never learned how to pour an English tea, nor was I practiced in the politesse of drawing-room conversation. I constantly had to remind myself that most unmarried young women of the early nineteenth century did not discuss politics, or any other topic that might betray a shred of intelligence; they were simpleminded when it came to financial and legal matters, blushed to the roots of their hair at the mildest sexual innuendo in conversation, and could not even call men's pants by their proper name, but must refer to them as "inexpressibles."

It irked me that I had so little chance to exercise my intelligence. Back in New York, as I rose through the ranks in an investment brokerage firm, my mind had always been challenged. I'd taken the demands on my capabilities for granted, and thrived on the stimulation. I was better versed in economics, the intricacies of the marketplace, stocks, bonds, and foreign exchange than were many of the polished Englishmen that now surrounded me. Yet all this had to be hidden from a society that expected me to tax my mind no further than the selection of ribbons for a new hat, or which dress to wear to an afternoon tea; while a male—Justin Pemberton, in particular—took control of my life, making all major decisions for me as though I were an addlepated idiot.

This same polite society wore another face: one of constant gambling debts, intrigues, affairs, mistresses, and other infidelities—all of which sordidness was supposed to be ignored, to be discussed only behind an artfully plied fan or closed bedroom door. I was placed in the awkward position of knowing precisely what was going on, but having to pretend to an innocence I'd left behind when I graduated from high school in twentieth century America.

Of course, there was a good side to the comparisons I was drawing between the two worlds. Here I was experiencing a slower pace of things, a more leisurely tempo. Being a guest at Warringwood House perhaps contributed to this feeling and set me apart from the less fortunate souls who had to work to put their daily bread on the table; but even the servants in the house seemed relaxed, and happy to give me a smile and a quick "good day" as I passed them in the halls. I felt as though I had embarked on an elaborate vacation—waited on hand and foot, chauffeured in a fine carriage on shopping trips, knowing that there was enough money in my purse to buy whatever I wanted and that, given my credentials, even the most exclusive shop would extend me unlimited credit. There were hours when I could secretly slip into the music room and experiment on the piano. Since no one else in the house was musically inclined, I could be sure of solitude as my fingers followed the notes of the old sheet music or played a more modern melody from memory. And there was time here for reflection. Gone was that harassed feeling of having more to do than I could accomplish in one day; of rushing through each hour with no time to consider just where it was getting me.

The unsettling thoughts that had surrounded me until the time of my departure for London no longer had the power to debilitate me. I still felt a terrible loss when I thought of my father's death, but I was learning to come to terms with it . . . building again. A new strength surged through my veins, perhaps because I needed it: in this strange world I could never be sure from one day to the next what the future held in store for me.

* * *

There was my first visit to Almacks to prepare for, and Caroline began pestering me to decide on a dress, the style of my hair, new shoes. She briefed me in detail on the notable persons who might be present, to whom I should cater and whom I could afford to ignore; what behavior was accepted under the rigid rules of Almacks—how many dances with each gentleman, and on and on.

I spent a busy hour each afternoon of one week in one of the small drawing rooms with a dancing teacher. Caroline was surprised when I'd mentioned to her that I'd need some instruction in the popular dances, but after I explained to her that New York society couldn't possibly be as up-to-date as London's, she understood and hired a Mr. Tidborough to rectify matters. Fortunately, dancing in any style came quickly to me, and soon I had Mr. Tidborough's praise and assurance that I would grace any dance floor in London.

Since I by no means fell into the "blushing miss" category of most first-time Almacks attendees, I had no intention of presenting myself that way. I put my foot down at white muslin, the traditional maidenly dress, determined to choose a gown far more in tune with both my modern background and my personality. In the baroness's wardrobe I'd found a sophisticated concoction of royal blue silk. Its lines were elegant, the long sleeves falling gracefully to my wrists, the material flowing like a waterfall from the high waist to my ankles. Once I'd tried it on and saw how the color and clean lines complimented my natural assets, I knew this would be the dress I'd wear.

That evening Jane dressed me with care. First the lacy undergarments, then the gown dropped gently over my head and fastened up the back, each silk loop over each silk-covered button. Then my hair, shining clean and shimmering with deep-red highlights, was piled on my head, a few soft curls left around my face and neck. For jewelry I wore only long sapphire earrings from the baroness's collection. A warm, rosy flush of excitement was high on my cheekbones and sparkled in my dark eyes. I'd touched my lashes lightly with mascara, and they seemed long and silky against the whiteness of my skin—a whiteness that swelled seductively above the low-cut bodice of the vibrantly blue gown.

Justin and Caroline were waiting in the front hall as I descended the stairs. Caroline was lovely in an ice-green gown that emphasized her ethereal fairness; Justin handsomely distinguished in the dark evening jacket, tight knee breeches, and white stockings. He glanced up. His eyes fastened on me in unconcealed admiration; drifted in deliberate appreciation over the length of me, from my head to my toes. Then the gray-green eyes came to rest again on my face. My knees turned to water. I forgot Caroline; was conscious only of the unexpected current between this man and me. It must have been a full minute before I could recover my poise and walk the rest of the way down the stairs.

I'd heard so much about Almacks—firsthand from Caroline and her friends; secondhand through twentieth century novels. I'd heard of the insipid refreshments, the moderate entertainment, the crush of some of the wealthiest and most influential people in Britain, and knew that it was the exclusivity of the voucher and the ability to show your face among the most select that made the place so sought after.

It was a heady experience for me to walk through the front doors, past the uniformed and powdered footmen; to peer into the main ballroom to see the

crowd of expensively dressed people gathered—a
crowd that was likely to increase until eleven, when
the doors would be firmly closed on any late arrivals.
As the three of us made our way across the room toward the patronesses standing in a group along the
far wall, I was stunned by all the glitter, the elegance. Jewels that dazzled the eye were worn as
carelessly as though they were mere trinkets. My
brain reeled as I heard the names and saw the faces
of people who were the very toast of their era and
would remain well-known personages into the
1980s—Beau Brummel, a suave perfectionist in
stark black and white; Lady Sally Jersey, brilliantly
vivacious; the duke of Wellington, fresh from his victory over Napoleon, making a brief appearance.

Caroline led the way through the crowd, nodding
and smiling to various acquaintances. Her husband
had dropped back to walk beside me, but he too had
many acknowledgments to answer.

As we approached the patronesses, Lady Sefton
greeted us affably and, since she had sent the
voucher to me, introduced me to the other two patronesses at her side. Princess Esterhazy gave me a
searching look from haughty, half-lidded eyes. Beneath her outward politeness, I could sense she
didn't like me, perhaps because I was older and more
sophisticated than the ingenues present; more
likely, Caroline later told me, because the princess
found me too attractive and my unexpected appearance into London society was causing too many comments. I tried not to let her veiled animosity bother
me, and answered with as much assurance as possible the two or three questions she asked about my
family in Germany and what connections we might
have in common. Since I could tell her that a ten-
year stay in New York had put me out of touch with

my relatives and their goings-on, she had no choice but to let the matter rest.

Lady Sally Jersey was something else—a well-preserved and gregarious woman, to say the least. She drew Caroline and me off into conversation for several minutes. Her sharp intelligence and piercing social wit were well known in London, though I'd also been told she could be an implacable adversary if crossed. I survived our talk unscathed, and actually thought from the twinkle in her eye as we parted that I'd made a better than average impression on her.

By now people were coming up to us on both sides, greeting both Caroline and Justin. I heard comments directed to Justin accompanied by firm handclasps, "Warringwood. Good to see your face. Thought tonight would be the dullest of bores. Join me later in the other room . . . I wanted to discuss this latest Whig maneuver." And to Caroline there were female welcomes; airy, frivolous conversations of parties and gowns and hatmakers and *on dits* circulating about fellow members of the elite. It didn't bother me that none of the women made more than the necessary overtures to befriend me. The men I'd been introduced to made up for the lack.

The musicians had tuned their instruments, and the first chords of a country dance were echoing across the room. Couples from either side of the floor moved into position. Thanks to Mr. Tidborough, I wasn't as nervous as I might have been to see Lord Frompton, a young baronet I'd been introduced to earlier, make his way toward me. He was fair haired, of medium height, and plain featured, but, as Caroline confided to me quickly behind her fan, he was one of the best dancers among the ton. His conversation was bright and stimulating, and I was able to respond as easily to it as to his excellent lead. When the dance ended and we walked off the floor together, he complimented me on my gracefulness and asked for a second dance later in the evening.

By now everyone in the room was aware of me. The curious stares were obvious. I saw Caroline's pleased smile, and the steady stare, less than pleased, of her husband.

As people drifted over to speak to us, the questions began. Lady LaFroy, a statuesque matron in her fifties with a rather bad set of teeth, began the assault. Her maroon-turbaned head wagged in disbelief when she heard me confirm that they actually had theater in rustic New York and fashionable shops too, and a certain number of paved streets. Then Viscount Trenton, a slim boy barely out of adolescence, with all of youth's curiosity for foreign places, monopolized my attention for fifteen minutes. He wanted full descriptions of the American wilderness and its inhabitants. Had I actually seen a native redskin? Was it really so dangerous to travel the roadways that one must always carry a pistol? I had trouble hiding my smile and was almost disappointed when he was interrupted by Sir Winsted. This sallow-complexioned and somehow seedy gentleman, though slyly cloaking the nature of his curiosity, pushed to the point of rudeness for details of my financial assets. I stumbled over my answers, not sure how to get rid of him politely, when Justin stepped casually over to place a protective hand on my shoulder.

"Ah, Sir Winsted. How is it we see you here? Last I heard, you were using all your energies in avoiding the ten-percenters. Or have you out-foxed the money-lenders after all?" The words were said in the mildest of tones, but Sir Winsted blanched pure white. Even I, with my limited knowledge of Regency England, knew that no gentleman of character wanted it known that he'd exhausted his credit to the point that he'd had to borrow money from that segment of the London business world known as the ten-percenters. Sir Winsted needed no other encouragement to turn on his heel and disappear into the press of bodies around us.

I looked up at Justin and smiled. "Thank you."

"You are quite welcome. You see, I can serve some useful purpose after all."

Justin remained steadily on watch, always hovering near by, scowling darkly when the single men, who'd by now heard that I was unmarried and rumored to be very "well set" financially, let their flatteries become fulsome.

Caroline drifted off to join a group of her friends. Though actually she, instead of her husband, should have been acting as my chaperone, I saw that she was in a quiet corner, and with her was a tall, handsome man in the bright-red uniform of the Guard. Judging from the apparent intensity of their conversation, I thought he must be a close and longtime friend of hers. Justin had noticed, too, and he didn't seem happy. But I didn't have time to figure out what it meant, because there was another man standing before me, asking for a dance, and I was soon out on the floor doing my best to negotiate the configurations of a country reel.

For the next three dances, I was led out by three successive partners, until finally, my cheeks burning from the exercise, I found Caroline, now alone, and the two of us went to find some refreshments and a place to rest. Justin had left for the anteroom where the gentlemen were gathered. After getting a glass of lemonade, Caroline and I went to another anteroom, where women were seated on couches and chairs. Men drifted in and out or stopped for a moment to talk.

Caroline was complimenting me on my success, telling me the gossip she'd gathered during the past hour.

"You know, I think Thomas Avery was quite impressed with you, and I learned tonight that he's come into a substantial inheritance . . . one of his uncles in the Midlands who found he had some rich coal deposits on his land and leased it for quite a fortune."

"Which was he?" I frowned.

"Marlena, how could you be so unobservant? The red-haired fellow in the canary jacket."

"Oh, him. I thought his striped vest would blind me—red and green with yellow. . . ." I shuddered. "Where do some of these men get their taste? But, of course," I said with a giggle, "it all went so well with his hair."

She looked at me as though I'd lost my mind. "What possible difference can it make what he wore? He's so full in the bank account that *you* could dress yourself in anything you chose. In addition to his uncle's holdings in the Midlands, Thomas himself owns estates in both Kent and Warwickshire."

"Those things do not concern me—"

"Excuse me, ladies."

At the sound of the deep voice, Caroline and I looked up simultaneously to see a beautifully dressed man standing before us, his face darkly tanned, and his hair black as a raven's wing. I couldn't believe my eyes! It was none other than the gentleman from the park—the rake and libertine Justin had warned me against.

"Please forgive me for interrupting what seems to

be a pleasant coze, but I have been most desirous of making this lady's acquaintance. Although I believe we have met, we have not been formally introduced. How are you getting on, Caroline? It's been some time since we last met. I trust I find you and Warringwood well."

"Very well, thank you. You have been out of London, my lord? I've not seen you at any of the gatherings." She seemed momentarily ruffled, her cheeks flushing.

"Just so." Through half-lidded eyes he looked down upon us. "Certain family matters called me off to Wales. You are aware, I believe, that my sister resides there."

"Of course. How is Leticia? It has been an age since we last saw each other."

"Very well. Enlarging her brood with every year and quite content away from the London whirl."

"You must remember me to her."

"I certainly will." He smiled again, displaying unusually fine teeth, their whiteness dramatic against the swarthiness of his skin. He was taller than I'd expected, and firmly muscled, if the fit of his dark jacket across his wide shoulders and around the tautness of his waist was any evidence. He looked to be somewhere in his thirties, and full of life, the creases in his face saying he'd enjoyed it all so far. The dark eyes were studying me with the same bold gleam I remembered.

Caroline suddenly remembered that he'd asked for an introduction, though her voice, when she spoke, seemed hesitant—and no wonder, I thought, recalling the remarks her husband had made to me about this man standing before us.

"Marlena, may I present to you the marquis of Radford. Lord Radford, the baroness von Mantz."

I extended my hand politely. He took it, dropping a light kiss on its back as was the custom. His voice was low. "Your servant, Baroness. It is indeed a pleasure to meet you. May I ask what fortunate occurrence has brought you to our shores?"

"Not fortunate. I've come in order to settle my father's estate, of which Lord Warringwood is executor."

"My condolences on your father's death. Since you are not in mourning, I presume it was not such a recent occurrence?"

"It was, but I do not believe in superficial affectations of grief. I mourn my father in my own, more personal way, as he wanted it."

"For which I can only admire you. I have never been fond of these meaningless conventions which society forces upon us. Your husband is with you?"

"I am not married."

"I see." Who could tell what was going on behind those dark eyes of his?

"You have been living in America?"

And at my amazed expression, he continued. "I wondered at your speech . . . such an unusual combination, and so obviously untinged by the Germanic. Yet it is not quite the same American accent as I've been accustomed to."

"You're acquainted with Americans, my lord?"

"I was there myself some years ago, visiting in New York as well as in some of your Southern cities, and your speech seems rather different, although I cannot quite put my finger upon it."

I could have done that for him, had I dared, simply by telling him that my accent was advanced more than 160 years beyond what he had heard. But I felt startled and upset. Not only had his ear detected the modern inflection in my speech that I'd been trying so hard to disguise, but he'd been to New York in the early 1800s and knew more about the city in that era than I did myself.

"I have spent the last ten years in America . . . in New York with relatives," I answered after a pause. "At the start of the war my father sent me abroad for safety."

"Interesting. Then you can tell me more about that country I so enjoyed on my visit there."

"I should be delighted."

"Ah, I hear the musicians tuning up again." His eyes had not left my face since his opening remarks to Caroline. "Would you be so kind, Baroness, as to honor me with this next dance?"

I didn't know what to do! Knowing Justin's feelings, I felt I should refuse. Yet there were no other gentlemen to whom I'd promised the dance, and to refuse him on any other ground would be obvious rudeness. Besides, the man fascinated me, regardless of what Justin thought. What harm could there be in one dance?

I glanced to Caroline. She was frowning; her fingers were clenched nervously. I gave her a small smile as if to assure her that her worries were unwarranted, then nodded to the marquis. "Delighted, my lord."

Still, I had qualms as I left the anteroom at the marquis's side and crossed the crowded ballroom to the dance floor. Had I been too impulsive in my decision?

The smile he gave me seemed sincere as he led me into the set. I reminded myself that I wasn't naive with men. Forewarned as I was, I certainly could handle myself . . . and any harsh words that Justin might later rain down on me. Just the same, the marquis' opening words were so frank, especially compared to the sugar-coated banalities of the other

tonnish gentlemen with whom I'd danced that night.
"So," he said, without preliminary, his eyes boring
down into me. "The damsel in distress. We meet at
last. Life *is* full of little surprises, is it not? I see my
first impressions are correct, and you are quite the
most interesting vision to enter the London scene in
many seasons."

Despite myself, my cheeks flushed at the blatant
flattery, though I held my eyes steady.

"And not another insipidly boring ingenue either,
if my guess is correct."

"I beg your pardon?"

"I mean that as a compliment. I have the greatest
aversion to feather-brained females just out of the
schoolroom." He paused. "I admit, on meeting you in
the park and knowing Warringwood to be a married
man, to wondering if you might be of a different per-
suasion altogether. You take my meaning?"

"Very well! I am not one of your demimondaines,
nor am I just out of the schoolroom."

"So I have gathered, much to my delight. Wipe
that frown from your brow," he unexpectedly teased.
"It mars the perfection of your looks, and I have not
tried deliberately to offend you. So you have spent
the last ten years in New York . . ."

He was an excellent dancer. He kept a steady flow
of conversation going even as our feet were working
out the steps of the dance. Very soon I forgot my reasons for irritation and was caught up by his witty
cynicism, the fresh unexpectedness of his comments.
We spoke briefly of my history and the circumstances that had brought me to England, but since I
didn't want too many questions in that direction, I
changed the subject to talk of his own background.

"And what can you tell me of yourself, my lord?"

"Call me Radford. My Christian name is Gervais,
though I've been told it does not suit me—not hard

enough for my character. I think I should warn you, by the way, that people are right. My character is not a pretty thing. I am the most dissolute hedonist, wild in my ways, inconsiderate in my habits . . . walking at the very edge of respectability." He grinned, a twinkle in his eye. "You see I do not bother to hide my indiscretions. They are there for the world to see. You should be aware that a close association with me is bound to cause speculation about you."

Completely intrigued that in his own words he was confirming everything Justin had told me about him, I laughed. "Then why are you here tonight? If you are as bad as you say, I cannot believe the ladies who give out the vouchers would let you through their doors."

"Ah, but you see they have no choice. With my wealth, I bring a certain *je ne sais pas quoi.*"

"Ah, but I know very well," I said, mocking him. "Despite your reputation, people see in you a certain excitement."

"Do you think that? Well, at least I have not yet been completely ostracized." His lips turned up reluctantly at the corners, as though he was trying to fight a smile.

"Now that you have told me of all your vices, I want to hear the real things about you."

"Yes, the substantialities. My family is an old one. We trace our roots back to Wales, where we were in power long before the Normans ever invaded these islands. Because of our isolation, we maintained that strength until the fifteenth century. Then came the English, and because we were adaptable to their ways, we found ourselves a niche and a title. We played the politics of the times, and have done the same since. We have mixed blood, been mediators, and in the process increased our holdings, to the point where I am now."

"Why the dark coloring?"

"There are stories of the ancient Phoenicians that came to the shores of Wales to trade for minerals and mix blood with the Celts."

"That was centuries ago."

"I am a throwback, you could say. My sister is fair haired, and her husband, too, though their children are as dark as I. It happens every two or three generations."

"All the more interesting."

"But let us get back to you. What is it I see beneath the surface that makes me curious about you?"

"I could not say."

"You have spent the last ten years in America," he mused. "Perhaps that is the answer."

"Yes, perhaps."

The music ended. He seemed disappointed as he took my arm to lead me away. "I would like another dance, Baroness, if you could fit it into your program."

"I believe I could."

"I will return. There are a number of people here I must see, and then too, I would not want you to appear conspicuous by receiving too much attention from the likes of me."

When the marquis left, I turned to Caroline. There was a scowl on her face.

"You dislike him," I said.

"Have you any idea with whom you have been dancing?" she asked incredulously. "No, of course you would not, since you are new to London—but *that*, Marlena, is the most notorious rake in all of England! He *would* wait for Justin to leave before asking to be introduced to you."

"The marquis told me his reputation was horrible." I didn't add that her husband had said the same. I wanted to hear her opinion.

"He was quite right, and how like him to come out front and tell you such a thing. It is a wonder any doors at all are open to him. His reputation is enough to make any decent woman blanch. . . . yet I cannot say I don't like him. He can, of course, be quite charming—perhaps that is why there are so many hostesses still eager to include him in their invitations."

"Fascinating."

She gave me an anxious look. "I certainly hope you are not taken with him, Marlena. The list of his discarded mistresses is long and famous . . . though I should not be speaking of such things.

"Women do tend to find him irresistible. I remember one young girl in her first season to whom Radford had paid some attention here and there—she actually tore at her own gown and caused a monstrous scene at one of the Cavendishes' balls when he turned his attentions to another woman. His reputation grew to the point mothers began steering their daughters clear of him despite his title and wealth. The man has no shame—parades his mistresses from Covent Garden in the park for all to see. He even brought one as his guest to one of the Jerseys' soirées. Of course, Sally Jersey laughed it off, but others did not. The latest *on dit* a few months back concerned him and Alaine Parsons—the earl of Medwick's wife. That affair almost came to gunpoint, and Alaine made quite a fool of herself, crying her heartbreak all over London and Brighton.

"And hardly any of Radford's other liaisons can be considered aboveboard. He was wealthy to begin with, but began dabbling in trade and shipping to make another fortune. Justin could tell you more about him in that regard than I."

"I do not believe I'd care to ask Justin," I said, and

grinned. Justin had already given me a very good indication of his opinion.

"Nor would I, but do take care for yourself, Marlena."

Which was precisely what I intended to do. Now that I knew so much of the marquis's character, I was sure I could handle myself intelligently where he was concerned.

It was late before he returned to claim his second dance. I'd seen his dark head from time to time about the room, mingling with the other guests. Despite what Caroline had said of his notoriety, it didn't seem to detract from the reception the marquis was receiving from the glamorous gathering. He was popular with the men as well as the women.

As he swept me into the dance—per the strict rules of Almacks, the one waltz I would be permitted that evening—he smiled. "Enjoying yourself, Baroness?"

"Oh, yes. This evening has been quite a novelty."

"And your obvious popularity has done nothing to diminish your pleasure, I'm sure."

"You have noticed?"

He chuckled, "And have you noticed the number of eyes watching you at this moment?"

"Should we pause now, while I count them and divide by two?"

"Perhaps we should, and do also remember my earlier warning to you."

"Nonsense. I'm sure that two dances with you cannot destroy my virtue . . . tarnish it slightly, perhaps."

"You know, my dear, I had been finding my life a great bore of late."

"Had you? With all your activities, that is difficult to believe."

"I see Caroline has been filling your ear."

"A touch."

"Nonetheless, my complaint is sadly true, and I should find it a charming relief from this diet of insipidity if you would permit me to pay my respects to you at Warringwood House one morning within the next fortnight."

I laughed up at him. "You're not serious?"

"Ah, but I am. I would never make such a proposal did I not mean every word of it."

"In that case, you are welcome to come—though I shall not hold my breath waiting."

"I see you think this is but a diversion for me."

"I should be a fool to think otherwise."

"Yes, well, maybe it is best your thoughts follow that pattern." The dance was over, and we'd begun walking toward the sidelines. "However, do believe me when I say it has been a great pleasure meeting you, Baroness."

As we returned to the spot where I'd left Caroline, I saw Justin had joined her. The two of them were talking together so earnestly, they didn't notice us until we were at their side. Caroline looked up and quickly stuck a smile on her face. Justin followed suit, but there was no warmth in his expression.

The marquis's and Justin's glances met coolly. It was obvious there was no love lost between them.

"How do you do, Warringwood."

"Radford." Justin nodded curtly. "I see you have made the acquaintance of my houseguest."

"Most delightfully so. I had not realized you had such connections in the German court, or I might have put an end to my rustications sooner and returned to London."

"Since the baroness has just arrived in town, it would have been to little point."

"Yes, she tells me you are executor to her father's estate."

"And her guardian, or did she neglect to mention that fact?"

The marquis raised a brow.

"You don't mind my clarifying, Justin," I interrupted, "that the guardianship is merely a quirk of the will, since I am fully of age and capable of managing my own affairs?"

"Tell the marquis whatever you wish. I was merely speaking conversationally."

"Well, I must say, Warringwood"—Radford smiled— "your handling of the Baroness's affairs thus far would appear exemplary. Almacks would, of course, be the place for putting her up to the highest bidder. I daresay by morning all London will be buzzing with talk of this new jewel and you will have a multitude of prospective bridegrooms at the door." He glanced nonchalantly at the gold watch on his vest. "Ah, but I must be going. I had no idea the hour was so advanced. Lady Caroline," he said as he bowed, "always a pleasure to see you. Baroness." He took my hand, but it was the glint in his eye that told his message. "Warringwood, I trust I will see you at White's or Brooks before long."

He was gone into the crowd before anything else could be said. Justin was livid. I knew he was only waiting for the opportunity to give me a lecture, but Lord Frompton had come up for the second dance I'd promised him. I was glad to avoid a confrontation with Justin, but I was tired too, and ready to call it a night.

Seeing no sign of either Caroline or Justin when Lord Frompton brought me to the side of the room at the end of the dance, I went in search of her, and found husband and wife talking to each other in undertones near a doorway.

"It is the same every time we are out," she was saying as I stood yet unobserved. "Or I should say, on those rare occasions when we *do* go out. You walk about with a frown on your face all evening, and then just as I am beginning to enjoy myself, you must rush us home!"

"Can I be blamed for frowning when I discover that you have made our guest acquainted with the marquis of Radford!"

"That was none of my doing, as I told you. He approached us and asked for an introduction. I could not very well refuse him, or help what followed. And he said he had met her before."

"I thought I made my meaning about him clear to Marlena on that earlier encounter, but perhaps she did not recognize him. Well, if need be I can handle the matter, and I believe the woman has some sense. I do think it is time we left, however. You have not been yourself these last months."

"Nonsense! I was just beginning to feel alive again. The prospect of escaping that stifling house several times a week is all I have ever needed."

"Allow me the ability to perceive when you are looking tired."

"I am *not* tired . . . only enjoying myself!"

"Caroline, you shall do as I say!"

I hurried away then, before I was caught eavesdropping, but it was only a few minutes later that Justin came to find me to tell me we were leaving. We collected our cloaks from the doorman and went out to the front steps to wait for our carriage.

Caroline icily avoided her husband, and when we climbed into the carriage, she sat stiffly in the corner, her profile turned coldly away. Justin's occasional glances toward her were unreadable. His looks to me were no warmer, but I was too tired to care, and spent the trip looking out at the city lights, sorry that I had overheard their conversation, yet amazed as I contemplated how much I'd enjoyed my night at Almacks.

SEVEN

I WAS DOWN TO BREAKFAST early, but when I entered the morning room, hoping to find Caroline recovered from her sulks, the butler came over to tell me Her Ladyship was indisposed and wouldn't be down. When I asked him what was wrong, he only said he'd been told Lady Caroline was ill.

Not knowing whether it was only a continuation of Caroline's sour mood of the previous night or something more serious, I went up to her room.

Her maid answered my knock and put a finger to her lips, then came out into the hall, closing the bedroom door behind her.

"I came up to see how Lady Caroline was feeling," I said.

"She's resting now, Baroness. A weary go she had of it this morning. Hate to disturb her."

"What's wrong?"

"Oh, the pains . . ."

"Pains? What kind of pains?"

"In the belly, Baroness. Comes and goes unexpected like. Not much she can do but take the drops the doctor's given her and weather it out."

"You've told her husband she's ill?"

"He was out. The butler will tell him when he returns."

"I see. Is there anything I can do?"

"No. The best thing's sleep. That's what the doctor says. Had these bouts the last year or so . . . always the same . . . always go away once she calms herself down. Meaning no disrespect—it's fond I am of the mistress—but this usually happens when things aren't going just as she'd want, and she was mightily upset last evening when she come up."

"Have you called a physician?"

"No need. He's left the drops for her to take. It's them that's easing her now."

"Well, call me if I can help . . . read to her, or whatever."

"That I will, m'lady."

She returned soundlessly to the bedroom, and I retraced my steps down the hall. A pain in her stomach . . . an ulcer?

Caroline and I had planned to go shopping that morning. Since I had nothing else in particular to do for the next few hours, I went in search of something to read. Among the odd fashion periodicals scattered around the drawing room, I found a romance from the lending library and went out to the garden, book in hand. The warm, clear morning air made it an inviting place, free from noise, free from interruption. I plopped down on the bench under the apple tree and opened to the first chapter. The scent of the flowers and the quiet droning of the bees had a hypnotic effect. I was startled when I heard the metallic snap of a latch and glanced up to see the French doors of Justin's study opening to let in the air.

He stood there for a few moments deep in thought, not seeing me where I was hidden behind the rose trellis. In a minute he turned and disappeared inside. Acting on impulse, I got up and followed.

I called to him from the doorway, my eyes adjusting themselves to the darker interior. "Justin? Are you free? May I come in a moment?"

He was standing by the bookcases and turned, startled, at the sound of my voice. "Marlena! I did not see you in the garden when I looked out."

"I was on the other side of the trellis. Is Caroline better?"

"Better?" He frowned, confused. "If you are speaking of the state of her temper, I have not spoken to her, so I have no idea."

"She's sick. Did Williams not tell you?"

"I slipped in the back way. I doubt he knows I am in the house. What is the problem?"

"Stomach pain, from what her maid said."

"Yes, I feared that would be the result of last evening." He sounded tired, worn. "She did not take kindly to my deciding it was time to leave."

"I shall leave you now, Justin, so you can go up to see her."

"She is no doubt asleep. Even if she were not, she prefers I remain away when she feels ill. There is no need for you to rush off."

"Oh."

He motioned me with his hand toward a chair. "It is early in the day, but can I offer you a glass of wine?"

"No, thank you."

"You have no objection if I partake?"

"No."

When he'd filled a glass, he came to stand before me. "My attitude must seem strange to you."

"Yes."

"Has Caroline told you anything of these attacks of hers?"

"I didn't realize she had them until this morning, but from what the maid said, they are frequent and the pain is severe. Has it occurred to you it could be a sign of something serious?"

"Of course it has occurred to me! And at the onslaught of her attacks I called in all the best physicians. Since no one of them discerned a rhyme or pattern to the attacks, each found her illness difficult to diagnose. But gradually, one by one, they came to me with the same remarks—they could find nothing physically wrong with my wife, only a high-strung nature and a delicacy of the nerves; perhaps a change of scenery, a quieter mode of living, and rest would restore her. I have tried each of these, to no avail. As you may have noticed, the quiet life is not precisely to Caroline's liking. Then I began noticing that these debilitating spasms of pain seemed to coincide with minor upsets—a disagreement with me that thwarted her plans, as last evening; my refusal to throw open the house to a continual round of parties; news that we would be departing for a stay at Pemberton Hall—all things that were contrary to her own wishes. Of course, Caro is not entirely to blame. I am not always the most sympathetic and feeling of persons. If only she loved Pemberton as I do . . ." He swung abruptly away so that his face was in shadow.

For a moment neither of us said anything. I watched him, lost in his personal trial, then said quietly, "I know you're not happy about my being here or the circumstances tying us together, but if there is anything at all I can do to help . . ."

"It is not my wish to involve you in the problems between my wife and myself." He still faced away from me; his tone was curt. "I have spoken to you as I have today only because I felt you deserve some explanation."

"I see." I rose. "Well, if you should change your mind . . ."

He didn't seem to hear me.

I felt the strongest desire to go to the broad back, lift my hands to his shoulders, and give Justin Pemberton a reassuring squeeze of comfort. In my mind's eye I saw him turning to me with a soft smile, touching his fingers to my arm—any sign of contact, of communication.

My inhibitions held me back. I stood there staring at him for several moments; then, feeling strangely inadequate, shut out, I silently left the room.

EIGHT

IT WAS A LIVELY SUMMER in London. With the Battle of Waterloo fought and won in June of that year and the threat of Napoleon at long last behind them, the population of England breathed a sigh of relief. The city seemed to sparkle with social entertainments; the Prince joining in and hosting grand parties at Carlton House—the Prince's elegant residence on the Mall, the exorbitantly expensive refurbishing and decorating of which, several decades earlier, had raised a clamor among the public—and at his outlandish Oriental Pavilion in Brighton. It was an exciting time for me too, as I tried to enjoy each moment to its fullest, knowing that at any moment my magical sojourn in the nineteenth century might end; wondering when, if ever, it would; storing away the memories to take back with me.

So much had happened in the days since my introduction at Almacks. I wasn't a stranger anymore in 1815 London, but quite a well-known personality in my own right and one who was becoming well acquainted with the ways of the tonnish world. It was increasingly difficult not to fall too deeply into the role of playing the baroness; to remind myself who I

really was and where I really belonged. I sometimes
felt I existed in a state of suspended animation. The
people around me were real, their problems real; but
my existence in their world was not real. Yes, it *was*
exciting—an experience unmatched—but though my
fears were subsiding, the uncertainty of my future
nagged at me more and more as each day passed.

One day in mid July, Caroline and I were in the
Green Salon accepting morning callers. Lady
Dunwithe had been in the room a few minutes before
with her eldest daughter, but at the sight of the number of men gathered there, her haughty brows had
risen. Her daughter was a dowdy girl whose frilled
yellow dress did nothing to offset the sallowness of
her complexion, and she attracted no more attention
from the men than a mildly curious look or two as
she entered the room. I wasn't surprised to see her
mother's nose flare.

Lady Dunwithe, of course, had come for no reason
other than to get a look at the much-talked-about
baroness living at Warringwood House. With her
quest for gossip satisfied, she stayed only a short
time before rushing off—probably to the drawing
room of her best friend with a luscious number of
juicy *on dits* ready to buzz off the end of her tongue.

Lady Dunwithe wasn't missed. As her skirts
brushed through the doorway, the butler announced
Lord Frompton, and on his heels Percivel Harriman,
an untitled but most interesting young man who had
hopes for the Commons.

Already in the room were several popular though
ineligible young dandies, startling in their rainbow-
colored apparel; a serious-faced viscount, up from the
country, who'd recently inherited his title and was
looking around for a suitable wife; and Captain
William Langely, the blond, handsome Captain of
the Guard with whom Caroline had been cornered

our first night at Almacks. I'd since learned that his friendship with Caroline went back to the days of her solitary country youth, and until their chance meeting in Almacks a few weeks before, she had not seen him in over five years. He'd taken a seat in the chair nearest hers, and it was obvious, at least to me, that the whisperings between the two of them went beyond the usual drawing-room inconsequentialities. But they were old friends who, I was sure, had much catching up to do; and it was good to see the vitality in Caro's eyes.

There was no loss for conversation amid the gathering as each man vied to make his impression felt strongest, or, if unable to get the attention of Caroline or me, settled for one of his neighboring males.

"I say, Rainey," I heard one young dandy utter to his posing counterpart a few chairs away, the points of his collar so high he could barely turn his head toward the fellow, "your man must be slipping . . . or else your glass is cracked. If that white aberration around your neck is meant to be a waterfall, I believe you have slipped a bit off the mark . . . or should I say, the fall."

A few masculine chuckles greeted the remark, but Rainey was quick to counter. "And I was just about to point out to you, Porter, that flowered waistcoats went out with the hare last March. Stripes are the fashion, my man." And he deftly drew open his jacket to reveal the bright green and red waistcoat beneath.

Other voices wagered on the outcome of the private fisticuffs match promised at Gentleman Jack's the following Thursday, and of the upcoming horse races at Newmarket.

I was laughing at Percivel Harriman's elaborately drawn comparison of peacocks and Englishmen when the butler appeared again at the door.

"My lord the marquis of Radford."

All eyes turned.

The marquis's eyes momentarily widened as he glanced about the room and saw he was far from alone in paying his respects. But it was only a second before his cool, suave manner reasserted itself. He smiled confidently, nodded to those he knew, then strode across the room to Caroline. "How do you do, Caroline. Allow me, on this lovely morning, to present my compliments."

"And the same to you, my lord. A pleasure to have you in our midst."

"The pleasure is mine; and permit me to give my greetings to your beautiful guest as well."

Caroline seemed uncomfortable, but did what was polite and nodded to Radford.

He turned and took my hand, then bowed and spoke in an undertone. "I am delighted, Baroness, when I find you in such lonely solitude, to be permitted to pay my respects. May I ask which of these airy, cosseted gentlemen has the honor of holding your interest? I would be greatly honored if you would name him, for I feel in need of rushing home to my rooms to reassess myself."

I grinned. "If you cannot behave properly, I shall send you away."

"Never do that, madam, for I fear you would be bored by my absence. I note that you have become quite the toast of the town. 'Incomparable' is the adjective most often used when your name is mentioned—as it is, often."

"You exaggerate. Besides, I'm too old to fall in that category."

"Ah, not too old at all, but polished. That is one quality so many find irresistible in you."

"Am I honored even to the extent that you number yourself among these admirers?"

"Considering the definite rapport we shared on our last meeting, I am surprised you must ask."

"Yet you have not exactly rushed over here to pay us this visit and further the acquaintance. It has been at least three weeks, has it not?"

"But there is my *reputation* to consider!" He smiled wickedly. "I cannot give the tongues too much to wag about. Of course, now that I see the fledglings who have gathered at your feet, I can understand your impatience."

"Is it your habit to flatter yourself so?"

He raised an eyebrow. "But I was about to say that this motley crowd is beneath your touch."

"Whereas you are, most suitably, within reach of that touch?"

"Let us just say I am mature."

"I do not know what concern it is of yours who I entertain."

"Impertinent, am I not? But I thought you had become accustomed to my peculiar way of expressing myself when last we met. You found a good deal of enjoyment in it as well, no? I had hoped you realized I am not such a hedonist as I lead the rest of the polite world to believe. . . . There *is* a heart under this sated exterior."

"I can believe that," I said thoughtfully.

"Then you are more perceptive than most." His dark eyes studied me until I began to feel uncomfortable.

"We are drawing attention."

"I was aware of that. Strange . . . I had thought my attention was given up utterly to you."

With a smile and a bow, he turned and retreated to a chair at the other side of the room, placing himself so that he had an unhampered view of me. His eyes, laughing again, fastened on me.

Ignoring him deliberately, I began conversation

anew with Percivel Harriman. We discussed the
campaign he was staging in his efforts to win a seat
in the next election. A devout Whig, he was well spoken and seemed to understand the needs and feelings of the working class men he would be rep-
resenting. Only because I knew that what would
eventually come to be in England through these lib-
eral policies was not all good, did I refrain from giving him my wholehearted support.

I was surprised when Percivel suddenly switched
the conversation away from politics. "You appear to
be well acquainted with the marquis," he said
mildly.

"We've met formally only once—at Almacks. I like
his wit. You disapprove of him?"

"No . . . I know him only slightly, though I rather
like him myself. I have often wondered why he goes
to such lengths to hide his talents."

"Oh?"

"Perhaps I speak out of line."

"I'm interested. Please continue."

"It is only bits of information I have picked up here
and there. Existing on the fringes of the ton as I do,
my only claim to fame being my political aspirations
and my mother's bloodlines as daughter to a baronet, I hear things that others might not. Radford is
quite a businessman. Perhaps he hides this because
anything smelling of trade is beneath the touch of
most of our polite aristocracy, but he is a success,
from what I understand—scrupulously honest too,
and conscientious. I have been down to the docks and
to some of his warehouses, talking to the workers. I
do not hear the discontent that is rampant among
the laborers in so many other districts of London. His
workers have very little to complain of, they tell me.
Their hours are good, their wages fair, and he has in-

stituted an incentive system whereby bonuses are paid on productivity. Needless to say, a man is more likely to work to his full capacity when it means a few extra shillings in his pocket. And though the marquis would appear to be living a life of sheer licentiousness here in London, his estates are some of the best managed in England. There is no bleeding of the land to pay for his extravagances."

"The stories of his extravagances cannot all be rumor," I speculated.

"That I cannot confirm or deny." We were interrupted by the sound of the drawing room doors suddenly closing sharply. Justin Pemberton stood on the threshold. He quickly scanned the group, and frowned for a moment as his eyes caught sight of Captain Langely sitting so close to Caroline. Then he came across the room.

He went immediately to Caroline, and smiled at her. "Well, Caro, I see you get on quite well. I'd not thought our humble home such a popular gathering spot for the beaux of Bond Street."

"Do not tease, Justin. It would not be seemly if I left Marlena unattended."

"I concur wholeheartedly, Caro." He glanced toward Langely, seated in the next chair, and spoke again, quietly, in a voice intended only for Caroline's ears. "What concerns me is the seemliness of my wife setting herself up as a flirt. It has not escaped my notice that not all the gentlemen present are admirers solely of our dear baroness."

I heard Caro gasp, but Justin had already turned away to face the assembled callers. "A pleasure, Percivel, Rainey, Broughton. Ah, Langely, but I thought you with His Majesty's Horse Guards. Are they not in Brighton at the moment?"

"You are correct. However, it is not much to the

point, since I have surrendered my commission."

"Have you? I have heard word of your uncle; I take it he is not in the best of form of late. You are his heir, are you not?"

A hush had fallen over the room.

The captain nodded. "My uncle being in his nineti-eth year, his present illness cannot be altogether un-expected."

"Quite so. Then with your expectations of title and estates, you must be making plans to settle . . . look-ing about for a bride. Perhaps there is someone in this household who interests you?"

Langely's face reddened, though he held his gaze straight forward. "I try not to rush my fences, my lord."

"I would give you that same advice myself. When one acts, it is always wise to look ahead to the conse-quences." Justin seemed about to say something more, then changed his mind. Still, there wasn't a person in the room who didn't understand the full in-tent of his words.

Justin turned his back to Langely and looked out at the other faces. He spotted the darkly clad figure of Radford in the far corner; the two men's eyes met.

"I must admit, Radford, to my surprise at seeing you here," Justin said mildly.

"I felt I should pay a visit"—Radford grinned—"and add my fair share to all the acclaim circulating about your two ladies."

"I trust you will not be offended if I say that this is not the type of house in which you usually pay your respects."

"By no means. My ways are well known, though on occasion I endeavor to mend them."

"You have chosen a most inappropriate time to do so."

Radford laughed. "Rest easy, Warringwood. A

morning visit is a bit early in the game to be pre-
dicting a suit."

The two men stared at each other silently, the grin
still on Radford's lips.

As Justin swung around to take a stance behind
Caroline's chair and my own, conversation began
again. About fifteen minutes later I saw Radford
rise. He stepped across the room toward us, paused,
and, smiling, inclined his head. "Ladies, it has been
a pleasure. You will excuse me if I depart, but I have
business to attend to." His tone was warm and relaxed; his manner indicated he wasn't the least disturbed by the sharp words that had just passed between him and Justin. "My thanks for your hospital-
ity, Caroline. And, Baroness, continued success on
your conquest of London." With a backward nod of
his head, he indicated the men seated behind him.

Hiding my amusement with an effort, I glanced up
at him. "I shall endeavor to behave myself, and
would give you the same advice."

"The point hits home. Let us see what I can do.
Warringwood, a pleasure."

"Radford."

The marquis bowed, turned, and strode away, his
long legs carrying him with easy elegance to the
door. With his departure, the room suddenly seemed
very quiet, almost empty.

Justin stood staring for several moments at the
closed door, deep in thought; then he dropped his
eyes, bringing himself back to his surroundings.

"Well, Caro, I too must leave. I have an appointment at White's. Enjoy the balance of your day, and I
will see you both this evening."

As his eyes, more green than gray at the moment,
rested on his wife, his warning was clear. His look to
me contained a message as well . . . but more than
just a warning.

* * *

The friendship between Caroline and me remained firm as we bustled about London together—shopping; visiting; driving in the park during the fashionable afternoon hour of five to six, with Caroline at the reins of her stylish two-seated curricle, a groom trotting sedately on horseback behind. We shared long chats in the drawing room after dinner when Justin wasn't at home, or in the garden in the mornings, sitting on benches amid the flowering beds and rosebushes. She was pleasant, gregarious, and so absolutely delighted that I was in London to give her some companionship. Yet some of my initial admiration of her sweet strength of character was slipping away as I was forced to listen to her continual small complaints about her life, her husband—his lack of understanding, his disinterest in the things that brought her pleasure, his every bad habit, however inconsequential.

I thought her criticisms were unfair. When I compared Justin to the other aristocrats I'd met, his finer qualities shone. I sensed, too, from my talks with him, that he would have given Caroline so much more if only she were willing to meet him halfway. Didn't she realize what a fortunate woman she was? Alone as I was in a society where most women my age were married, I sometimes felt the emptiness . . . a twinge of envy that I tried to suppress as I wondered how it would feel to be held in a man's arms again, know I had his love and protection. It had been a long time for me since my last love affair. Didn't Caroline too need that warmth? Then again, I'd never been in the privacy of their chambers to see what went on between them. Against my will, my mind had often wandered into that forbidden territory. Did they forget their daily quarrels? Did he take her in his arms, try to soothe away her complaints, draw her down onto the sheets of the bed beside him? Did his hands caress her skin, work the tension from her neck, pull her closer?

To think any further brought me a pain I didn't understand. But even I, who had good reason to be at odds with the man, had to admit he was making an effort. He took us around town, to a garden party, to a flower show in the park, to a reception at Carlton House—a never-ending dinner entailing course after course of rich food and a stream of superficial conversation in a room that, in keeping with the Prince's taste, was too warm for comfort. It seemed the Regent was too occupied with preening before his visitors even to notice his guests' discomfort. But at least I met him, in a fleeting introduction amid the crush of others waiting for the same privilege; heady for me, since I was actually face to face with and speaking to this self-indulged Prince whose future I knew as he did not. He was everything I'd read about him in another century—at that point still only chubby, smiling, affable, extravagant, good and generous to those around him when it struck his royal whim to be so. Still, as far as depth of character went, he paled beside Justin and the few other serious-minded noblemen I'd met.

I saw a look of pure perseverance on Justin's face that evening. He was not one of the Prince's set and had made no secret of his disapproval of the Prince and his frivolous brothers. Yet he was with us, as he had been on every other evening since my introduction to London society, taking his wife's arm, making polite conversation with people I knew he considered absolute bores.

On the morning rides, it was still just Justin and I, though I don't suppose I minded Caroline's absence very much. It was good to be alone with him—I didn't allow myself to consider the reasons why; but there was something to be said for cantering through the morning mist, speaking only when either of us wanted to. Gradually, the tension between us was easing, and an understanding growing to take its place—an understanding that neither of us acknowledged, but only accepted. It was there in a shared look, the crooked smile of sympathy he'd give me from across a room when I was trapped in a tedious conversation. In the morning solitude in the park, he was opening up about himself, telling me of his political ambitions, his plans for Pemberton. Underlying all his talk of dreams for the future, there was a disquieting air of unhappiness about Justin.

He was particularly somber one morning, and I spoke up. "You are very quiet. Would you rather cut our ride short?"

My words startled him out of his introspection. "No . . . of course not. Forgive me, Marlena, it is only that I have a great deal on my mind."

"Has it anything to do with me and the guardianship?"

"As difficult as it may be to believe, I have managed to accustom myself to the situation." He smiled wryly. "It is something else altogether."

"You and Caro?"

He looked over sharply. "She has said something to you?"

"Nothing directly."

"I see."

I expected an interval of dead silence. Instead he continued in the tone of a man anxious to lift some weight from his mind. "I suppose living in the house, you must have noticed something is wrong. Caro and I are two very different people. When I first saw her, I found her a lovely, sweet thing, shy but charming. With her background and country upbringing, I thought her perfect for the life I had in mind for us at

Pemberton . . . my lovely bride, later a family of
lively children. I have my political interests too, as
you know, and business that brings me to town, but I
have never been content to spend my life drifting
from sporting party to gaming table, drawing room
to tea party.

"When we were first wed and she told me of her desire to see a bit of the social scene, which was so new
for her, I escorted her to every rout and party in
London. There was not a single event at which we
were not in attendance. I know of naught that was
accomplished except to wear us both to the bone. You
see, she found me a rather dull escort." He shook his
head slowly. "Perhaps if there was a child to occupy
her time and thoughts. . . . But that is another
story."

He broke off abruptly, and seemed angry with himself for having spoken so frankly.

"I've offered before," I said quietly, "but if there is
anything at all I can do to help . . ."

"I thank you, but there is nothing you could do.
This is between Caro and me. Now—I believe it is
time we started back. I have become quite maudlin,
and had better direct my thoughts to the several
business engagements I have this morning."

Pressing his heels to his stallion's flanks, he
started off at a brisk trot. The subject was closed.

For a moment I stared after him, noting the proud
angle of his head, the straight set of his shoulders.
Then I too spurred my mare homeward.

The three of us went out a few nights later for a mu-
sical evening at Lord and Lady Newbury's.

The twenty or so guests were congregated in the
rear drawing room, and since the night was fair and
warm, they'd spilled out through the open doors into
the lighted garden beyond. A small stage had been

set up in the corner of the room, surrounded by a
semicircle of light chairs; a table of refreshments
was along the side wall. Footmen circulated with
chilled champagne.

In the confusion of greetings, I lost sight of Caroline and Justin, but since I was by that time acquainted with many members of the London elite, I
wasn't uncomfortable.

The musicians came to the stage at nine-thirty,
causing a stir in the room and a dash for seats. I saw
Justin standing by the doors, a glass of champagne
in hand. Caroline wasn't with him, and I guessed
that she'd wandered off with one of her women
friends, with whom I'd seen her earlier. As the crowd
settled, I glanced among the seated heads. I didn't
see her. Justin as well was scrutinizing the room.

When the music began, I fought the urge to crane
my neck around to see if she had appeared, or if
Justin was still alone by the door. Finally I dared a
glance. There was no sign of either of them, but during a brief break in the music as the musicians
changed scores, voices could be heard from the direction of the garden. I could pick out Justin's deep
tone; Caroline's higher pitched one sounding stri-
dent.

I tried to pay attention to the rest of the performance, which was a good one, but my mind was out
in the garden, picturing in vivid color what might be
going on.

It seemed an eternity before the instruments were
lowered, the flutter of applause dwindled off, and
people rose to their feet. As the guests began to dis-
perse toward the refreshment table, Justin emerged
from the semidarkness of the garden with Caroline.
His hand held her elbow firmly; his face was tight-
lipped and hollowed. Caroline's face was pale, wide-

eyed, but she said nothing as Justin motioned to me and then called for our wraps.

I fervently wished myself somewhere else when the carriage started off and I noticed the glares Caroline and Justin gave each other. The short journey might have been bearable if Caroline had kept her silence, but she didn't. We'd gone about a half a block when she lashed out at her husband.

"Well! Are you satisfied, Justin, now that you have made a spectacle of us all? What could you have been thinking of, rushing us off as if there was something appalling in my having a friendly chat—"

"That will be sufficient, Caroline! Recall that we are not alone."

"Marlena's presence is of no matter. She will hear it all soon enough in any event. And she can only have been as mortified as I at your behavior. Sneaking out into that garden, spying on me! Dragging me off as though I were a child! Is it not enough that I must be cooped up in that house? Am I not allowed even the smallest freedom?"

"When your actions fall within the bounds of propriety, you may do what you wish," he exploded, "but what I witnessed between you and that cad fell far short!"

"Langely was only offering me a bit of sympathy . . . which I receive so little of anywhere else."

"Yes, I am sure you've been reading him quite a tale, dear wife; however, I do not consider a fevered embrace the proper manner of showing sympathy to a married woman."

"You are cruel and unfeeling!" she cried. "You care nothing of my own sufferings."

"And what might they be?" One angry brow lifted over his narrowed eyes. "It appears to me that nothing one does for you is sufficient in your eyes. What is it you want? That I allow you a free rein . . . let you have your head so that you may ruin yourself in the speediest manner possible? Unfortunately my pride gets in the way of such action. I am a man, and, as you seem so eager to forget, your husband! Recall that you are not the only member of this incongruous duo who has had much to endure!"

"And who was it who deceived me into this marriage . . . took advantage of my innocence—"

"Enough! If you have anything further to say to me, Caroline, it will be said in the privacy of our chambers! You have done more than is necessary already this evening to embarrass both myself and Marlena. Do not make matters irreparable!"

"If I wish—"

"I said *enough!*" His tone was so harsh, I expected him to rise from the seat and shake her. Apparently she thought the same, because she cowered into her corner, staring at him as though she couldn't believe her ears.

At the house, waiting for no one, she ran up the stairs, presumably to lock herself into her room. I would have gone up to bed myself, to hide my embarrassment at having been witness to the scene between them, but Justin laid a hand on my arm, forestalling my departure.

"Marlena, you will forgive us, I hope. I cannot apologize to you sufficiently for that scene you should never have been made a party to."

I dropped my eyes.

"I could have left her alone to her own foolhardiness—I *should* have, I suppose. But something—"

"Please, there is no need to explain. My sympathies are with you."

He looked worn to the bone. He let out a ragged sigh. "I have thought often these last weeks of how different it might have been. At this point you must be sorry you ever set foot within this house. No . . . do not comment on that. I would rather not hear the truth. Good night, Marlena."

"Good night."

I saw a bleakness in his eyes, and turned from it to climb the stairs; his gaze lingered when I turned again to wave a last good night.

I felt that sadness; understood the feeling he was conveying: if only things had been different, and we had been free to find how deeply we might care for one another . . .

NINE

IT APPEARED the differences between Justin and Caroline went much deeper than I'd suspected. My ears were picking up stray bits of servants' gossip, which at first I refused to believe—a conversation between two chambermaids on the oddity of the mistress's and master's sleeping arrangements; Caro's personal maid confiding to the housekeeper: "There'll never be a child under this roof, Meg, the way Her Ladyship's behavin'. Meaning no disrespect, but it's just not right, her denying her husband his rights."

From what the gossip told me, I supposed Caroline had never cared for the sexual side of her marriage; had used it as leverage in getting her own way. Rumor had it that the two had not shared the same bedroom for over a year. When her husband had refused her some whim, she'd reciprocated by denying him her bed on some pretext or other—a severe headache, an attack of stomach pain, the selfishness and inconsideration she perceived in his character—until finally, in disgust, Justin moved to rooms in another part of the house. No hints were ever dropped of his having a mistress, though I began wondering, on those many evenings when he was out of the house,

if it was really business that called him, or the arms
some beauty of London's demimonde.

I was glad that our social life was so busy; glad
that Justin now maintained an aloof attitude. It kept
the two of us at a safe distance from one another.
Justin didn't accompany Caroline and me as often as
he had, so we attended the parties alone. Though she
was several years my junior, the ton considered
her, as a married woman, to be an acceptable
chaperone—a fact that struck my sense of humor.
Though I was terribly disillusioned with the new
face of Caroline I was seeing, I maintained the pretext of friendship.

We saw a lot of Radford during those weeks—at
Almacks; during intermission at the opera; at a couple of the dinner parties we attended. He paid no
more attention to me than he did to the other
women, limiting his conversation to the light repar-
tee that set him apart from other London gentlemen,
most of whom were almost fawning in their flatteries to me. I knew that nothing he said could be taken
at face value, yet he was interesting, a diversion who
helped take my mind off Justin, and I enjoyed his
company. We established an unusual friendship; one
that made no demands on either side.

Gradually, though, he began singling me out. He
would suddenly appear at my side when I'd wandered away from the crowd for a moment, or bring
me a glass of punch, or intervene when a group of
dandies surrounded me or I was caught in a conversation with someone who wasn't quite "above the
touch." I thought of Percivel Harriman's words to
me as I began seeing for myself the more private side
to the marquis—the side he kept so well hidden from
the world. I asked him about his business enter-
prises, and without apparent reluctance he told me
how his ventures had begun as a lark to get himself

out from under his father's domineering hand. He'd kept the purchase of his first cargo vessel a secret until he was in a position to present his father with an account statement showing a healthy profit—to prove to both of them that he was capable of surviving without reliance on the estate purse strings.

His father was devoted to his family, though he ruled them all as a dictator. Radford was the only son. He'd had two sisters, but the younger had died of smallpox in her early teens. His older sister had married well, to an earl, and now lived in Wales on her husband's family estate, happy with her children and the tranquility of country living. Both his parents had been respected members of the nobility. They were wealthy, had an impressing lineage, and came up to London for the season, yet remained devoted to each other without indulging in the liaisons that were so common among other members of their set, until his father's death ten years before.

Radford had already proved himself by then; had tripled his initial investment in purchasing his first cargo vessel. He had succeeded at impressing his family, though, despite taking pride in his skills, they otherwise held to the traditional values of looking down their noses at trade.

Then there'd come a bad time in Radford's life. I was amazed that he told me about it, but he did, in sketches. He'd fallen in love with another man's wife—the wife of one of his closest friends. She let him believe she'd give up everything for him. On that promise he went to his friend, swallowed his feelings of guilt, and asked that the man give his wife the divorce she sought without dragging all their names through Parliament and hell.

Suddenly, though, after Radford's confessions, she backed down. She denied to her husband she'd ever had a part in a private relationship with Radford.

Her cool denial made Radford seem a fool. She broke his heart, and since she was also cunning and beautiful enough to convince her husband to swallow her every word, Radford left for the Continent quickly, spent a few months there, and returned an embittered man. His belief in love was lost, as was his best friend. He determined then the course that was to be his future—that of a dilettante and rake. Since the affair had been kept so secret, very few in London knew the reason for his departure or his changed behavior.

So here was Radford's own version of the incident Justin had described to me—and what a different perspective it put on things.

It wasn't only these confidences about himself that began to change my opinion of him. He treated me as a woman, not a decorative piece with a cobweb brain. I spoke my mind, talked of politics, dared to tell him that I despised sewing or any of the other pursuits on which most women centered their lives. I had to be careful with him, though, and avoid applying too much of my twentieth century knowledge in our talks. He was sharper than most and probably would catch the smallest hint that I was something other than I pretended to be.

Justin, on those now rare occasions when he was abroad in society to witness Radford's attentiveness, looked at me darkly, but said nothing, though I sensed it was on the tip of his tongue to do so. Lately his temper was very short indeed. Caroline had continued showing an incautious interest in Captain Langely. So caught up was she in her finaglings, she seemed uncaring of the hurt she was inflicting on her husband, the slap to his male pride. He was ready to explode, and I didn't blame him. It pained me just to see the expression on his face when we'd arrive at one of the society gatherings and Caroline, who'd been withdrawn and pouty to that point, would suddenly smile brilliantly as she spotted Langely, and within a few minutes work her way through the crowd to his side. Justin deserved better. What was Caro about? Not only was she hurting her husband, but gossip was spreading like a rampant disease.

I wasn't so naive that I didn't realize there was also gossip—though not malicious—about Radford and me. For him to be spending as many hours with any one woman of the ton as he was with me, didn't go without notice. Polite society was accustomed to his consorting with demimondaines, but unused to his associating habitually with any one woman of his own class. "What are his intentions?" was the question in all their minds. "What is he up to?"

Everything went smoothly enough until one sultry morning in August. I was sitting in my room at the desk before the open windows, trying to find a breath of air. My task at hand was answering a letter I'd received from New York a few days before—from the baroness's aunt and uncle. The letter had come as a shock. In my absorption with my own difficulties in this 1815 world, I'd somehow forgotten that the real baroness had a life; that there were people out there concerned for her welfare. When the butler had handed me the letter as I'd crossed the front hall, returning from a shopping trip with Caro, I looked at the postmark and felt stunned. Then, breaking the seal and reading the contents, I'd felt a strange sense of guilt. How could I have forgotten the Aunt Eva and Uncle Andreas Marlena had mentioned in her diary? How could I have not considered that they would have expected some word from her on her safe arrival in England? It took me several days to compose a response, not knowing how reassuring to be when I didn't know myself if they'd ever see their niece again . . . any more than I knew whether I'd see the twentieth century again. In the end I finally composed a letter I thought the baroness might have written, telling them of a safe journey, the thrills and excitements of London; of the Warringwoods, the stipulations of the will.

I was finishing the last paragraph when there was a knock on the door. At my call, Jane entered.

"Begging your pardon, Baroness, but His Lordship sent me up. He'd like to see you in his study."

"Now?"

"It's what he said." She looked bashful.

"Did he mention why he wanted to see me?"

"No, m'lady, just that I was to ask you to come right down."

"All right, Jane, you can tell him I'll be there in a minute."

She hurried out. I rose from the desk, straightened my hair in the mirror, and left my close room for the even stuffier hallway.

The library doors were closed as I approached them across the downstairs hall. There was no sign of Justin's man, so I went to the heavy doors and knocked lightly.

"Who is it?"

"Marlena."

"Come in."

He was seated behind his desk, but rose as I entered to cross the room, and shut the door behind me. He didn't sit again, but came over to stand before me as I took a seat on the leather-upholstered wing chair. Restlessness and anger vibrated in the air about him.

"You wonder why I have called you here?"

"Yes. We saw each other this morning and everything was fine. Has some problem with the estate suddenly sprung up?"

"The estate? Nothing of the kind, though I suppose what I have heard might affect it in the long run." He stood, hands clasped behind his back, glaring down at me.

"I have just returned from White's, where I received the most interesting piece of information. Perhaps you have some idea of its content?"

"Since I've never been to White's, I am afraid not."

"Then let me enlighten you. As I walked through the front door of the place early this afternoon, I was aware of a stir at the betting book."

He began pacing, turning every so often to check my reaction; his resonant voice echoed against the walls of the room. "Since I was there the night before and laid all the wages I cared to place, it was of no matter to me, until I suddenly heard a loud chorus calling my name. 'Ah, Warringwood, just the man we wished to see. Give us your advice.' The fellow who spoke loudest was old Brason's boy, a rascal I've known since he was in leading strings—and surrounding him were some men going back to my Eton days, to say nothing of the Austrian prince and Lord Lamb listening to every word. 'Which shall it be? Will Radford do it or not? There is five hundred already laid that he will make the baroness an offer within the fortnight—another five laid that he will not.' And then to have Brummel, a man with whom I am on good terms, turn to me, laughing, as though it were all a huge joke—'Well, what say you, Warringwood? You are her guardian. Does Radford stand a chance? I should be willing to lay a few quid down that you will withhold your consent.' "

"Justin!" I was digesting his rapid-fire words. "This is all nonsense. Just a bunch of young and drunken fools with nothing else to wager on."

"You and Radford have apparently given the *beau monde* every reason to speculate!"

"He is a friend. I have no thought of carrying the relationship any further, and I'm sure neither does he. He is not the marrying kind."

"I am so glad your perceptiveness had made you cognizant of that. Being so astute in your evaluation of his character, then, you have not failed to appreciate that his intentions are less than honorable."

"Radford has made no move in *that* direction either. He has been considerate, and a good friend. But if he should get out of line, I am quite capable of handling myself."

"You are deluding yourself if you think for one moment you will have anything to say in the matter should Radford decide to play his hand."

"If this is what you brought me here to discuss, I will leave now."

"No, you will not!" I got no further than lifting my weight off the cushions before he was towering in front of me. "You will see no more of Radford! When next you come across him at a gathering, you will advise him firmly that his attentions are no longer welcome; that if he persists, he will answer to me. Do not deceive yourself, either, into thinking that you will be able to sneak about behind my back. Should I discover this is what you are doing, I will not hesitate to detain you bodily in this house, and will allow you out only under the chaperonage of one of my most loyal footmen."

"You could not do such a thing!"

"Not only *could* I do it, under the conditions of my guardianship, but I would take great pleasure in it."

"I cannot understand. Why are you so angry? You've heard talk of some foolish bets, but I've done nothing to warrant them—or such treatment as this at your hands."

"Because of your precedents and the fact that you have spent most of your youth in a rough and unciv-

ilized country, you have been granted far more le-
niency than any English girl of your station! It is
time you realize that."

"But I am no girl. I'm a full-grown woman!"

"You are unmarried and under my guardianship.
It is all the same." He ran his fingers through the
thick red-gold of his hair.

"There are times, Justin, when I think you must
despise me."

"Whatever gave you that idea? Actually, I think
you can be a rather charming creature—despite your
unbridled tongue. What I do is in your own best interests. I will not countenance any suitors for your
hand until the year is out. They will be sent off as
speedily as they arrive with a bug in their ears!"

"Not so long ago you had me convinced you
couldn't get rid of me soon enough. I'll be glad to
pack my bags and find other lodgings."

He swung from me and began to stride about the
room. "You try my patience!"

"And what of *my* patience? I hate the bonds of this
restrictive arrangement! But it seems there is no
way out for me."

Deliberately, he turned his head away. "If I remember correctly, this conversation was instigated
with the purpose of warning you from Radford."

"We've progressed beyond that point, my lord."

"Don't call me 'my lord'!" he roared irrelevantly.
"My name is Justin."

"I still haven't had my answer."

"What answer do you want? I will not permit you
to move from under this roof, so put the thought out
of your head. You are a woman. Why must you persist in thinking and acting as a man? There are matters in which I know best."

"It is just as I thought."

"The only thought to keep in your mind is that

from here on out your relationship with Radford is at
an end. Beyond that . . . oh, damn, I do not *care* what
you do! Perhaps if I were wise, I would send you off to
Radford and wish the best to both of you!"

"If that is quite all," I said, fuming, infuriated,
"then I have things to do."

"Yes. Go . . . begone. Get out of here!" His temper
was equal to my own.

As I strode angrily back to my room, I cursed myself for having allowed my emotions to become so
firmly entangled with this man. How dare he dictate
to me! And what kind of idiot was I still to feel this
indefinable attraction to him? Already I was searching my mind for excuses for his behavior; ways of
smoothing his ruffled fur. Regardless, I was not
about to take his ultimatum sitting down.

I was a modern woman. In my own world I would
walk out the door rather than let any man dictate to
me. But of course the truth was, my hands were tied;
I was forced to acquiesce.

Where after all, could I go now? I'd saved something from my monthly allowance, but not nearly
enough to pay for a respectable house or to feed and
support myself indefinitely. There was the real baroness to think of, too. I liked her. Assuming my time
in this early nineteenth century would eventually
end, I didn't want to risk her inheritance or leave her
any other manner of disaster to untangle. I decided
to put a word of warning in Radford's ear the next
time I saw him.

In spite of the festivities for visiting royalty, the
summer heat had gotten to the ton. Most of the elite
crowd had left for Brighton during the previous two
weeks. Since I knew Radford had remained, I hoped
to see him that evening. I'd take him aside then, discreetly.

Caroline and I left for a dinner party at the
Conlins' at eight. Justin had told us he had another
important appointment and wouldn't be attending. I
imagined this news made Caroline very happy, especially when we walked into the already crowded
drawing room to see Captain Langely, in conversation with Percivel Harriman. Also there were Lady
Jersey, who'd come alone because her husband was
in the country, Lord and Lady Aleford, Lady
Fontane and her daughter Meredith, another lady
and her daughter I didn't recognize, the host and
hostess and their own daughter of marriageable age,
a number of eligible bachelors, and several persons
of lesser nobility. Having surveyed the room and
found no Radford, I was cursing my luck when, just
at that moment, the butler announced his name. As
beautifully dressed as ever, Radford stepped into the
room.

Easily over six feet tall and slim, he looked magnificent in the cherry-colored jacket and fawn
breeches, and with his jet-black hair brushed carelessly in the windblown style, his tie immaculately
white and elaborately fashioned, he would have
turned heads anywhere. Our eyes met and we exchanged knowing glances; then he came forward.
Compliments were passed around, and the light conversation continued. Three more guests were announced, and finally we were called in to dinner.

I didn't have a chance to talk to Radford in the
other room, but I was surprised to discover I'd been
seated beside him at the table. Perhaps Lady Conlin
was amusing herself by trying to fuel the current
gossip. On my other side was Percivel Harriman.

After the first course had been served, everyone at
the table was engrossed in either talking or filling
their mouths, and I was able to say to Radford in a
hushed voice, "I must speak to you privately later.

We cannot leave the room, but perhaps after the gentlemen join us in the drawing room, we could slip into a corner unnoticed?"

"Why, Baroness," he chuckled slyly, "I am intrigued. May I ask the occasion of the honor?"

"I had a small lecture from Justin this afternoon."

"Did you? About what, may I ask?"

"Let us talk about it later. Given your whiling ways, I imagine you can meet me later without drawing too much attention."

"A simple task."

The rest of the meal was pleasant, with Percivel keeping me busy with chatter on the political front, and Radford, his eyes laughing, doing his best to throw only the most teasing comments my way.

After the ladies had retired to the drawing room, the men remained at the table barely long enough to savor their port. It was my guess that there were too many male hopefuls who didn't want the young ladies at the party to remain out of their sight for too long. Although he would have been most embarrassed to think anyone was aware of his feelings, it was obvious Percivel had a crush on Meredith Fontane, a pretty girl who, although quiet, had a sharp intelligence and pleasant conversation mandatory in the wife of a man in his career. There were other men, too, who had lost no time in aligning themselves with the single women. Fortunately I managed to escape the usual circle of admirers, probably because, in my preoccupation with finding a chance to talk to Radford tonight, I'd appeared cool and disinterested.

Caroline and Langely drifted off to a small sofa by the fire to lose themselves in talk, which had the immediate effect of raising eyebrows throughout the room. As usual the two of them seemed oblivious of their surroundings. I wondered at the behavior of the captain, who in other respects seemed so conventionally aboveboard. How could he publicly involve himself with a married woman, at the risk of his reputation and hers?

I continued to avoid all but the lightest conversation, roaming around the room until I saw the others were engrossed. Then I caught Radford's eye and moved as inconspicuously as possible toward a bookcase in the corner. I paused before it to study the volumes. In a moment I heard a voice at my ear.

"Shall we begin our discussion, Baroness?"

I didn't move my eyes from the shelf. "Yes. No one is near by?"

"Not to my knowledge. I left Sally Jersey with Lord Aleford, who is sure to keep her ear and attention for a while. The rest we need not worry about, so caught up are they with familial love—mamas, papas, and offspring included."

"Good. What I have to say needs privacy."

"I would wish for a more private place than this; however, since your message seems of the utmost urgency, I will put up with the inconvenience." He reached from behind me to pull a book from the shelf. "Our dear Miss Austen. Have you read her?"

"Yes, and think she is excellent, though I would not expect you to share that opinion."

"True, romantic morality is not one of my stronger suits. But this is not what you brought me here to discuss."

"As I said before, I had a talk with Justin today. It seems he has heard some rumors about us and is not particularly pleased. Of course, when you consider that he heard the rumors flying over the betting book at White's—in the form of a five-hundred-pound wager that you would make an offer of marriage to me within the fortnight—I can sympathize with him."

I heard a delighted chuckle.

"You were aware of the wagers, my lord?" I asked, wishing I could see his face.

"No, but it comes as rather diverting news to me now. I was wondering when the wind would come up."

"He has told me I have to stop seeing you."

"But you are in my company at this moment."

"He allowed me one meeting in which to explain the situation."

"*Allowed* you? I should not thought you one to accept such generosity as that."

"Well, I would not, except that he is holding the will and this guardianship nonsense over my head. I have no intention of snubbing you, of course, but we shall have to do our talking when other eyes are not watching."

"Would it not be simpler," he interrupted mildly, "to break our relationship altogether?"

"If you wish."

"You know I do not wish it. You are the most interesting bit of womanhood to come my way in a long time."

"Well, I wanted to warn you."

"Let us go back a bit. How can he have this power over you? What is this about his guardianship, and the will?"

"I have never told you all the details. They are complex, and unfortunately there is no way for me to get around them." I went on to summarize the baron's wish for his daughter to marry Justin Pemberton; the guardianship; the year's waiting period; the stipulation that the baroness couldn't enter into any other relationship until the year's end without forfeiting her inheritance. "And Justin intends to carry it out to the letter. He says that if I do not stop seeing you, not only will he restrict me to the house with one of his footmen as guard, but he will force you to answer to him."

"Is that so?" Radford's tone, though subdued in volume for the sake of our privacy, was hard and angry. I looked over my shoulder to find him staring into space, a deep scowl on his forehead. "Warringwood goes beyond himself! I answer to no one, and I would not have believed you to be a coward, Baroness; nor did I think you so weak-willed you would let another make your decisions for you! You are a fool to bend to his threats."

"Radford! I am neither a coward nor a fool!"

"You are behaving remarkably like one—or is there something here you are not telling me?" His tone was speculative, his eyes cunning.

"Of course not." But I swallowed quickly. If he only knew how close he was to the truth . . .

"Well, he is mad if he believes I will allow him to dictate *my* actions. And you are of age, are you not?"

"Yes, but—"

"Then he has no right in the world to restrict your movements."

"Do not make him out to be such a villain." I was torn between my feelings for Justin and my unwillingness to hurt him, and my agreement with what Radford was saying. Still, I had to remind myself that I was an imposter and must try to behave as the real baroness might.

"He *is* a villain if he tries to control you in this manner!" Radford argued, his voice low enough so others couldn't overhear.

"In his anger he overreacted."

"How can you possibly defend him?"

"It is because you dislike each other so much that—"

"*That* is an understatement, although he is the one who initially provoked the argument after that unfortunate affair I mentioned to you. He never could see my side, and it is difficult for me to feel any warmth in my heart toward a man who deliberately snubs me and treats me with contempt. However, that has nothing to do with what we are discussing."

"It does! His dislike for you prompted his anger. If another man's name had been linked to mine, I'm sure he would not have reacted so harshly."

"I should be flattered," Radford quipped sarcastically.

"You are impossible."

"No, it is *you* who are impossible." He studied me, frowning darkly. "So what are you going to do?"

"I've enjoyed our friendship and see no harm in continuing it . . . but discreetly. Our meetings will have to be such that others do not see."

"And if I do not agree?"

"Then our friendship has to be at an end." I almost choked on the words; self-sacrifice went against my grain. Yet if I was to keep peace with Justin and protect the baroness's future for her ultimate return, I had no choice.

Radford was silent. I knew he was watching me as he turned the problem over in his mind, but I didn't have the courage to lift my eyes to his.

"Very well," he spoke at last. "I see if I wish to continue this stimulating relationship at all, it will have to be on your terms."

I stared at him, amazed that he would agree with me.

"Surprised you, did I? Or perhaps you would have preferred that I politely back out."

"No."

"Of course, I am not particularly polite when it does not suit my purposes, and putting a full stop to our relationship does not suit my purposes. I cannot very well protect you from your foolishness if we are not on speaking terms."

"As I said before, I am not foolish!"

"Blind . . . weak-hearted."

"You are insulting me!"

"I *thought* that might bring a show of your real spirit." His deep laugh rang out. "So we reach an agreement—not one that is entirely satisfactory, to me; however, we will work on that." With a devious smile, he lifted my fingers to his lips. "Until the next time we meet behind the potted plants . . . though I have a feeling you will soon be removing to the country."

"What do you mean?"

"Considering the season, his wife's behavior of late, and his desire to get you out of my company, that would seem Warringwood's next move. Have you been to Pemberton Hall? It is quite lovely, you know, down on the Sussex coast."

"Justin has spoken of it."

"Yes . . . well . . . I see Sally Jersey is watching us with considerable interest. I shall pretend to be the gentleman I am not and leave you now. But we shall meet again soon—*that* I promise."

He turned and strode with casual grace across the room, and for the moment I felt very much alone in the world.

TEN

RADFORD HAD ACCURATELY CALCULATED his opponent's next move. Justin met me in the downstairs
hall two mornings later with an ebullient grin, so in
contrast with the worried frown that too often
creased his well-molded, aristocratic features. He
took my arm and began walking with me. I could
barely believe the gesture; was acutely conscious of
the heat of his fingers on the sleeve of my gown.

"Lovely morning." He smiled down at me.

"It is. Wonderful for a ride in the park."

"Ah, but as I was just going to advise my wife, I am
afraid you will have to reserve a part of it for pack-
ing. We will be leaving for Pemberton tomorrow
morning."

"So suddenly?"

"I think it is high time we left the city, and I have
estate matters calling me."

"But how long will we be away? I shall need to
know what to pack."

"Several weeks. At least until September. You
will miss nothing in London. Almost everyone has
already left town and will not return until fall, and
then only for a brief period, after which

most—ourselves included—will retire again to their country seats for the holidays. You will find amusement at Pemberton, Marlena. I have a fine stable, and we are near enough the Channel to enjoy the cooling breezes."

Together we headed toward the breakfast parlor. "By the way, I want to apologize for my tirade the other afternoon. I spoke with Lord Jersey last evening. His wife was explicit in describing to him the scene that passed between you and Radford—how, following a brief conversation between the two of you, you were not noticed to exchange so much as a glance the balance of the evening, and Radford appeared in a dark and thoughtful frame of mind, barely hearing the comments passing in the room around him. Let me compliment you on your promptness in carrying out my advice. I take it you made it clear to him his attentions were not welcome in the future?"

"Yes," I replied, telling only a partial lie.

"Good. Shall we go into breakfast? I feel it is going to be a delightful day."

Arriving downstairs the following morning, I found the front hall in utter disarray—leather-bound trunks and bandboxes piled here and there, servants rushing madly around on last-minute errands. Caroline was standing to the side of the hall, cheeks flushed in anger. I wasn't surprised she was upset about the projected trip. In Sussex she would be out of easy reach of Captain Langely and all the other gay entertainments so readily available in London or Brighton, and I had a suspicion Justin wasn't disposed to opening his Sussex estate to constant partying.

Finally she and I were hustled into the light traveling carriage, its brass fittings gleaming, and four matched bays harnessed, stamping, between the shafts. The servants would follow in a heavier dray coach with the luggage. Justin didn't make his appearance until the last moment; no doubt a wise move on his part, in view of his wife's mood. As we climbed into the carriage he only nodded to us, passing by to speak to the driver. His final instructions complete, Justin returned past the windows, heading toward the rear of the procession and his waiting horse. The coachman slapped the reins, gave a call to the horses, and we were off.

After several minutes spent in deep silence, Caroline turned to me. "Really, Marlena, I cannot like the fact that Justin has rushed us off in this manner. He knows how I despise these sudden trips. The least he could have was allow us to take a small house in Brighton for the summer. But no, that would not suit him, and he will not allow me to go off alone. He can be so inconsiderate." She lapsed again into silence, her mouth tight. "Well, you at least should enjoy the country."

"I am looking forward to it."

"I must warn you, the local gentry are all staid, their dinner parties the greatest bore. Of course, with Brighton not far off, perhaps Justin will allow us to drive in for some shopping." There was a momentary sparkle in her eyes, which she quickly disguised.

So Captain Langely was to be in Brighton. "The riding must be excellent at Pemberton."

"For those who indulge. There is little else left but walking among the gardens to relieve the tedium . . . an uninspiring jaunt when one knows them all by heart. Justin will be out on numerous estate matters visiting the tenants. One rarely catches a glimpse of him but at the dinner table." Her mouth had gradually gathered itself into a pout.

The trip might have been more tedious for me if I hadn't been so delighted with the scenery beyond the coach windows. We'd opened them to let in the air, and everything outside was lush, green and gold, fresh smelling; rolling farmland and quaint villages nestled between the hills. Since we'd left London so early, there was no need to stop except for lunch and two changes of horses at the bustling, picturesque post houses along this much-traveled route.

Being gentry, we were afforded preferential treatment at each of our stops, the yard boys running to our leaders' heads and unharnessing them while Justin, Caro, and I were escorted to a small private parlor in the inn for refreshments. By twilight we were rolling through the stone gates of Pemberton Hall, down the graveled drive to the wide front door. I was delighted with my first view of the rambling three-story Tudor mansion surrounded by rolling lawns and ancient oaks. The house was alive with activity. The head groom and the butler came forward at the same time to greet us as we stopped. Footmen came down the steps to take the luggage. Once out of the carriage, I felt the breeze caress my face, bringing with it the scent of the not too distant sea. Although Justin had come down on his own mount, he was with us, dismounting before the steps, handing his reins to one of the grooms and coming to help us two ladies to the front door.

He spoke to the butler, and gave instructions to the grooms for the stabling of the horses and to the footmen for the unloading of the luggage. Then, smiling, he led us up the front steps through the front door.

"Caroline, I have put Marlena in my mother's old room, since it is close to your own."

"Have you spoken for dinner?"

"I advised Merwin we would be wanting it in an hour."

"Then let us go freshen up, Marlena," she said. "Later I will show you the house, and tomorrow the grounds. I do want to inspect the flower beds I had laid out in the spring, and the rose garden . . ." With these words we disappeared up the staircase, well-lit by candle-filled sconces placed on either side.

I was entranced by the house. It was Elizabethan—low beamed and hospitable, but huge. Caroline led me upstairs and to the right down a long hallway, then to the left into another corridor whose architecture seemed to be of a more recent date than the rest of the house. She told me that the wing we were in had been added by Justin's father in the Georgian style of high ceilings and light-toned wall coverings. She paused before a set of doors near the end of the hall, opened them, and motioned me in.

"This is my room. I shall take you to yours directly. It neighbors my room and is connected by a small dressing room. I must say that I am amazed my husband has put you in his mother's room. In my memory he has never before so honored a guest at Pemberton. However, it will be convenient for us. These last four rooms are part of a suite—first my room, then yours, then a sitting room, and lastly the master bedroom, all joined by connecting doors. Oh, do not raise your brows . . . Justin does not sleep there. He continues to use his old rooms. As I said, this wing is new, replacing the original central wing. The family sitting and drawing rooms are to the front of the house, the guest bedrooms in the wings. Downstairs are the dining rooms, the formal drawing room, the library, and the great hall, which makes a tremendous ballroom, should we ever have occasion to use it as such. I shall take you through some of the house tonight—at least on the ground floor. And perhaps you will play the pianoforte for us. I overheard you a few times in London, hidden behind the music room doors to play when you thought no one was listening."

"I thought that was my secret."

"You play exceedingly well." For the first time that afternoon, she gave a small smile. "I hope you won't refuse to play a tune or two—there are so few other entertainments here in the evening."

"Your husband has an interest in music?"

"None that I know of." She dropped her purse on the dressing table and led me toward the connecting door. In my bedroom too, candles were burning in readiness for my arrival. It was a lovely and elegant room, done in gold and moss green, with a fireplace along one wall and a velvet day bed beside it. Sheer draperies hung from the canopy of the four-poster bed opposite. The wallpaper was a gold fleur-de-lis on white; the curtains at the wide windows echoed the gold. The plush carpet was white and moss. Everything was as it should have been—soft and summery, warm and feminine.

Caroline led me off into the adjoining sitting room. Here too the candles were lit, and revealed a room of auras both masculine and feminine. The colors were deeper, more vibrant; yet there were feminine touches, in the delicate Sheraton furniture, the Limoges porcelain pieces, the cozy placement of the couches before the hearth. I wondered what the last room in the chain, the master bedroom, held, but Caroline didn't lead me that far. She moved back into my bedroom. "I hope the luggage has been brought up. Do you wish a bath?"

"There is not a great deal of time."

"I thought that myself. My husband does not like

to be kept waiting—though he will probably be in good spirits this evening since it is his first back at Pemberton."

Forty-five minutes later Caroline and I met in the hall and walked down together to the dining room. It was a long, low-ceilinged room, with dark beams against white walls. Fireplaces stood at either end, each large enough to hold half a tree. There were no fires on this warm summer evening, but I could picture flames licking up into the chimneys. A shining refectory table that could easily have seated thirty was the predominant furnishing in the room; placed about it were genuine Elizabethan carved high-backed chairs. On the walls were images of hunt scenes and pastoral villages, all original works, old and pleasing to the senses.

Justin was already there. I saw him at the other end of the room examining a painting—a new one, perhaps; he seemed to be studying the signature and the brushwork. He turned when he heard us.

"Ladies, how prompt. You must be as famished as I—and Marlena, wait until you taste Guillaume's delicacies! Caro, I have a notion to bring him to London with us. Come, shall we be seated? I have just been studying this new landscape. Quite good, don't you think? The artist is John Constable, an unknown, but he shows much promise."

I'd never seen him in so effusive a mood, open and smiling and talkative. If this was what a trip to his home estates did for him, I would prescribe that it be taken regularly.

Justin sat at the head of the table and Caroline and I to either side—together, a small offering to the huge table before us. A candelabrum set between us blazed with twelve lights, all reflecting from its silver surface. The dishes were the finest French china, the cutlery Sheffield sterling, the wineglasses old crystal.

As the first course was served and we began eating, Justin talked of some of the improvements that had recently been made to the house, restorations to the west wing and maze. He mentioned to Caroline a possible trip to Brighton and had her glowing. To me he praised the stables. He noted that he had a mare whose spirit was in tune with my own, and suggested we take a ride down to the coast to a neighboring village that boasted an original Norman church.

What had happened to him? I was stunned, but didn't push my hopes up by thinking his good spirits would last for long.

Justin didn't stay at the table for his port that night, but joined us immediately in the formal drawing room, where Caroline had taken me after a brief tour of the downstairs rooms. The drawing room was almost square, with the usual huge fireplace to one end; the walls a combination of white plaster and paneling; the draperies, upholstery, and carpeting done in darker, Elizabethan colors; and the antique furniture either of that era or from the later William and Mary period.

The most modern furnishing in that room was the pianoforte, which I guessed to be of fairly recent design, a Broadwood with pedal action and a longer keyboard than the harpsichord; yet from its setting in the far corner of the room, it blended with the decor.

Caroline renewed her request that I play. Hesitantly, I rose. There was no point in refusing; she would only press. Glancing briefly at Justin as I took my place on the bench, I noted the curious lift of his brows. There was a Haydn piece before me. I opened it and began, soon forgetting my nervousness and the two people listening. But the Haydn seemed too

staid, my tastes ran more to Chopin or Beethoven—
and the former had yet to put a note on
paper. At least Beethoven was alive and composing
during this era, and although my listeners had probably never heard his work, I knew I wasn't being too
incautiously impulsive in choosing to play it. At the
conclusion of the Haydn piece, I let my fingers slide
naturally into the "Sonata Pathétique."

They were both silent when I finished; Caroline
with her eyes wide; Justin with his cup lifted halfway to his lips. I played well—training had done that
for me—and knew the feeling of the music had come
through.

Justin studied me, his eyes seeming to go gray as
he did so, reaching unfathomable depths. There was
admiration in them, and something else—an intensity of feeling I both dreaded and desired.

ELEVEN

THE FRESH AIR was invigorating after so many weeks of city smog and dust. The sun shone on us from an almost cloudless sky. Justin and I often took long rides across the parkland, he speaking freely with a quiet pride of the various beauties of Pemberton and the workings of the estate. He explained the tenant farms and the distribution of the profits of the yearly harvest, pointing out the importance of the lay of the land: this low-lying piece was well suited to crops because of the thick topsoil brought up and left behind by spring floods; that higher, woodier area was more conducive to grazing cattle or sheep. Each farmer was responsible for his own acres, but Justin kept a careful watch over the whole, maintaining a friendly and fatherly tie with those who looked up to the master of the estate for guidance.

As I looked over at the straight-shouldered form riding beside me, appreciating the elegance of Justin's profile and the love of his land that glowed in his eyes, I pondered the still-growing depth of my sentiments for this man—sentiments that had survived our sometimes noisy disagreements. I was

learning to respect and empathize with him more
and more. And I'd grown almost certain it was not
only my imagination that sensed a reciprocation of
those feelings. There were signs, signals: a touch of
his hand unnecessarily long on my waist as he
helped me mount, a tone of voice, a gaze that seemed
to take in every feature of my face when we were discussing some impersonal matter.

There'd been visits from neighboring gentry to
break the days and evenings, a small dinner party
with card playing afterward. I found myself falling
into the relaxed country routine with an ease and enjoyment that itself disturbed me. I was becoming too
much a part of this world, forgetting who I really
was.

On an especially balmy afternoon, Caroline and I
left the estate grounds and headed off down the road
to the coast, she in a light curricle and I on horseback. The road was a fairly well frequented one, and
we'd already passed several fellow travelers. I
wasn't surprised to see two more horsemen approaching, but was astounded by the out-of-place fa-
miliarity of their faces. One was Captain Langely
. . . and the other, Radford! I hadn't seen him since
the night in London when I'd told him of Justin's decision. At that time Radford hadn't mentioned any
plans for leaving London, so my surprise was doubled at seeing him now. And what in heaven's name
was he doing with Langely? I hadn't known them to
be close friends.

There was no question of Caroline's reaction to the
surprise encounter—it was utter jubilation. And
with her eyes riveted on Langely, she lost all awareness of anything else. That I—or even Radford—was
a witness to her joy obviously didn't enter her mind.
I knew this meeting wasn't the sort of thing I wanted
to be an accomplice to even inadvertently, especially

with Justin's wrath hanging over both his wife's head and my own, but the shock of seeing Radford in such an unexpected place outweighed my common sense.

As Caroline and Langely moved off together up the road, deep in conversation, I halted and Radford drew up abreast of me. His black stallion was handsomely matched to his hair and his riding habit.

"Baroness," he exclaimed with mock amazement, "is this not a surprise? Meeting you here, of all places."

"Innocence doesn't become you, Radford. As astonished as I am to see your face, I suspect there is some method behind this meeting. I had not noticed you and Langely were anything more than casual acquaintances."

"This is true, but rummaging about Brighton, where I went for lack of anything better to do after you quit London, I happened to run into the man—and knowing him to be the light of fair Caroline's eyes, hastened to better our acquaintance. Our friendship has progressed well since that time, yes?"

"Admirably, but then it probably would have made little difference to you if you cared no more for him than for a stick in the straw. As you have said, whatever suits your purposes . . ."

"Yes," he said, and smiled. "Yet I would not let myself be too upset by the means, Baroness, for here we are—and did I not promise we would meet again soon?"

"You could just as easily have run into Warringwood riding down this road. Your memory is not so short you have forgotten that aspect of our agreement?"

"There is no law forbidding me to have business in this part of the country. As a matter of fact, I have a close friend not a far distance from here."

"Male or female?"

"Which would you prefer?"

"I just hope Caroline does not carry tales."

"And incriminate herself? No, I doubt that will be the case—hence my reason for bringing the captain. Cannot you see their lips moving in silent conversation, their eyes observing nothing but each other?"

"You have absolutely no conscience."

"Only when it suits my ends. But we are wasting time in fruitless debate. Shall we remain here or continue down the lane?"

"Let us proceed, but stay behind and out of earshot of Caro and Langely."

"My thought exactly."

We rode on at a slow walk. I was a wreck. True, there was no real fear that Caroline would talk, but we might as well have asked the rest of the world to come take a look. Almost immediately two farm boys came ambling up out of the pasture and paused to say good day; then a cart with a farmer's wife and daughter perched on the seat was trotted by—and all four people were tenants of Justin's. On the heels of the farm cart, another carriage passed by carrying the dowager Lady Carlisle, known to be the biggest gossip in the area; and not two minutes later we were forced to the side by a doctor's carriage rushing full tilt down the road on its way to an emergency.

Well, if not quite the whole neighborhood ten miles around would learn of Radford and Langely's meeting with Caroline and me, Justin Pemberton surely would. I cringed mentally as I pictured Justin's raising the roof when we got home—and the worst was that I did not want to hurt Justin. My pride still smarted at his dictatorial attitude toward Radford and me, but I hardly wanted to put myself in his bad graces. There were too much sympathy in my heart for his predicament with his wife; and then there was my own fascination with him, try though I did to push it to the back of my mind.

Finally I said to Radford, "This is no good. If you have not noticed, half the population of the coast has seen us. Either Warringwood will be out after you and the captain with a gun at sunrise, or I'll be restricted to my room for the next two weeks. Caroline has made her own bed—if you will pardon the expression—so I will not worry about *her* . . ."

"If it will serve your state of mind better, then let us get out of the spying crowd and into this next wood."

"No. My only choice is to head straight back to Pemberton . . . and somehow get Caroline to come along with me."

"You are wasting energy and breath. Come!" He grabbed my mare's bridle.

"For God's sake, Radford! I am *not* going into these woods with you. Let go of my bridle. A few frank words in Caroline's ear, and I should not have much trouble getting her home. Once we are there I shall think of something to convince Justin, if he hears any rumors, that it has all been a mistake."

"You are doing nothing of the kind. We will have a pleasant ride through the wood and meet the two lovers at the next bend."

"Pleasant? With my heart in my throat?"

"Oh, come, Marlena, you are not unsophisticated. The damage has already been done, if any has been done at all. Aside from which, I have no intention of seducing you . . . 'tis neither the time nor the place. What do you say? A nice trot and, when we reach the meadow I see ahead through the trees, a race across the pasture, over the fence, and onto the road."

"Oh, very well, but brace yourself, because if you think I intend to let you beat me across that meadow, you are mistaken."

"This stallion has not yet known defeat. Would you care for a wager?"

"What do you have in mind?"

"If you can get your mare over the fence before me, you may have my stallion for a week—provided, of course, you can explain him to Warringwood. What would you care to wager in turn?"

"Oh, Radford, if you win, you can have what you want . . . *if you can get it!*" But I had signaled my mare as I spoke those last words, and already we were several strides ahead of him and doing well. My mount was long-legged and over sixteen hands, and a fair match for Radford's stallion.

We thundered over the grass. I glanced back once to see him behind me, his stallion's nose closing at my flank; but I wouldn't let him have the best of me. I spurred my mare to greater speed, and the fence was only yards away. If I could get over it before him . . .

But he was gaining, and as I felt my mare gather for the jump, I saw him beside me; it was close. She was over. Her forelegs touched the ground, but his stallion was just that one instant faster. I saw his midsection beside my mare's forelegs and knew I'd lost.

I was fuming when we reached the road.

Radford turned his mount and, with a wide grin, trotted back toward me. "Well, I won, and have come to call the bet."

"I cannot imagine what you mean."

"Your words, if I remember them correctly, were, 'You can have what you want if you can get it.' Am I wrong?"

"I only meant you should get what you want from life," I prevaricated.

"One of the things I want may be you, Marlena."

"I will never be another in your string of mistresses."

"Have I asked that?" he laughed. "Actually, I was thinking of something else altogether."

"Oh?"

"Yes." He studied me. I dropped my eyes; not sure why, only knowing I found something unsettling in those brown eyes.

At my continued silence, he spoke again. "Have you really given thought, Marlena . . . serious thought . . . to your guardian's motives in keeping us apart?"

"What do you mean?"

"Come now, we've touched on the subject before. At least I have tried to hint it to you. You are a wealthy and beautiful woman. My lord Warringwood, for all the upstanding gentleman he is, cannot be blind to your charms. The thought must have passed through his mind what a lovely adornment you would make to his bed. Are you not totally in his power?" He lifted a brow.

"How can you say such a thing, Radford! To be insinuating such foul nonsense—"

"It is because I am your friend that I speak out."

"And what other motive have you? With your history, I wonder that you can have the effrontery to condemn anyone else!"

"Whatever you think of me, I am giving you good advice." His expression now was deeply serious, and his eyes remained on mine. "And there is your inheritance, too."

"The whole idea is preposterous! Justin hardly needs my money, and he has never hinted that he wants me in his bed!"

"And methinks thou protesteth too much." With a piercing look that struck far too close to home—how could he begin to imagine the many times I'd dreamed of Justin; fantasized what it would be like to have his naked form playing against my body under the sheets, or on the grass of a secluded meadow—Radford suddenly reached across the short distance between us. His strong arm went around my shoulders; his mouth came down on mine. Our horses fidgeted beneath us, but that didn't waylay him as his lips seared their message into my brain.

In his own good time, he released me, and stared across at me. His kiss was still hot on my lips. My face flamed, my senses spun.

"Think of that instead," he said huskily, "when you wander through your daydreams. It will bring you far more gratification."

"How dare you!"

"You should know I would dare almost anything. And I should hate to see you waste yourself on such as Warringwood."

"So it is a game—a competition. I am no more than a potential conquest—something to fall to the highest bidder!" I was doubly angry because Radford's kiss had stirred something inside me; I'd thought for a moment that he was sincere.

"You are far more than a conquest, Marlena. I hope someday you will change your opinion that I am a rogue and your guardian is your defender."

"And what have you done to make me change my mind?"

His gaze was steady. There was no hint of guilt or embarrassment in his features. He was cool, calm, while I felt my own cheeks flushing. "That is something you will have to see for yourself," he said.

"I thought I was your friend . . . worthy of some respect."

"You have my respect, *and* my friendship, *and*—"

"With special privileges!" I interrupted.

"If you are looking for an apology for the kiss, none is forthcoming."

I spun my horse away, too furious and confused to say more.

"Marlena!" It was almost a command, but I was already cantering off, pounding up to a surprised Caroline and Langely.

Somehow I managed to pull Caroline from her dear captain and get us headed homeward.

Radford sat on his stallion a few yards away, watching. There was a slight smile on his lips at my obvious efforts to ignore him, and that infuriated me further.

Caroline and I had little to say to each other on the ride home—no explanations, no questions. She was caught up in her dream world, and I had worries of my own. Why had Radford come? Why jeopardize our friendship when I knew a serious attachment was the furthest thing from his mind? Then there were his comments about Justin and my feelings for him. He'd hit too close to home, and I didn't want to think about how deeply I was entwined; how strong an attachment I'd formed for my guardian—a married man, out of reach.

My worries didn't leave me as the days passed. I waited in trepidation for Justin to learn of our meeting, for his wrath to come down on Caro's head and mine. Yet much though I quaked each time I passed him in the hall or met him in the stables, he only smiled at me and paused to talk for a moment about the estate, about guests who had come by, about my plans for the day and whether I was enjoying myself. Difficult as it was to believe, apparently no gossip had reached his ears.

Radford's insinuations too were often in my thoughts. I didn't believe for a moment that Justin

was after the baroness's fortune; nor could I believe
he would seriously contemplate luring me into his
bed—he was too much a gentleman to break the un-
written rules of his guardianship . . . But if he ever
did approach me, would I refuse him?

Not long after that we received an invitation from
Squire Ganthan, Justin's nearest neighbor, whose
lands met his along one long boundary. The squire
and his wife would be holding their annual lawn
party, and if we would forgive the shortness of the
notice since the squire hadn't been aware we were
down for the summer, we were all invited to be his
guests two days hence. Caroline was matter-of-fact
about this proposed entertainment. I had a feeling
she knew the captain wouldn't be there, and thus her
lack of enthusiasm. Since she'd been unsuccessful to
date in persuading Justin to let us take a day trip to
Brighton, she'd been irritable and short tempered.

The squire had said the occasion was to be in-
formal, more a picnic than a party, but the festivities
we saw when we reached his home were a far cry
from my definition of a picnic. Long tables were set
up across the back lawn under a huge red-and-white
striped canopy. Rustic benches and tubs of wild flowers were placed randomly under the trees to give the
impression of an unaffected woodland setting. A
portable fountain near the tables bubbled forth a
stream of champagne, which the guests were already
catching up in long-stemmed glasses. Near the doors
that opened into the drawing room at the back of the
house, a wooden platform, surrounded by potted
shrubs, had been constructed for dancing later in the
day.

Neither Caroline nor Justin seemed at all surprised by the elaborate effects, but it was my first
taste of the frivolities of Regency country life. Of
course, in London there'd been glitter and glamor

aplenty, but I'd expected it there, in a city of mansions and elegant town houses.

It seemed the Ganthans had invited anyone of any importance in the surrounding twenty miles to be their guests, and many people had traveled so far as to require they spend the night.

Carriages were still coming up the drive as we moved under the canopy to the refreshment tables and began filling our plates with delectables ranging from a whole quarter of roast beef and several whole hams, to fresh vegetables and jellied side dishes, to warm breads, to dainty French pastries and candied fruits. Justin brought champagne to Caroline and me and led us to a bench. We ate, concentrating more on watching the crowd than on conversing. What a picture of ease and merriment surrounded us: the ladies strolling across the green velvet lawns in high-waisted dresses of colorful lightweight materials that wafted in the breeze, elegant wide-brimmed bonnets tied over their curls, parasols opened and held high to protect their complexions from the bright sun; the gentlemen in fitted breeches, long-tailed coats, snowy cravats, and top hats moving leisurely beside them; the sound of laughter and low-toned conversation blending with the trills of the birds in the treetops. Caroline's eyes began to take on animation. It was a relief to see the sullen expression wiped from her face. Justin stayed with us until we had finished eating and one of the numerous servants had taken our plates; then he wandered off, having spotted a friend who'd come up from Brighton with his wife. Caroline soon saw some of her own friends and began tugging at my arm.

"Look, Marlena—Martha Hillyard and Jane Stanton. What luck! They have both let houses off the Parade in Brighton for the summer. I must hear the news."

I followed, not sharing her thirst for gossip, but enjoying the gaiety that permeated the gathering as the crowd spread out over the sun-dappled lawns.

The hours passed quickly, and as the sun began dipping over the hills, lanterns were lit; they were hung from the branches of the trees and strung up around the tables and the dance platform. Music drifted out into the dusk, and people began moving slowly toward its source. As I stood on the sidelines watching the dancers, unexpectedly my arm was caught by a young man I'd met in London. He pulled me up unceremoniously onto the dance floor, and soon, laughing, I was being jostled through the steps of a country reel. When my partner dropped me at the side at the dance's end, apologizing for the informality of his invitation and thanking me warmly, I barely had time to fan my face before the squire's eldest son, a man of about my own age, drew me out with him for the next set.

Justin stood, still with his male friends, under the trees, his face reflecting the lantern light. Caroline was some distance away from him, but I spotted her brightly flowered dress and the luminesence of her clear complexion as she smiled up into the faces of the many male admirers she'd gathered during the afternoon. I looked back at Justin; saw that his eyes, too, glanced in the direction of his wife, but his expression was that of the greatest disinterest. Always before, the sight of Caroline flirting had stirred some disapproving, irritated reaction in him.

My confusion increased when I saw him walk forward, step up onto the platform, and approach me. The dance with the squire's son had ended, and I stood by the railing, leaning one arm against it. Justin stopped before me. He bowed his head slightly, and smiled, though it was only a slight

turning upward of the corners of his lips; a serious
smile.

"The first waltz of the evening, Marlena. I am
wondering if you would honor me."

Justin didn't dance—at least I'd never seen him do
so in the time I'd known him, not even to oblige Caroline. Yet here he was, asking me, and I was dumbfounded. My surprise must have shown in an uncon-
scious widening of my eyes as I looked up at him.
"But . . . but, of course, I'd be honored."

"I am delighted."

His hand reached forward to take my own. We
turned, moved forward, and mingled with the other
couples. He was completely confident as he put one
hand behind my back, took my right hand in his, and
stepped into the rhythm of the dance. In the back of
my mind I thought how fortunate it was that the
floor was crowded. I soon lost my nervousness and
began to enjoy the strange and exciting new sensation of close contact with his body. Up to that point
there'd been no more between us than the occasional
handclasp, a hand on my elbow as I walked across a
room, a leg into the saddle. My reaction to the new
closeness was instantaneous. I fought the impulse to
tighten my fingers around his, press my face closer
to his neck, touch my hand to the golden curls that
lay along his collar. I told myself nothing was meant
by the tightening of his arm on my back so that I felt
his fingers pressing very unconventionally against
my ribs; the squeeze of his fingers around my own
was my imagination.

He said little except to ask how I was enjoying the
ball, but I felt his warm breath on my cheek, and in-
haled the scent of lavender spice rising from his
heated skin. As he drew me closer so that my breasts
were tight against the hard muscles of his chest, his

lips touched my hair. I was trembling, and sensed he was too. When the music ended, he smiled, and touched his lips to my hand; his eyes searched deeply into mine, and then he turned and walked off to rejoin his male friends.

I was so shaken, I stood frozen to the spot, unaware for several seconds of what was going on around me. It was the jolting sight of Radford's dark eyes meeting mine as he came through the doors of the drawing room into the lantern light that startled me out of my trance. His eyes seemed to accuse: I saw you with Warringwood. . . . What are you doing, Marlena?

I couldn't acknowledge him, though his expression seemed to ask just that. What was he doing here? I should have expected him to be invited—he was an influential lord staying in Brighton—yet somehow the thought hadn't crossed my mind. And after his behavior and my obvious anger at our last meeting, I didn't think he'd search me out.

Radford maintained his stance just outside the back doors of the house, partly in shadow, staring at me where I stood at a disadvantage—directly in the lantern light. He smiled at me slowly, a brilliant flash of white teeth; winked; looked hard toward Justin.

I forced my features to remain unflinching. Another country dance was beginning. Fortunately the couples moving toward the dance floor partially blocked Radford's view of me. I took that instant to turn my head quickly to look at Justin. He'd seen everything and was now glaring at Radford with an anger that at least matched his antagonist's.

As the evening progressed, so did the tension. Radford never approached me—though he might as well have, the meaning in his eyes was so obvious.

As I wandered through the crowd, trying to lose myself in the milling bodies, it seemed that no matter where I looked, Radford was there, his lips parted in a smile. He'd nod his head and almost salute me in those seconds before I had an opportunity to turn my head. Why was he doing this? Why deliberately provoke Justin? From the grim set of Justin's lips when I caught sight of his face, it was clear what he thought.

Justin didn't approach me again. Despite all the beauty of our dance, now he kept his distance; there was little doubt he was construing the situation between Radford and me to be something it wasn't. I tried to catch his attention, to smile and convey my wish to talk with him. He only dropped the lids over his eyes and moved away.

We left for home shortly after twelve. Justin said nothing to me in the carriage. I longed for some understanding look, a hint of the feeling that had passed between us while we danced. I saw only a cold, hard unapproachability as he stared at the cushioned wall of the carriage.

The moon winked at us from behind a cloud as we came up the drive of Pemberton and halted before the grand front entrance. Justin brusquely ushered Caro and me out of the carriage and up the steps into the front hall. Then, as the butler took our light shawls, Justin strode off to his study, and Caroline and I went directly up to our rooms, parting at our bedroom doors.

After undressing and washing my face, I climbed under the folded-down sheets. I lay there distraught, but sleep wouldn't come. My thoughts were churning, my muscles tense. My heart overflowed with hurt and confusion. Justin's soft attentiveness earlier that evening had broken through the wall I'd been so determinedly constructing around my emotions. I'd allowed myself to respond to him. Now his cool rejection left a void in my heart.

No matter which way I turned on the now warm sheets, I found no comfort, only an ungiving mattress and a pillow that had become a well-pounded lump.

About two in the morning, hoping that movement and a stiff shot of brandy might act as the sleep inducer I needed, I rose. I took it for granted that I would find what I was seeking in the library.

It was not easy going as I slipped from my room through the moonlit halls. Here and there a nightlight burned, and I found my way to the staircase without mishap. I slid round the corner of the downstairs hall to the room I knew was as much Justin's domain as was his study in London. There was a candle on the hall table outside the door. I lit it from the matches by its side, then entered. Bookcases covered every wall. The tall, small-paned windows bordering on the terrace let in enough light so that I could see quite well. I walked beyond the desk to the small sideboard standing along one wall. Here was what I had expected—a decanter filled with amber liquid. Unstopping it, I took a glass and filled it half full, then went to one of the chairs and sat down to a moonlit view of the park beyond. It was mystical in the soft glow—the evenly spaced oaks casting lightgray shadows on the silvery lawns between them, the moon and stars bright in the deep lavender above.

My thoughts whirled round and round . . . first to Justin, then to Radford . . . then to myself and the circumstances that trapped me. I was not a baroness. I did not belong in this maze. I did not know how to cope, which way to turn, what action to take, where my feelings lay. I was no more or less than Monica

Wagner, a middle-class American woman—reasonably intelligent, surely, but even more surely unprepared to deal with the problems now facing me. I'd only wanted to carry through with the charade, living on the fringes of it all, my emotions uninvolved, until my time came to return to my own world and my own problems. But I was growing more and more uncertain that time was coming; it was impossible to remain a bystander. I was frightened, afraid of my own weaknesses—especially my inability to hold my real identity in the forefront of my mind much longer; afraid of where the future might find me.

I left the library as the moon was moving across the trees. I thought it must be very late, but I didn't care. Leaving my empty glass on the table by the chair, I slipped through the moonlit room to the double doors and back into the hall. The hallway was dark. The light I'd been counting on to guide me up the stairs had guttered out, and only the dimmest of illumination came from some source along the hall at the top of the stairs. I cursed myself for not having taken the candle from the library, for the shadows were long. I trembled slightly when I reached the dark at the top of the stairs, turned to the right for a few strides, then stepped nervously down the corridor leading to my own bedroom.

There was one light flickering in a wall sconce all the way down at the end, and there, somewhere in the distance, was my door. First I would have to pass a great number of other doors and several darkened alcoves. I was a fool, I reprimanded myself, to wander about so late at night. I wouldn't do it again.

Suddenly a door opened. I saw a flash of light dance into the corridor; a figure. I knew Caroline was asleep in her room far down on the opposite side—and this was no woman, but a man of tall stature. A servant? I could think of no reason for a servant to be about at that hour unless mischief was his purpose. I didn't know whether to bolt back the way I'd come, retreating again into those dark, gloomy expanses, or to face the man head-on. He'd seen me, at any rate, and now appeared to be looking directly at me. It had to be a servant—the house was too well locked, and too well protected by two great mastiffs that roamed the grounds at night, for a burglar to chance entry.

I took a few slow steps forward. As I did so, the figure moved, the light from behind him glancing across his features. It was Justin. But that fact startled me at least as much as it relieved me, for what was he doing up at this hour, and why here in this corridor, giving every appearance of having lain in wait for me?

"You are wandering late at night, Marlena." His voice, after all the stillness, reverberated against the walls. He stood before me in a white shirt unbuttoned to partly reveal his chest.

"I could not sleep. I went for a walk."

"Strange to think of someone roaming about this great manse as a sleeping tonic." He had taken a few steps to close the distance between us; now he reached out a hand to take my forearm.

"I couldn't think of anything else to do. I went to the library to sit by the windows for a while."

"And had a brandy."

"Why should you think that?"

"I saw you, and have waited here for your return. Had I been aware of your liking for strong spirits, I could have had a supply left in your room."

"It seems you have had a few brandies yourself."

"As I have. You cannot sleep? What is it that disturbs you?"

"Only my own restlessness, but I shall be fine. And what keeps you up?"

"The same . . . restlessness."

"To the point of sneaking around empty rooms and scaring me half out of my mind?"

"But as I told you, I was waiting for you, and what more logical spot to do so than from my own chambers? Were you not aware these were my rooms? I realize the situation between Caro and me might warrant my removing myself to the farthest corner of the house . . . however, she is quite safe. My desire is long gone."

"You need not tell me about such things."

"No, I need not."

I tried to pull my arm away.

He held it more tightly. " I was wondering if your insomnia was not more the result of a nagging conscience."

"There is no reason for my conscience to bother me."

"No? After you have deliberately thwarted my wishes and seen Radford behind my back? I am well aware that the two of you were out riding together and my wife rendezvousing with her dear captain the other afternoon— I have heard the news from many lips. And if you think that little farce you put on for my benefit this evening deceived me, you are a bigger fool than I. He virtually raping you with his eyes; you pretending to play the innocent! Do you want him that badly, Marlena?"

"You are completely misconstruing the situation. If you will let me pass, I want to go to bed."

Instead of releasing his hold, he drew me closer, until my chest was pressed against his own and I could feel his warm breath on my face. "Why do you find his attractions so much greater than mine? Oh, no—don't bother to answer, I'm afraid I am aware of the reason. . . . It is that rakish air that excites your blood—While I have been allowed to present only the face of respectability."

"For God's sake, Justin, what are you saying!"

"Tell me you have not been aware of the attraction that has existed between us from the start. Tell me you did not feel as I did tonight when we were dancing. And in the days before that—an understanding, a knowledge I tried to disguise in harsh words."

"This is the brandy talking—not you! In the morning . . ."

"Tell me." His fingers had come up to caress my cheek. His voice was no more than a soft sigh. "Tell me you do not want to feel my touch . . . do not enjoy this contact of our bodies . . . do not want me to do this . . ."

His head dropped down, his lips seeking. At first it was just a butterfly caress, a tentative brush of mouth upon mouth to send tingles over my skin; then the kiss deepened, growing more intense, devouring, until our lips were parted and our tongues meeting hungrily. I heard his deep moan, felt the firm, hard strength of his body buffeting me. My thin nightgown was no insulation against the heat of his hands as he pulled me closer. I felt weak, unable to resist; all the logical reasons in my mind why this shouldn't happen suddenly dissolved.

"Finally tonight I've found the courage to speak to you as I've wanted to for months." His hips pressed forward. "Oh, Marlena, I want you . . . I want you so much. Come with me to my room. We need each other, will be good for each other."

"No . . ."

"We are a man and a woman. And we *belong*."

"I can not!"

"Why?"

"No good can ever come of it. It does not matter what I feel or you feel . . . can you not see that?"

"No! All I can see is a chance for some happiness in my life, and there has been little enough of it; these last years. Even our fathers saw that we were meant for each other."

"The finaglings of old men." My voice was breathless as I fought the impulse to go to him. "You told me yourself you would not have done what they said."

"How could I have known how I would come to feel about you? Come, Marlena, please . . ."

"No! I cannot!" I pushed myself away from him. In his surprise, his arms loosened, and I slipped away from him, turned, and stumbled down the hall to my room. Shaken and unable to see clearly, I flung myself through my doorway, closed the door behind me, and fell back against the wood.

I stood there like stone a few minutes, the scrolls of the woodwork pressing into my back, then sank into the chair by the fireplace and buried my face in my hands. I felt such a longing inside; such a deep desire. All the yearnings I'd tried to push to the back of my mind were suddenly there, revealed, and I knew I could no longer force them from my consciousness. I wanted him so much that I knew if it hadn't been for my confusion and the unexpectedness of it all, I would have gone with him; lain in that bed of his; joined myself to him and loved him.

TWELVE

GOLDEN MORNING LIGHT slipped in warm and brilliant to wake me with the cock's crow. I sat up against the pillows, and everything that had occurred the night before was there again before my mind's eye, just as it had happened a few hours before. I felt my muscles go weak with the remembrance of our ignited emotions; of Justin's arms around me, of his kisses. But it was wrong, so wrong. Not only was he a married man in a world where divorce wasn't condoned, but I was a woman from another century whose path should never have crossed his. There could be no future. Circumstances . . . endless circumstances forbidding me to move: a world not my own; a year of guardianship to wait out; a man's love I couldn't accept; a lack of independent resources; the knowledge that any day I might be gone, yet was forced in the meantime to continue playing a game of appearances lest all fall down on my head. Only the instinct to survive and an avid curiosity to discover what lay beyond the bend could keep me going.

On other days, when I'd resolutely paid little attention to Justin's whereabouts except to notice whether or not he was at the dinner table, he'd always seemed to crop up around a corner. Today, when it seemed every thread of my existence was linked to him, when even the lightest mention of his name in conversation was enough to send a tremor to the pit of my stomach, he was nowhere to be found. I suppose he'd had as much thinking to do as I, and, for obvious reasons, needed to avoid me.

I waded through the afternoon, fiddling with as many odd and meaningless tasks as I could find to occupy the hours. Finally, my restlessness having become too much for me, I had the mare saddled and went off for a solitary ride across the parkland.

Justin didn't appear at dinner either; he'd sent a message that he would dine with a neighboring landowner he was visiting on business. I could barely force my mind to concentrate on Caroline's ramblings, especially when nearly every thought that crossed my mind was a betrayal of her friendship. But why should I feel so torn with guilt? Wasn't she carrying on a clandestine affair of her own and betraying her husband painfully and cruelly?

Finally she became irritated with my distracted responses and, signaling the footman to take away the tea things, told me that she would spend the rest of the evening in her room with an engrossing novel.

Sleep was the furthest thing from my mind, and I wandered out into the moonlight. The mellow glow from the windows of the house left a reflection on the grass behind me. The warm night air was soft, filled with the summer smells of new-cut hay, the sea, the rose garden.

I walked alone, pausing under one of the spreading oaks to stare out at the dimly illuminated landscape. My yearnings had become a dull ache; an ache I hoped with each passing day would subside, then dis-

ppear. I remembered other hurts I had known and
ow, gradually, they'd healed.

I must have been out on the lawns at least thirty
minutes when I sensed something behind me. I had
heard nothing—no movement, no sound—but I
urned. Justin was standing in the shadows, watch-
d. How long he'd been there, I didn't know.

"Did I startle you?" he asked softly. "When I was
oming in from the stables, I saw you out here alone
nder the trees." He was only a few feet away, yet
eemed uncertain whether to come closer. We stared
t each other, each hesitant to move.

At last he spoke, almost in a whisper. "I want to
pologize for last evening. I stepped beyond the
ounds."

I stared at him, unable to say a word.

"Have you nothing to say? Can you forgive me?"

"Yes."

"I am so sorry, Marlena. Everything I said I
meant, but none of it should have been said at all."

"I understand."

Perhaps nothing more would have happened if
ustin hadn't reached out a hand. "Come, let me
alk you in." As his fingers closed warmly about my
rm, something sparked between us. He looked
own at me, and in the next second pulled me
gainst him.

With that contact of our bodies, his arms tight-
ning, there wasn't anything either of us could do
ny longer to fight the desire that flamed between us
ke a bonfire. Suddenly reason didn't seem impor-
ant: nothing mattered, only the two of us.

I watched as he lowered his golden head; welcomed
is lips. His mouth was firm, soft, enticing. His arms
rushed my body against his own. Our lips parted for
long, deep kiss; he whispered huskily.

"Marlena, please, don't say no again."

We were on the grass, slipping down together into its softness, two lonely, searching people striving to find comfort in each other.

His fingers touched my cheek. "How can I think of right or wrong any longer?" he whispered. "I only know I need you."

His body pressed against me with all its need. His long legs entangled with mine. His broad chest was a sweet heaviness on my breasts. The scent of him aroused me as I buried my face against his neck and felt the stubble of beard on his cheeks. His fingers slipped beneath the bodice of my gown and hungrily loosened the fastenings; he searched for, then caressed the warm white mounds. I moaned at his touch, ripples of pleasure flowing through me; knew I wanted him as much as he wanted me. As his hands moved down my body and over my hips, his lips blazed a trail of kisses across my neck, down to the deep cleavage of my breasts, where they lingered. He pressed his hips against my thigh. I could feel his need, bulky against the constriction of his pants. Then he was lifting my skirts, drawing the lacy underwear down over my legs and feet, his hands moving to my inner thighs to tease me in dizzying swirls, drifting ever upward until my flesh was alive, yearning.

In answer to the soft cries of pleasure I could no longer restrain, his hand went to the fastenings of his breeches, hastily slipping the buttons, pressing the tight cloth down over his hips and thighs. I felt his warm, bare flesh against my palms as he freed himself and moved over me.

"You're so soft, so lovely," he moaned.

Then he was entering me, full of fire, urgently. Reaching beneath my hips, Justin lifted them to meet his for the pleasure that had been denied him for too long. I felt his efforts to hold himself in check,

to prolong the ecstasy. Then, finally, with one last
thrust, he groaned, a tremor coursed through his
body, and we clung together.

It was many long minutes before we moved. He
lifted his head and touched his lips to my forehead, to
each cheek. "I love you. From the moment I laid eyes
on you, I knew I wanted you."

I studied his face in the moonlight. He'd turned to
his side, his arms still wrapped about me. My hand
slid along his back, getting to know the feel of him;
over his taut muscles, across his broad shoulders,
down his arm.

"You return my feeling?" he whispered.

I was afraid to tell him how much; afraid to think
of what we'd done.

He must have sensed my fear. He turned his head.
"You do not regret this night? It has been inevita-
ble. . . . Each day when I saw your face, I knew the
feeling was growing, tried to hide from it behind unfeeling treatment of you."

"I've felt it, too. But you are a married man. There
can be no promises, no future." I lifted my hand to
touch his cheek.

"My marriage to Caro has been no more than a fa-
cade for years. There is no longer any love . . . if ever
there was, in the beginning. I am a man, Marlena. I
have needs, feelings. I know what it *is* to love. I cannot continue being tied to a sterile, passionless relationship when I know there is something so much
more beautiful within my grasp."

"And how long do you think you would be happy
living behind a veil of subterfuge, with a wife you
can present to society—and a mistress behind closed
doors! I would not want that kind of existence."

"There are ways." He kissed my forehead lightly,
and gently squeezed my fingers in an effort to reas-
sure me.

"Not divorce."

"Many would say I had just cause."

"You're my guardian. I am living as a guest under your roof and your wife's! You would be ostracized."

"Does it matter what the rest of the world thinks?" But the look in his eyes was not devoid of pain.

"Someday it may mean a great deal to you. You have your position, your future career to consider. Little would be worth the price of losing them both."

"By the time a divorce was final, we would be old news, not worthy of drawing-room gossip. A new scandal will have arisen."

"There are other people to think of besides ourselves."

"If you are referring to my wife, can you really think I would waste a moment's sympathy on her?"

"She deserves some consideration."

"Then let it come from another source. I am not about to throw away my happiness—I have waited too long for it." He rolled onto his back, and pulled my head against his shoulder. His eyes gazed upward at our leafy canopy, rays of moonlight sneaking through here and there between the branches. "Marlena, when Fate takes a hand as it has with us, there is always a solution."

I'd always denied the existence of Fate, yet now I wondered if such an entity existed; was my master. How else could I explain my strange journey to this world, into the arms of a man I would never have met had my life continued along its normal course? And what was I doing falling in love, carving such a deep impression on his emotions and my own, when at any moment that same capricious Fate might snatch me back to my own time?

"I realize I am asking a great deal of you," he said intently. "I am not blind to what may happen to your name and reputation, but we will be cautious. I will protect you until that day we can make our relationship open to the world. I love you, Marlena, completely and without reservation. I want you to understand that. . . . It does not even matter to me that there was someone before me." His voice caught for a second. "Did you love him?"

"It seems such a very long time ago now . . . a different world altogether . . ." But Justin's words had disappointed me; served as a sharp reminder that I was living in an era in which men had one set of morals for themselves . . . and another for women.

Perhaps he had noticed my reaction, because his fingers tightened on my arm; he sighed. "We have found each other. That is all that matters."

THIRTEEN

I BEGAN THE NEXT MORNING humming a gay song; felt buoyant all the rest of the day. And although I didn't see Justin until dinner, except to exchange a wave of the hand with him from a distance as he rode out to see his tenants, I moved about almost dreamily, in a world where no stark realities were manifest.

When I arrived in the drawing room for a glass of sherry a half hour before dinner, he and Caroline were already there. The sour look on their faces told me that conversation hadn't gone well before my arrival. Had he told her about us? No, he wouldn't be such a fool. But had she seen us together? Was she suspicious?

It was with difficulty that I reduced the wattage of my smile as I gazed across the room; but since Caroline's back was toward Justin, there was no need to temper the warm look he returned to me.

I sat down opposite Caroline on the couch. Justin handed me a glass of sherry.

"Well, how has your day been, Caro?" I asked.

"The usual tedium," she complained, "though from the little I have seen of you and Justin this day,

I gather you have each had a diverting time. Fortunate that some of us, at least, can get out of this house for entertainment."

"The carriage is always at your disposal," Justin remarked, "should you wish an airing beyond the grounds of the house."

"An excellent notion, should there be anywhere for it to carry me. You know I do not get on with these rustic neighbors of ours, and since you forbid me Brighton, there is nowhere I wish to go."

"Let us not go into that now, shall we? You have but a brief time more to endure, then we are off to London again—though were it not for the business that calls me back to town, I would be tempted to extend our visit. The air and rest seem to have agreed favorably with you, my dear. I trust there will not be a relapse."

"I do not know what you are speaking of," she replied sharply. "You must know as well as I, I am bored to tears."

The butler entered to announce dinner, and saved Justin a reply.

Though only a small distance separated us at the dinner table, as I sat to his right, it might have been a mile: we both watched the tone of our voices, what we said; tried to behave in the same manner we had in the past, as though nothing had occurred to transform our relationship. His eyes strayed every so often to study me, then quickly returned to his plate. He paid no more than perfunctory attention to Caroline, who had become loquacious all of a sudden on the subject of Pemberton, talking of a change of decor in the Blue Salon to the new Greek revival style, and of possibly finding a new housekeeper, since of late Mrs. Crane seemed "not the least inclined to follow one's wishes." To all of this he nodded agreeably when I knew perfectly well that the Blue Salon con-

tained some of the family's most prized heirlooms
and that Mrs. Crane had been with the household before Justin was born and was a greatly valued re-
tainer.

Soon enough the meal ended. We all went to the
drawing room, and after tea had been served, Justin
asked if I'd join him in a game of chess.

Caroline rose at that moment. "I believe I will retire. I am not feeling quite well."

If she expected this to solicit a sympathetic response from her husband, she was disappointed.

Out of politeness I turned toward her. "Is this
something sudden? You seemed all right at dinner."

"Only a slight stomach pain coming on."

"I'm sorry," I said. "Let me know if there is anything I can do."

Justin was setting out the chessboard, placing the
pieces in position, paying no attention whatsoever to
his wife, though her eyes were riveted upon him.

Suddenly her smile was very sweet. She turned to
me. "As a matter of fact, perhaps I would feel a bit
better if you would read to me for a while. There is a
novel of Mrs. Radcliffe's I did want to finish, but I
fear the strain on my eyes would only make my head
ache. Would you mind, Marlena? I am sure Justin
can amuse himself in his study as he does most every
other evening."

I threw an aggrieved glance at Justin. "No . . . no,
of course I would be happy to. . . ." There was nothing else I could do.

The glare he was directing toward his wife was
vile, but if she noticed it, she chose to ignore it,
smiling at me instead. "These are the times it is
most wonderful to have you here. Good night, Justin.
I trust you will sleep well. Come along, Marlena. I
will have Margaret lay another log upon the fire."

I hadn't even time to say good night to Justin,

managing only a quick smile over my shoulder as I was shuffled out the door.

My heart sank; I knew this was a portent of things to come, a sign of what the days ahead would be like for us. I foresaw furtive glances, smiles of secret meaning behind Caroline's back, stolen moments and whispered words, lies, excuses, and through it all, frustration, never being allowed to show our love in the open or to be as close to each other as we longed to be. The freedom of an honest relationship wasn't to be ours, and I suddenly felt overwhelmed by the deceit of the act I was perpetrating with Justin—and the precariousness of my position in the household.

I had no close contact with him until late the next evening, and then only for a few minutes. We would be leaving for London soon, and I had a feeling I'd find it more difficult to be alone with Justin then, in a smaller house, with less privacy, when the three of us would be expected to go out in the evenings—at least Caroline would expect that, and if I suddenly began to refuse, it could only seem odd. Justin, of course, could restrict her entertainments as he'd threatened to do before we left for the country, but now he no longer cared if she misbehaved. Her continued misconduct would be perfect fuel for his fire should he ever decide to press for divorce.

He wanted me to come to his room, and oh, how I longed to! But Caroline was a light sleeper, as I'd discovered since our coming to the country, when, on several occasions, I'd wakened during the night to hear voices beyond the wall and known she was up, with her maid in attendance. The chance would be too great to take. If she should be awake, and come to my room for some reason and not find me there . . .

We made do with long, frustrated embraces behind

his closed library door, a flood of words that had been dammed up by our usual inability to speak freely to each other, a promise, a touch of impatience from him at my stubbornness, a hunger that went beyond it all. And we shared an underlying sadness at the circumstances that surrounded us.

Though Justin and I were happy now, here in the country, even with our rides across the parkland, a few stolen episodes deep in the center of some secluded wood, there was always the fear that someone would unexpectedly walk up on us. We weren't children who could innocently follow our heart's desire without fear of the consequences.

We arrived in London to an unusually sultry heat that was relieved only by the promise, from a distant rumbling, of thundershowers to clear the air.

The days went forward as they had before. Summer drew to a close, taking with it the heat, and gradually the ton began drifting back to town for the "little" season. Justin and I had our quiet moments together early in the morning on our rides in the park, and later in his study sipping coffee while the rest of the house still slept. But the strain I'd anticipated was there all around us.

Caroline seemed a new person now that she was back amid the glamor of city life. She chattered on excitedly until my ears rang. All her plans—Almacks Wednesday, Covent Garden Friday, tea at the duchess of Lancaster's Thursday—didn't she ever tire of that same old round? Of course, Langely was in London, and his presence amid the whirl of social life was all the motivation she needed.

Justin went out with us at night, playing the role he despised. Yet despite his efforts at appearing the solicitous spouse, gossip was again rising . . . and this time the hushed whispers were about the trio of

Justin and me and his wife. Not that Justin and I did
anything deliberate to incite gossip. Perhaps it was
the way he looked at me; his apparent lack of interest these days in his wife's continuing flirtation with
Langely; the way our bodies met in a dance—or even
the fact that he danced at all, often singling me out
as his preferred partner. When two people are in
love, much though they may try to deceive themselves into thinking they are hiding their feelings
from the rest of the world, the emotion is there in
every action and gaze, and I was caught up in such a
whirlpool of infatuation, I wasn't thinking—only reacting.

Although Caroline and Langely were carrying on
their affair with at least a modicum of discretion, always leaving people guessing, unsure whether
they'd actually stepped out of line, Justin and I knew
better. One night I came across them in a back bedroom in the Cowpers' town house. We were there for
an evening reception, and suddenly I found the
crowd suffocating. I excused myself to go upstairs to
freshen up, and got lost among the long corridors. As
I moved down a semidarkened hallway, hoping it
would bring me back toward the center of the house,
I heard voices, carefully lowered yet unmistakable,
coming from along the hall directly in front of me. I
would have turned and ignored the sounds if I hadn't
at that moment been passing a partially open bedroom door. The light from the hallway, penetrating
the dark of the room, glanced off the figures of Caroline and Langely closely entwined on the bed. It was
an intimate embrace, his hand, slipped under the
bodice of her gown, gently caressing her breasts; her
soft voice urging him on. For a second I stood frozen
in shock; then, embarrassed at witnessing such a
very personal scene, I retreated on silent feet. What
kind of fools were they? Didn't they care at all about

ing caught? Yet, when I thought about it, were
ustin and I acting differently?

Risking everything, Justin came to my room a few
ghts later. I heard a light knock at the door just as
was about to blow out my candle. At last we were
one, had our privacy, could be what we wanted to
e to each other. I gloried in his tall, golden body
iding naked against my own; his broad chest
gainst my breasts, his long legs wrapping around
e beneath the sheets. And we made love to each
her as after a long thirst, deeply and almost with-
ut relief until the early hours of the morning. I'd
llen asleep with his arms wrapped around me;
oke only as I felt him stirring, lifting himself on his
bows and surveying the dim light seeping in from
hind the curtains.

"Almost dawn. I must go, Marlena."

I was only half awake, gazing at him through
eepy eyes. "Already?"

"I go to my solicitors this afternoon. I have already
t the appointment to discuss with them the terms
ad possibilities of instigating divorce action."

"You did not tell me." I sat up quickly. "Are you
re?"

"I would go to the ends of the earth to sanctify my
lationship with you . . . to allow us to be together
we were meant to be."

"Love is a fragile thing. It does not always stand
 to a beating."

"Ours will."

I touched his face, feeling a pang of uncertainty.
efore, he'd only talked about a divorce. Now that he
as taking action, I was suddenly frightened . . . for
th of us.

That afternoon, while my stomach churned as I
ondered what was happening with the attorneys,
aroline and I went to the dressmaker's shop in Old

Bond Street, and looked over the many bolts of fine cloth as she tried to decide which would be the most suitable for a new afternoon dress. When finally she'd selected a fabric, decided upon the style, and had her measurements rechecked, we climbed into the waiting carriage and headed back through the busy traffic to Upper Brook Street. Since she'd just bought a new gown, Caro was, according to her nature, in an excellent mood. I wasn't, and was having trouble keeping my attention on the thread of her conversation as we waited at the corner of Piccadilly for a tangle of carriages to clear and allow us room to pass.

An unexpected change in her tone, though, alerted me.

"I begin to believe my husband finds you quite charming," she said lightly.

"Oh?"

"Or did you think no one noticed?"

"I'm afraid I do not understand you, Caro."

"Strange that he has suddenly acquired an interest in social activities . . . in dancing. Why, I can no recall him ever taking the floor with me, except a our marriage ball—and then only for a moment for tradition's sake. Now he seems quite anxious—or have you coaxed him out of his shell?"

"I am sure it is coincidence. Caro, all you would ever have had to do was ask him to dance."

"Perhaps. Margaret has told me she has heard you two talking in his study in the mornings."

"Occasionally. We have coffee there after our ride."

"And late at night also?"

"Not to my remembrance."

"Let me make one thing clear to you. There may be many things on which Justin and I do not agree, bu he is my husband, and I have no intention of allowing any woman to come between us. He is your guardian, and you are a guest in my house. Need I remind you of that fact?"

"That is hardly necessary. But remember, too, that I am a full-grown woman and my own mistress. I take orders from no one."

"Are you threatening me, Marlena?"

"Nothing of the kind. You started this conversation, Caro. Draw your own conclusions."

Her words had amazed me. Why was she suddenly so possessive of Justin? Was her self-esteem so weak, she needed both Langely and Justin? But, of course, her husband was an earl of unlimited resources. Langely had nothing—no title, no wealth, nothing to offer until his uncle died. Then too, I should have had the insight to realize that greed was part of human nature. Very few of us will give up valuable possessions except out of desperation.

That night I found Justin alone, standing out on the terrace behind his study, as was often his habit, smoking a cigar.

I came toward him across the grass from another doorway. Hearing my approach only as I came upon him, he was startled until, in the dim light, he recognized me.

"Marlena," he spoke quietly, "but this is pleasant. I had not expected to see you until our morning ride."

I went directly toward him, and took his extended hands. "Justin, she knows. We had it out this afternoon. She had no really damning evidence in hand, but she is suspicious. Her maid must watch every move we make. The gossip you and I have both heard around town must have reached her ears too, and started her wondering. The thing that puzzles me, though, is why she even cares, the way she has been behaving."

"The reason is obvious," he responded wryly. "I have put the riches upon her back and the food in her mouth. I am almost certain she never planned on this affair with Langely to be more than a dalliance—something to take her mind off the horrors of living with me and to sate the sexual appetites that must have been tormenting her since she refused me access to her bed two years past. But what did she say to you?"

"A number of things. She has noticed that we dance together, when you have never danced before; our talks in your study. I denied the evening meetings, but she has drawn other inferences as well. I think she was trying to tell me that she has no intention of letting you go, or of closing her eyes to our relationship. She reminded me that I was a guest in this house, and your ward."

"She would do that. Caroline is not stupid, for all that she often appears to have moths flying through her brain."

"What are we going to do?"

"Nothing, for the moment, aside from what we are doing. I have my spies as well. She may be wary of us, but if I know her inclinations, she will not be able to keep herself long from the side of Langely. And once she makes a false move, I will have all the evidence I need."

"I liked her so much when I first came here," I said sadly.

"As I did, obviously, upon our initial meeting, but first impressions are not always sound bases for one's judgment. Of course, Caro is not all wrong in this. I have given her cause."

"Certainly not cause to justify the ends she has reached."

"And mine are more honorable?" He lifted his brows. "She may have veered off course before I, but I have long had the thought in the back of my mind. . . . I only waited for the right woman to come along to prompt me to action. And I have been dreaming of you since the day I met you; fantasizing holding you in my arms whenever I please, taking you to my bed every night—fantasizing *your* having been the woman standing in the country garden the day I met Caroline. No, the fact of the matter is that Caro and I are not well suited to each other. With another man she might very well have been the picture of complacence; we both might have found happiness rather than a need to look elsewhere for the salve to soothe our souls. I carry my own guilts."

His arms went round me then, his hands on my shoulders grasping me tightly. The irises of his eyes were fires reflecting the deep emotions churning within him. "This is my second chance, Marlena. One chance, which not many men have, to try again when they have the wisdom of themselves and the world to do the right thing . . . both for themselves and another. I don't want to give up this chance to be with you. I love you. I want you beside me and will do everything in my power to make you happy. But I pray I have not been overly selfish in thinking of my own happiness when not even the news I have today from the solicitors is heartening."

"What did they say?"

Justin suddenly became very businesslike, but his voice was tired and there were lines etched in his forehead and between his brows. "I must have her followed, spied upon for some concrete evidence—"

"But we have that. I saw them together on the bed at the Cowpers'."

"I am afraid you will not be counted a reliable witness. If you had raised a stir that night and others had rushed up to see the same . . ."

"I have cursed myself for not doing that, but I was too shocked to think clearly."

"I know. Do not fault yourself. Had I been the one to come upon them, I doubt I would have thought ahead. However, I must accumulate some evidence, and then it must be weighed to see if it is worthy of divorce action. All this will be made difficult now that Caroline is aware of our own liaison; she will be on her toes. If we do accumulate evidence, then a decree from Parliament will be necessary after both sides are heard. The weight is on my side only because of my position and her unwillingness to provide me an heir. There are enough loyal retainers in this household who know the facts and who I can call on as witnesses, should there be any need. If I can gain concrete proof of her adultery, though, none of this would be necessary. Needless to say, my solicitors did everything in their power to talk me out of it. When I pointed out that my chances of begetting an heir were nigh on impossible since my wife refused me my marital rights, they went so far as to suggest I ply her with wine and champagne one night, and seduce her and have my way. Then once the seed was planted, the child born, there were always mistresses . . ."

I had to smile. "Did they suggest what to do if no child was born from the first encounter? I doubt Caroline is fool enough to allow that kind of approach too many nights. Though perhaps that is what she has needed—a show of force."

"That, too, I have tried, with a very detrimental effect on my ego. To be treated with abhorrence as though one is a predatory monster does not heighten male arousal."

"Oh, Justin!" I said, laughing. "There are too many women who could only wish for such a man as you! You could have the world at your feet."

He took my chin in his hands, a twinkle in his eyes, "Or find a variety of mistresses?"

"You already have one very loving one."

"Marlena, I do not think of you as a mistress. Only as the woman with whom I wish to spend the rest of my life."

"Be that as it may, it will not be easy."

"When I asked you to return my love, I anticipated a difficult road," he said quietly.

But later, alone, I wondered if he really understood how difficult it was going to be—if either of us had the strength to survive and overcome the obstacles with our love intact. Was I being selfish in falling head over heels into our affair, encouraging him? Was my love strong enough to warrant the sacrifice he was willing to make?

FOURTEEN

IN AN EFFORT to starve the gossips and reduce his wife's own conjectures, Justin didn't go out with us socially as often as he had before. Since, as it was, he and I had so little chance to be together, this added restraint was a burden; but then, it had a double purpose. Away from Justin, out from under a watchful eye, Caroline was more likely to step over the edge; give Justin the evidence he needed. He was giving her the rope with which to hang herself.

A discreetly dressed man now often appeared in our vicinity. Whether Caroline noticed his presence and suspected he was in Justin's hire, or whether she had suddenly acquired a bit of wily wisdom, it was impossible to tell, but she too was behaving with more circumspection. She had her captain, but if there were secret trysts and garden meetings, they took place when others were not around to observe.

Although on the surface Caroline and I put up a civil front, beneath it there was a disquieting hostility between us. There would be no recovering the warm, open friendship we'd shared during the early weeks of my sojourn.

When the mood seized her, she would make double-pronged comments to annoy me. "I see Radford has not yet made an appearance in town. Perhaps he too noticed a new light in your eyes."

"Radford's a busy man. There are no ties between us."

"Yet I think he stays away for a different reason."

"I fail to see what reason of any kind he would have to avoid me."

Her eyes narrowed, "Perchance you underestimate me, Marlena. There is a very obvious reason—and the three of us are living in the same house."

"And what of Captain Langely?" I couldn't help thrusting.

We were at that moment interrupted by the butler announcing a morning guest, and because Caroline turned her head as soon as the butler opened the door, I couldn't read her expression.

I tried not to let her vindictive words bother me. True, I hadn't seen Radford, but given all his interests, legitimate and otherwise, I wasn't surprised he had business elsewhere.

It was almost impossible now for Justin and me to have a moment alone, even the smallest conversation, without fear of being spied on. I'd caught Caroline's maid listening outside the study door. She claimed she'd dropped something on the carpet and was trying to find it. Justin wanted to dismiss her, but what good would that have done? Caroline would have found a substitute elsewhere in the staff: not everyone, surely, was uncompromisingly loyal to Justin.

We longed that much more for the comfort of each other's arms; for words of love and reassurance. There were a few stolen opportunities, brief and frustrating in their desperation, both of us too pent up from the waiting and worrying for our thoughts and feelings to run free. When we were out together, obviously I couldn't make it evident to the rest of the ton that my interests were set on Justin. I was forced to keep up the pretense of flirting and dancing with eligible men; and there were quite a few still interested—those who thought that my reluctance to tie myself to an eligible lord in the initial months of my first season made me that much more tantalizing. I began to believe in the old adage that a woman should let herself be chased until she caught the man; certainly these men loved the challenge. The few times Justin accompanied Caroline and me, he watched their hands on my arm, imagined the words they tried to whisper in my ear, saw me smile and answer them. I had only to look into his leaden eyes to know the agony he was suffering.

We'd been back in London four weeks. A ball that Caroline last June had connived Justin into giving in my honor, was scheduled for the following week. Obviously it was now an affair Caroline planned more for her own enjoyment than for mine, but we maintained the surface amenities anyway, and the activity of preparation was a welcome distraction from my problems.

There hadn't been an occasion in recent memory to match that of the earl of Warringwood's opening his home to all of the ton. Justin's father had entertained, and lavishly, but his son, never. Nearly every one of the invitations sent had been accepted, and because of the large crowd expected, Caroline and I had quite a few late errands to run. We went to the draper's shop in Bond Street. I'd gone in with her, but I became bored and uncomfortable in the stuffy shop as she haggled over the color of the linen cloths for the buffet tables. I went out into the street to stand beside the carriage to wait for her.

Lost in thought, I paid no attention to the crowd passing by—until I heard the low tones of a familiar voice in my ear.

"A penny for your thoughts, madam."

I jumped.

"Is that so much to ask? Perhaps I should have offered my fortune." Radford lifted his hat and smiled—that half-cynical smile that was his trademark. "Baroness . . . pardon me for startling you. It was too tempting an opportunity to let pass."

"Radford. This is a surprise."

"Yes. It has been some time, has it not?" His dark eyes studied me, serious above the smiling lips. Everything about him was the same—the magnetic promise of excitement, the worldly charm and allure; the dark-brown jacket and immaculate white cravat looking ever so much better on him than on the foppish dandies who thought themselves to be the epitome of style. "I was just leaving my tailor. You had a pleasant time in the country?"

"Very nice. You stayed on in Brighton?"

"No, as a matter of fact, I did not. I left shortly after that country party at which we saw each other. There seemed little point to my remaining on. You take my meaning, I presume." His voice was everything it should have been for an unexpected chat on the sidewalk, yet I knew something of Radford's ways. . . .

"It wasn't the nicest trick you played coming to the Ganthan party."

"Something in my system persuaded me it would be a diversion. And a diversion it was, though not quite as I expected."

I could have said a great deal more to him about his behavior in the Sussex woods, but I had a feeling he was waiting for just that comment from me, so, perversely, I changed the subject. "Are you planning a long stay in London?"

"That would depend on several factors. There are matters I must pursue."

"I see."

"I would gather you have been pursuing a few of your own."

"I miss your meaning," I said vaguely.

"I think you take it very well. However, if you wish to play the dunce, I shan't persist."

"My intelligence has never been lacking . . ."

"No, but your common sense and the ruling of your emotions leave much to be desired."

"You do not know me well enough to make a statement like that."

"I know you better than you believe, and though I have been in town only twenty-four hours, the gossip has reached me. It would appear you have taken the ton by their ears again, though not in as sweet a vein as last time, perhaps. It is understood your guardian is taking extremely good care of you. Ah, but there is no point in dwelling upon such insubstantialities. I have set people to talking often enough myself and still enjoy the polite company.

"I was wondering, Marlena, now that I have the joy of seeing you again, whether you might join me in a ride in the park . . . tomorrow afternoon? I will not suggest that I meet you at Warringwood House, since such a meeting could only bring unpleasant repercussions—but at the gates at Hyde Park Corner? At half past four, shall we say?"

"I do not know, Radford. We are preparing for a ball at Warringwood House . . ."

"I have received my invitation."

"Have you?"

"You seem surprised, but you could not have

thought your guardian's sweet wife would omit my name from the guest list? Such action would be in very poor taste, since so many are waiting to mark my presence."

"Yes, the matrons will die of curiosity as they shield their daughters from the sight of you. But your presence will be a welcome insurance against tedium for all present, I am sure."

"Then at the park gates at half past four?"

"No, I think not . . ."

"What are you afraid of?" he taunted. "I had not *really* thought coward's blood ran in your veins."

"It is nothing to do with that."

"No? Or since our last meeting has your guardian strengthened his ties upon you?"

I dropped my eyes, afraid I'd give the truth away. "I shall see you at the park gates tomorrow afternoon."

He raised his hat, nodded in satisfaction, and set off. For some reason I wanted to reach out my hand to stop his departure, but he was gone too quickly into the crowd tramping along the street. Only a few seconds after his back disappeared, Caroline came from the draper's, and with a word to the driver, we left for home.

The three of us were there for dinner that evening, seated about the huge table in the dining room, all the candles lit, the fire blazing, for now, in late September, the evenings were growing chill. There wasn't much in the way of dinner conversation. Justin and I looked at each other; Caroline watched. We quickly averted our glances.

He reached for the salt. "Well, Caro, things are progressing well for the ball?"

"Extremely so—only a few arrangements yet to make. I have requested Maintly to have flowers brought up from Pemberton. You have no objection?"

"No. Whatever decorations you need to make the place suitable."

"As I thought. You will be pleased to hear that nearly every invitation I have sent out has met with an acceptance. Even the Jerseys will be here, though they will be coming in from the country, and the Seftons and the duke of Clarence may even attend. The Esterhazys informed the duke of the fete, and he expressed an interest. It would seem he is an admirer of our dear Marlena." Her eyes turned in an arc toward me; they were alight with malice.

"We will not discuss such things at this table," Justin intervened.

"I cannot see why not. He is eligible, and it is well known that he is now searching about for a suitable wife. How much higher could Marlena look than to a royal duke?"

"Quite so. Now that he has gotten a dozen illegitimate brats off Mrs. Jordon, he suddenly realized he requires some legitimate ties. I will not see Marlena coupled off with such as he."

"It would be one of the best connections she could make."

"Caroline," he warned, "you get carried away with yourself."

"Well, at any rate, to have him attend our ball is something of a feather in our caps."

"In yours, perhaps. I am not impressed with such things."

We left the dining room shortly thereafter and had our tea. Caroline left for her room, and I stayed on awhile with Justin. Hardly believing our luck, we were careful, as we had to be, in our conversation.

Standing by the fire, he poked a few of the logs to a brighter blaze and spoke in a hushed voice.

"Can I come to you tonight?"

"It is too risky. I've heard footsteps past my door these past few nights."

"Whom do you fear? Caro's maid?"

"She would be the first."

"I can rid the house of her, as I have said before."

"Still too dangerous . . ."

"My man will lie through his teeth to swear I have spent the night in my chambers, snug beneath my own bedclothes."

"And his testimony would mean nothing if other eyes saw you elsewhere."

"Oh, Marlena, my love, you worry too much."

"But I have to. One of us must. You are trying to gain evidence against her. How will it look in Parliament should it turn out the other way round?"

"She still sees Captain Langely. The man I have engaged is gathering evidence. It is slim to this point, but there will be more. They are wary now . . ."

"Will it ever be enough? As you said yourself, Caroline has no intent of carrying this affair with Langely too far. She needs you for her position and support."

Suddenly his voice took on a cooler tone. "I hear Radford is back in town."

"Do you?"

"Have you come across him?"

I lied; I hated myself for it, but I hadn't the heart to tell him the truth. "No."

"Caro tells me she has invited him to our ball. A farcical affair it should be, would you not agree? Everything appearing before the world exactly as it is not."

"It is only a ball . . . a few brief hours during one evening. We shall get through it."

"I suppose it would waylay the gossips if you appeared civil to the man."

"I had not given it a thought. And there is no saying he will even approach me. It has been some time." Fortunately, Justin swallowed my words without question.

But by the time I went to my room for the night, my mood had become melancholy. Was it just the nerve-racking tension in the house, the frustrating circumstances of our relationship that were wearing me down? Justin repeated his request to come to my room . . . almost pleaded with me . . . but I remained firm. For that night, at any rate, I wanted to be alone. Everything suddenly seemed too much for me.

The following afternoon I met Radford. I left the house for the stables almost eagerly, hoping to escape my oppressed mood. Caroline was in her room feeling under the weather, suffering from the spells she'd been having too often lately, though she wouldn't expound upon her malady even upon my most sympathetic pressings—and here I did sympathize with her. I remembered that first terrible attack of hers shortly after I'd arrived; had noticed recently the deepening shadows under her eyes, the increased pallor of her skin. But perhaps it was just worry over her captain and the intolerable situation in the house. Justin had left that morning for his usual business rounds. No one expected him until shortly before dinner.

As I entered the park, my eyes searched for Radford among the dashing array of horsemen and the press of gleaming carriages with their stylish occupants. I didn't see the rider on the prancing black

stallion until he hailed me from across the roadway.
I lifted my hand, and he came trotting forward, exquisite in his horsemanship, erect, masterful. "I
wondered if you would come," he remarked.

"You imagined I would not?"

"Commitments are often made to be broken."

When I said nothing further, he turned his mount
and led us down one of the paths. I was well aware of
the eyes of the tonnish crowd all around us, alert,
watching; for why else come to the park at the fashionable hour if not to gossip, see who was with whom
and perhaps latch on to a new *on dit?* I didn't want
word of my meeting with Radford to get back to
Justin. He'd be angry, and I'd have to make explanations I didn't want to make. I nudged my mount toward one of the less-frequented rides.

"Let us get out of this spying crowd, Radford."

"So, things have not changed. Still we must sneak
around." The double meaning was clear from the
tone of his voice, but I deliberately made myself ob-
tuse, and offered no response.

"When must you be back?" he asked.

"In an hour. You have not told me, Radford, where
you've been these last weeks."

"In Wales, visiting my sister."

"It must have been urgent business, to call you off
to such a domestic scene."

"The christening of my godson. You see, my sister
persists in trying to make a respectable man of me."
He grinned.

"But then she lives so far from London, perhaps
she does not know your darker side."

"She misses very little. These are her small efforts
at opening my eyes to the benefits of the married
life—settling down and getting a few offspring of my
own."

"She sets impossible goals."

He lifted his brows. "Do you think so?"

"It hardly matters."

Scowling, he studied me thoughtfully. I didn't like his penetrating look, and to avoid it I kicked my mare into a canter and moved ahead of him. We'd ridden a considerable distance, to a section of the park I'd never visited. The shrubberies were lush, the trees mature and broad limbed. Radford didn't follow immediately, but when I was forced to slow the pace, he drew up alongside.

"You cannot run from your troubles, madam," he said suddenly, perceptively. "Is there something you wish to say to me . . . something you are hiding?"

"I have nothing to hide."

"The rumors I mentioned earlier?"

"I thought this was going to be a friendly visit." My voice was short.

"As you say." He was silent for a moment as we walked the horses. "There is a lovely garden just beyond these hedges. Have you seen it?"

"When did you develop a love of flowers, Radford? It does not seem your style."

"Oh, on one of my evening walks I came across this spot. Wonderful what the night air will do for one."

"And a bit of muslin by your side. Have your mistresses, then, acquired an aesthetic interest in the wonders of nature? Or perhaps their brand of horticulture is somewhat different from mine?"

He laughed. "You really should put a curb on that tongue of yours, Marlena. One day you will offend someone. Would you care to take a walk through the garden?"

It seemed a strange invitation coming from Radford; but why not?

"We can leave the horses here." He gestured toward the iron fence to the side of the bridle path, dismounted, and came around to help me; then, securing the horses' reins, he took my elbow and led me through the gate.

It was a beautiful spot, just as he'd said. We strolled in silence for several minutes along the circular graveled path, on either side of which were bountiful manicured beds of mums and late marigolds.

"You are indeed pensive today," Radford said softly.

"I was only admiring the flowers."

"Or avoiding a conversation you find unpleasant," he suggested.

"I am not avoiding anything."

"I really dislike nagging at you, you know . . . but you have a knack of late of doing things to raise my ire."

"That would not be a problem if you stopped listening to the stories society concocts."

"In this case I might advise you to do the same. I do not suppose your sharp mind has missed the intent of this particular gossip."

"I have heard it all."

Suddenly he turned on me. "And this is all you have to say? Has your self-esteem slipped so low that you would consider making yourself that man's mistress?" I had never before seen Radford frankly, unironically angry.

"I've indicated nothing of the kind."

"Yet the idea does not appear to arouse you to indignant fury as it would have done several weeks ago. What has happened to you? You realize I speak up only because I think you are worth so much more than to ruin yourself on this sordid affair!"

"You are mistaken, Radford." I laughed to throw him off the track. "You have been too long in the sun. Shall we find a shady spot for you to recover?"

"This is no joke, Marlena! I am quite serious. We

have been through this before, and I think you know I am speaking to you as a friend—a well-meaning friend."

"You should have enough to keep you busy with your bits of muslin and opera ladies without worrying about me. Ravona Wilde, isn't it, the actress? Your newest mistress? And before that it was Pamela of the sweet voice; you provided her with a house in Chelsea. But you see I have not meddled in your affairs, so why should you try to meddle in mine?"

"Have you considered that for you I might give up the others?"

"Ha! With your predilection for wandering, I would never believe it possible. No, Radford. You are not a one-woman man. In less than half a dozen months, you would be regretting your decision."

"That remains to be seen. I am giving you good advice with only your well-being in mind."

"And I suppose your actions in Sussex were a sign of your deep sincerity."

"I was wondering when you would get to that. So, you are still angry."

"You could at least apologize."

"As I told you, I have no intention of apologizing for an incident you enjoyed as much as I. If you were not so blinded by your devotion to your guardian, you might very well see that!"

"This conversation is growing old, Radford. I am tired of being preached to, and will thank you to keep your remarks about Justin to yourself." I started to turn away.

His hands gripped my shoulders and swung me around toward him. "Perhaps it's more than words you need—only actions get through to you!"

"Do not be a fool."

"I am never a fool . . . never."

His fingers bit into my skin so hard that I winced. I tried to draw away, and he forced me against him. I saw the anger in his eyes, the pride. Then his mouth came down hard, bruising, seething with power and passion. One of his hands gripped the soft skin at the back of my neck; the other forced me close so that I felt the hammering of his heart against mine. Only in the last seconds of the kiss did his lips relent, gain a tenderness.

Then he was pushing me away, his dark eyes staring into my soul.

"Wake up, Marlena!" he growled. "Take the clouds from your eyes." Then he turned on his heel and left.

Shaken, trembling so badly I had to clench my hands together, I stared at his broad back in utter disbelief as he strode across the grass to his horse, mounted, and without looking back, galloped away.

FIFTEEN

THE BALL was a success. We had cleared the large upstairs drawing room—its dimensions more than amply large enough to hold the mob. Only a few chairs
had been left, and one long table for liquid refreshment. Food was provided in the dining room on overflowing tables: cold canapés, hot meats, sweets,
breads, fruit, coffee and tea. Champagne was served
throughout the evening, unliquored punch, and, in
the library, harder refreshment for the men. There
was an orchestra for dancing, and in the salon, card
tables had been set up for those more interested in
that form of entertainment.

Justin, Caroline, and I stood on the reception line
greeting the guests as they entered. It seemed an in-
terminable time before Justin signaled the musicians to begin. The room was overflowing with
laughing, glittering people; anticipant, curious
about the goings-on between the members of this unusual household. I wondered if Justin felt the same
tension as I. And what of Caroline's thoughts?

Then the music began; a waltz—a daring move on
Caroline's part, opening with a dance that wasn't
yet entirely accepted in London. Justin turned to me,

extending his hand, seemingly oblivious of the suddenly widened eyes of the guests nearest us. I tried to
wag my head to him in warning. Either he missed
my message altogether or decided to ignore it, because he came forward. True, the ball was in my
honor, but with all the gossip that had been going
around about us . . .

Justin Pemberton's wife was left standing alone as
he led me onto the floor; pulled me close with a look
in his eyes that said he'd dismissed all other human
beings but me from his mind; no longer cared what
vicious tongues would say. His eyes, the soft, private
smile, and the firm pressure of his hand on my back
told me everything.

And it may have told the rest of the room as well,
because we danced on alone, out of either our guests'
politeness or their shocked startlement; not until
several measures had been played did the other couples join us. I was conscious of the sudden blanket of
silence dropping over the room; felt the stab of
watching eyes; sensed the mental clickings as people
found their speculations confirmed.

I couldn't wait for the dance to end. Didn't Justin
feel the tension that held me tight as a bowstring?

Caroline, smiling viciously, met us at the side of
the floor and immediately went to her husband to
take a possessive hold on his arm. Soon several
others gathered around us, including none other
than Sally Jersey. My heart was in my throat, and I
found it almost impossible to speak. I noticed Sally
Jersey studying me speculatively. Unexpectedly, a
few moments later she drew me to the side.

"You surprise me," she said bluntly. "I had
thought all these rumors no more than a bag of
wind."

I swallowed. "I am not quite sure of your meaning."

"Come, now. I speak of Warringwood and you."

"Lord Warringwood is my host."

"You have not answered me."

"No, I have not, my lady, because I do not know exactly what you are asking."

"For goodness' sake, call me Sally. Your rank is no less than mine—nor would the size of your fortune warrant such modesty. Now, what is going on? Last I heard, your interests were in another direction . . . one that had my blessing. I cannot believe you such a fool to throw over the attentions of Radford."

"Radford is no more than a good friend; but at least he still is that, as far as I know."

"He has made you no offer?"

"I have never expected one from him."

"But I should warrant Warringwood has not hesitated to make advances, and has had them favorably met."

"He is a married man!" I answered, choking out the hateful words and feeling every inch the hypocrite.

"From what I have heard of his wife's behavior of late, he has had ample provocation to look elsewhere." She glanced across the floor to where Justin was standing. "Handsome gentleman—not that he mixes often in polite company. Your father's executor and your guardian, is he not?"

"Yes."

"Considering the size of your inheritance, that gives one much to ponder."

"How would you be aware of the size of my inheritance? It is not publicly disclosed information."

"No, but my husband has a friend at Watkins and Witt who let it slip that the Baroness von Mantz, orphan and heiress to approximately"—she lowered her voice—"one million pounds, was presently abiding in the earl of Warringwood's home until the end of the year as a stipulation of her father's will . . ."

"You have said enough, I think."

"Have no fear. These words were uttered in confidence to my husband at a private table by a normally trustworthy man who was half-tipsy with the brandy my husband had been supplying him all evening. My husband has a reputation for discretion, and neither have I reached this place in society by flapping my jaw when it should remain closed."

"Thank you for that."

"My only concern is for my friend Radford. I have known him a good number of years. His reputation is not savory, nor are certain of his activities. Beneath it all, he is generous hearted, a gentleman and someone I would not hesitate to trust with my life. I also know he thinks a great deal of you and had thought you intelligent enough to have perceived all this."

"I am aware of his qualities. There has been no reason for secrets between us."

"Apparently there are one or two secrets too many."

"I think you're reading more into our relationship than there is. It is no more than a friendship, for both of us."

"I wonder if Radford will agree. It would seem he has been a bit behindhand in his evaluation of the situation." She turned her gaze to the crowded room. "A pleasure to have you in London, Baroness." With that she left me.

A moment later Justin walked over. "You and Sally Jersey had a nice chat. You are well acquainted, I see."

"Just slightly."

"Is that so?" He was speculative. "What had she to say? You seem upset."

"We should talk later, Justin. We have been seen together too much already tonight!" My nerves were utterly on edge. I could only give him a pleading look; then, spotting Percivel Harriman standing a few yards away, I hurried off.

Smiling, Percivel took my hand. "Your ball seems to be quite a triumph."

"So good to see you, Percivel. And how is Meredith?"

"She is well, very well."

"Is she not here tonight?"

"Oh, yes, over at the other side of the room. She wanted to come to speak to you, but you seemed so engrossed in conversation."

"I should love to see her. It has been so long . . . and, Percivel, am I jumping the gun by wishing you well—the two of you?"

He crimsoned; so unlike Percivel, who could have delivered a political diatribe before the prime minister without blushing. "We were thinking of the spring."

"My best to both of you. You always seemed so well suited. Yes, bring her over."

When he did, the three of us fell into a quiet discussion.

Radford hadn't made his appearance yet, though it was characteristic of him to arrive well after the rest of the guests. I'd been thinking about him a great deal the last few days, and my fury at his behavior on our last meeting hadn't abated one bit; had been refueled, in fact, by my remembrance of my own response to his kiss. When he did enter, I wasn't near the door, and saw him only from the distance as he went directly to Caroline. He then turned to Justin. The two men appeared civil, but only barely. I was glad I couldn't hear the terse courtesies exchanged.

Radford began winding his way through the crowd, calling out greetings where necessary, until he spied Captain Langely. They met each other with a firm handclasp and an honest smile. Perhaps I'd misjudged Radford in thinking his friendship with Langely in Brighton had been purely selfish, but at the moment I had no inclination to give him a kind thought. Justin, who was watching the two men with a steely glare, seemed ready to explode. It was bad enough that his wife had invited her lover to a ball under his very roof, but to see Radford and Langely together—his rivals in turn for the affections of his wife and his mistress—must have been a blow to his pride.

Another set of dances began. The attention of the crowd was diverted as dancers took to the floor. I saw Sally Jersey watching me again. She looked over toward Radford, then back to me, her meaning obvious.

Justin approached me. "I see your old beau has arrived."

"Who might that be?"

"Remember to whom you are speaking. There is only one who turns my innards to steel."

"All right, yes; I see he has come."

"Will you dance with him?"

"I seriously doubt he will ask."

But that was precisely Radford's next move. He was talking to Lord Ashford near the refreshment table. They parted company as Justin left my side, and Radford headed determinedly in my direction.

He stopped before me, a twinkle glinting in his eyes.

The nerve of him—the absolute gall of the man! After leaving me stranded in the park (and it had taken me some time and a lot of aggravation to mount the sidesaddle without help), he could walk over now as though nothing had happened!

"Baroness. I have not had the pleasure yet this evening of presenting my compliments to you. You are looking as beautiful as ever. Red peau de soie becomes you admirably." His gaze swept over the low décolletage of my gown.

"Radford." My voice was ice.

He chuckled. "Not still angry with me, are you, Marlena?"

"I am furious, and if this were not a public party, I would tell you precisely how much."

"Would you?" The grin never left his lips. "Can you be so very angry as the result of something you enjoyed so very much?"

"Why . . . *you* . . ."

"Temper, my dear. You *are* the guest of honor, and I was just about to ask if you would do me the honor of stepping out for this next country dance with me."

I stared at him in amazement, but before I had the time to get the words of a refusal out of my mouth, he took my arm and started walking me toward the floor. "I thought this a good maneuver to break the ice. One turn about the floor with you and, of course, I will behave most decorously for the balance of the evening."

"As if you could find such behavior within your powers. How dare you leave me in the park!"

"Oh, so it is *that* that upsets you? I thought perhaps it was the kiss. Now, now, Marlena—slapping my face in these surroundings will only bring you unwanted attention."

"Sometimes I could strangle you!" I forced a smile for the benefit of the other dancers.

"I'm sure you could. The feeling is occasionally mutual, but tonight I intend to be the perfect gentleman."

"I pray."

"You can be sure. One must gauge each move carefully in a game where your opponent has gathered his forces against your queen."

"You are obviously not talking about chess; still, you will have to clarify yourself."

"I had a word or two with Sally Jersey after my arrival this evening . . ." He grinned as the movement of the dance drew us apart. When we were rejoined, his expression wasn't so sweet. "So you have decided to confirm to the polite world that you have become Warringwood's mistress?"

I gasped. "Sally Jersey has gone beyond herself! I never verified that to her."

"She said as much, however—took your lack of a strong denial as sufficient proof."

"It is no proof at all."

"Do not lie to me," he growled. "When did it happen?"

"I refuse to dignify your impertinence with a response."

"In Sussex? Yes, of course. The three of you in his great house, and his wife not caring. It was when you returned to London that the rumors began. It is just as I suspected. I could curse myself for a fool for taking myself off to Wales!"

"If you do not this instant cease speaking nonsense, I will walk off this floor! I have said nothing. Your imagination has done that."

"Would that I could believe you."

"It hardly matters to me whether you do or do not. If your intentions toward me had ever been honorable, you might have something to say."

"Marlena, you know perfectly well I have tried to tell you on several occasions of my admiration for you—your intelligence, your charm, your love of life. There are not many women I would honor with such a compliment. You have so much in your favor, why are you throwing it all away on Warringwood? Perhaps he has some finer qualities I am too prejudiced to see, but he is still using you." He paused, spoke more quietly. "Can you not believe I care enough about you to think of your happiness?"

The exigencies of the dance separated us again, and there was no further opportunity to talk before the music ended. Radford led me off the dance floor, yet he hesitated a moment over my hand. His dark eyes looked deep into my own. "Marlena. Think about what I have said." Then he bowed and walked away.

Before anyone else could approach me, I left the party for a few minutes of quiet in my room. As angry as I had been with Radford moments before, his last words had a ring of sincerity. I'd always considered him my friend, trusted him; and despite his stolen kisses, I felt I could still do so. I had to admit that we had a great deal in common, that Radford understood me better than anyone else I'd met in London—even Justin. His words were prompting me to think clearly for the first time in months; to remember who I was, assess where my impulsive actions were leading me; to take a second look at my feelings for Justin.

When I returned to the ballroom, they were announcing the last waltz before intermission for supper. I didn't want to dance and, instead, had planned on going over to talk with some of the guests; but Justin caught me as I crossed the room, and led me to the dance floor.

I knew that Radford's sharp eyes, as he stood watching near one of the doorways, would not miss a trick—not the movement of Justin's lips as he whispered in my ear, the look in his eyes, the squeeze of his fingers as they held mine tightly. Shortly before the waltz ended, Radford left for the night. But his had not been the only eyes watching. I knew this evening would be the topic of conversation for many days to come.

SIXTEEN

AS I EXPECTED, tongues wagged following the ball. A long item in the *Gazette* society column described the event and told how "Lord Warringwood and his beauteous ward behaved in a quite warm and friendly fashion during the waltzes they were seen enjoying together. It would appear they have reached a very interesting level of understanding. One wonders how the Lord's wife is adapting to the whole."

But it was as we entered Almacks the next Wednesday that we felt the sharpest stabs. Heads turned as the three of us came into the room, Justin between Caro and me, one hand on her arm and the other on mine. I ignored the stares, until later, when I was frozen in my steps by the bold smirks I saw on several women's faces; few bothered to disguise the looks behind their fans. Most of the men who approached me smiled with a certain unspoken suggestion; still others made comments that would have been more appropriately directed to one of the notorious demimondaines. Though the snubs hurt, I was more concerned about what the scandal would do to

Justin. In the past few months he'd gained a very strong standing among his Tory friends. There'd been rumors of his being the prime candidate to rise to the leadership of the party. I'd been aware of his delight with the prospect; enjoyed the look of proud accomplishment in his eyes when he spoke to me privately of his hopes, of the work he wanted to do in the conservative cause.

Yet in the days that followed, Justin, smarting from Radford's behavior at the ball, the unspoken challenge, seemed to throw caution to the winds —pulling me aside publicly at the Esterhazys' political reception when I became engrossed in conversation with one of the foreign diplomats; forgetting his usual care in front of the servants and showing his feelings for me in the tone of his voice, the possessive touch of his hand on my arm. Where before we had amiably discussed the happenings of our days, now each evening he demanded a detailed account of my actions during every hour we were separated. When, one morning, Caroline decided she didn't feel well enough to accompany me to the hatmakers' to pick up a bonnet I'd ordered, Justin immediately decided he would drive me. My protests were useless, and we were seen alone together in an open carriage in Bond Street by half the gossipmongers in London.

The scandal grew worse, and I was beginning to feel engulfed; the situation was entirely out of control. I pleaded with Justin to take a care. He couldn't seem to understand how out of hand his behavior had become, and thought my anxieties stemmed from the slights I'd received since the ball.

Overwhelmed by my worries one dreary October day not long after, I knew I had to get out of the house for a while. Caroline was in her bedroom with her dressmaker and wouldn't miss me, but I didn't

feel like walking in the park, where I would have to
take my maid. I thought of Hookham's Library. I'd
run out of reading material and had a few books I
should return. Justin had left the house earlier in
the closed carriage for some business appointments
and his club. I decided to walk, since I didn't want to
take the time to have the stablehands harness the
smaller cabriolet. It wasn't all that far to the library,
and the exercise would be good for me. Putting on a
high poke bonnet that matched my blue serge braid-
trimmed cloak and leaving a brief message with the
butler, I escaped out the front door to the street.

The rooms of the library weren't crowded, and I
could browse among the shelves at will, taking books
that interested me to one of the reading tables. The
next hour passed quickly as I lost myself in the pages
of the volumes, relaxed, and temporarily forgot my
worries. At the end of the hour I'd selected four books
to bring home to read, signed them out, and stepped
through the paned glass front doors of the library to
the street.

The gray-blanketed sky looked ominous as I hurried homeward through the crowd on the bricked
sidewalk. I'd gone only a short distance when the
first huge drops of rain began to fall with all the
promise of a downpour. I knew I wouldn't make it
back to Warringwood House without getting thor-
oughly soaked, and when I spied a hackney cab up
ahead discharging a passenger, without thinking
twice I ran forward and signaled the driver. Jumping into the dry interior, I gave the driver directions
and leaned back on the dirty, worn seat. At one time
it had been black velvet, but the nap was long gone,
rubbed through almost to the stuffing in places. That
didn't bother me in the slightest; I was out of the
rain that was striking the cab roof with a vengeance.
I pitied the poor driver up there on his open box seat,

and the horses clopping over the slippery wet cobble-
stones.

Soon enough the hackney was at the steps of
Warringwood House. I dropped a generous fare in
the driver's hand, feeling sorry for his soaked mis-
ery, then hurried up the stairs to the door. Before I
reached it, it was flung open, and Justin stood on the
threshold.

"Where have you been!" he roared as I ran into the
hallway.

"I left a message with Williams. I went to
Hookham's."

"In a hired hack!"

"Well, no, I walked over. But with the rain, I had
to have some conveyance back."

"And you went alone, without your maid or any
other escort!"

"Yes, why?"

"It is totally unseemly! I thought you would have
had more sense. You are not to leave this house
unescorted again! Do you not think society has
enough to talk about?"

"And whose fault is that!"

"I obviously do not blame you for the gossip, but
there is no need to make it worse!"

"Why are you making such a fuss about my going
off to the library alone? Certainly Hookham's is entirely respectable. I have not heard recently of any
woman's being molested within its portals."

"That is not the point. I do not want you wandering around London streets alone! Anyone could ac-
cost you."

"I was walking through a respectable neighborhood. Whatever I encountered in this district I'm
sure I could have handled."

"Don't be ridiculous! You are a woman . . ."

"Or do you not trust me?"

"I want to know where you are and what you are doing, and if you leave this house, I want some respected servant in attendance. You are going to be my wife, and I want you behaving in a suitable manner."

"And aside from choosing my activities, are you also going to select my friends?"

"When your own judgment seems to be lacking."

"Oh? I'm not wise enough to make my own decisions?"

"For a woman you are quite intelligent."

"Indeed."

"And once we are married and you settle down to wifely duties, I am sure your headstrong streak will disappear."

"I had not realized I was so faulted."

"You must admit you are a trifle outspoken at times . . . which you can easily rectify if you put your mind to it."

"Is that so!" I couldn't check the anger rising in my voice.

Justin suddenly became aware of the curious eyes of the servants standing in the shadows of the hall. "Workmen are repairing some shelves in my study. Let us go into the morning room to finish this discussion."

I preceded him into the morning room. To the side of the room away from the French doors I turned to face him.

"Justin, I think we should clear the air. I am not a little doll to be put on a pedestal and told to dance and perform at your will. I am a woman with opinions of my own. I will not be dictated to, nor will I allow you to make me a possession. I will not be told when I can stay in this house and when I can leave it. If in *my* judgment a destination of *my* choice is a safe enough one to attain, I will go to it—escorted or unescorted, at *my* discretion. I will not heedlessly be cosseted with maids and grooms. You have no right to question my every movement; I do not question yours. If there is any love between us, it has to be based on trust, and trust has to work both ways or it does not work at all."

"Trust is not the question. No woman is allowed such liberties! Except your harlots and ne'er-do-wells. Is that what you wish to be?" The color was high on his cheeks; equally high on my own.

"You know perfectly well I am neither!"

"Yet you seem determined to behave like one. You know I love you, yet you do not heed my better judgment . . . you fight me every inch of the way."

"Your wishes are sometimes unreasonable. Today was the perfect example." Despite my anger, now I was almost pleading with him, thinking there must be some way to get him to understand.

"You are a woman. It is up to the man to make the decisions, to provide and protect!" His voice was hard and angry. "Obviously this situation, which is difficult for both of us, is doubly hard on you. We will discuss this later when you have better control over your temper."

He walked hurriedly from the room, and I ran up to my room, furious. I threw my reticule on the dressing table so that it slid against the crystal vials and dangerously rattled them; then I sat on the edge of my bed and stared unseeingly out the back windows. After all our love, after all we'd shared, Justin hadn't changed his opinion of me one iota since lecturing me when I first arrived in London. He didn't want me for what I was. He wanted a conventional nineteenth century woman willing to be led and dominated; a woman with no strong opinions of her own, who would always bend to a man for guidance. How dare he lecture me as he had? Wasn't I suffering as much as he? The scandal bothered me, though I'd told myself often enough that it didn't. I couldn't stand to hear my name degraded any longer, live with the tension, bear the sneers and sly remarks. I'd meant no harm; had only been swept up in a loving relationship.

Now even that relationship wasn't what it should be. I was suddenly seeing things as they were without the rosy distortion of passion to blind me. I could no longer continue sliding along. As much as I still cared for Justin—and the love we'd shared wasn't something to be blotted out of my mind that quickly—I knew the differences in our opinions were widening the gulf between us, destroying the love. My feelings had not remained unchanged.

Today's painful experience had forced me to see that I'd forgotten the truth about both my feelings and my position. I didn't belong here; had no right to be meddling, no right to be loving, caring, interfering in and obstructing the course of lives that had been patterned before my arrival. I was encouraging the hurt by pretending a future that didn't exist.

It took several days for these realizations to sift down and become sorted into sensible patterns in my mind. When I was certain I saw things clearly, I knew I'd have to talk to Justin . . . tell him our relationship couldn't continue as it was. It waited only for the right opportunity.

On the fourth day after our angry encounter, he and I were to go out for our usual morning ride in Hyde Park. I was waiting in the hall at eight-thirty precisely and trying to build up my courage, to formulate the words that would tell him everything I was feeling. Yet, when he came down the stairs, his smile of warm and anxious greeting forestalled my

speech, and in the mews, where the grooms were
waiting with our saddled horses, there was no privacy. Justin helped me mount, and all the way into
the park, across Park Lane, through Grosvenor
Gate, I thought of how to broach the subject. It
wasn't until we had cantered down the wide, pow-
dery length of Rotten Row, up to the Serpentine, and
turned to walk our mounts for a moment, that the
words were forced from my lips.

"Justin, I must talk to you."

"Talk." He had put his horse into a trot, and I followed suit.

"What I have to say is private. Can we get off the
Row?"

"No one is around this early in the morning to
overhear."

"Just the same, can we walk our horses there, under the trees?"

"If you like." He turned his stallion onto the side
trail. "What is on your mind? Not our disagreement
the other day? Marlena, I was concerned, beside myself when I saw you coming into the house out of a
hired hackney. You have to understand how I felt. I
didn't mean to be so harsh, but surely you can see—"

I didn't let him finish. "It is much more."

"I do not understand."

"Justin, I've been doing a lot of thinking the last
days. I am not sure exactly how to say this, but I'm
not happy with the way things are going . . . the
strain in the house, the deceit, the scandal, the way
you have been treating me. I have begun to realize I
do not feel the same about you, about us, as I did. I
can not keep rushing blindly along in this affair, let
you ruin your good name . . . when I'm no longer
sure I want what we would have together."

"What are you saying!"

"I am saying that it must now be over between us.

I can not continue on. I would be deceiving you . . . and myself."

The shock on his face was profound. He didn't understand. He hadn't imagined my thoughts had been leading me in this direction. He stared at the intractable expression on my face . . . my only defense against weakening; his hands gripping the leather reins as though he would snap them between his fingers.

"No!" he roared as the truth sank in. "I do not believe it! Why? Everything in the world could have been ours! I have been so happy! I thought you were as well. How can you so foolishly let mere social pressures rule your heart? Is it so cold? So devoid of the overflowing warmth I thought I saw there?"

"It is not cold, and my decision was not made solely because of the scandal. We are not the same; we don't want the same things. You are asking more of me than I can give, and we would end up hurting each other."

"I was feeling no pain. Only joy . . . hope . . ."

"Which would have been bitterness and hate before we were finished if I had to force myself into a mold that was not me."

"You cannot mean this, Marlena!"

"I mean it. I wish I did not have to mean it, but I do."

"No!"

"Please, Justin, try to understand. There is so much at stake. I am not trying to hurt you, but my feelings are just no longer strong enough to warrant the scandal, the gossip, the ruination of your career."

"You would end this beautiful love we have had?"

"And it *has* been beautiful, Justin, I admit that . . . but it has changed, at least for me. We failed to think ahead. We saw only today, and the moment's gratification. You were not thinking clearly of the future, your career. We knew we had to have each other—yes, of course I felt it as much as you—but we never stopped to look at each other carefully enough."

"I was not just thinking of the sexual side, Marlena." The fire in his eyes told me he meant that. "I saw you for the woman I had always wanted."

"But as recent events have demonstrated to my satisfaction—a most *unhappy* satisfaction—you do not see me for myself. Think, Justin! Is the woman you've always wanted what I am? Or are you making believe I have those characteristics?"

"I *thought* I was finding everything I ever wanted."

"I can never be what you want. I realize that more with each day that goes by." I was thinking of who I really was, and why this man I'd loved could never fully understand my meaning. Much though he loved me, he would never accept as anything except fantasy, the truth that I had arrived from another century. "There are other reasons," I said finally, "why it has to end. I cannot explain except to say I think I am doing the right thing."

"After all we have shared—this dagger's thrust! Marlena, there *is* something you have not told me. What is it? I know it is more than a cooling of your feelings. Is it another love? Radford? You love him more than you do me!"

"No."

"Then tell me!"

"I cannot. It has nothing to do with love. It is just something that binds me."

"I do not understand."

"And I do not expect you to. Just believe that I'm doing what I have to do."

"I will not give you up that easily!"

"Perhaps it would be better for both of us if you would let me find another house in London, as I suggested many weeks ago. I could bring in a woman as a companion—"

"No! You will not leave my roof. I want you near me, in the event you should change your mind. This is too rash; too sudden . . . you will come back to me."

"No."

"I will continue with the divorce proceedings. By spring—"

"*No*, Justin. I mean what I say!"

"You cannot!"

"Yes." But strength was weakening; I had to leave him. As I turned my horse, his hand reached out.

"Wait. Stay a moment. I shan't press you further. Just do not leave me yet."

"There is nothing else to say."

"You tell me your reason for ending our relationship is not another love—but will you continue to be friendly with Radford?"

"I have not thought of it. I suppose I will, though we are not on the best of terms at the moment."

"What do you feel for him? More than friendship?"

"I have never thought of him in other terms."

"Yet I am sure the same cannot be said about his feelings for you."

"Must we discuss it now? You let the thought of him eat at you—and there is no cause, nor any benefit." I looked into the sea-green eyes, at the firm chin and the proudly set shoulders, and remembered, and a flood tide of love flowed through me. Was I doing the right thing, giving all this up? Yet I was not going to give in.

"I am still your guardian . . . can still make use of those powers."

"I hope you will not assert them."

"Does all we have shared together really mean nothing to you?"

"You know it means much."

"Then I will tell you something, Marlena. You are sometimes a hard woman, too independent; sometimes soft as a nymph and passionate. As much as you seem to think to the contrary, I love both women. But I am a man, and I will not lower myself to beg. If you should decide you want me after all, it will be you who must do the telling, for I will not come to you again until you show me you are willing to accept me . . . I will not give up hope, either."

SEVENTEEN

JUSTIN AND I retreated to a ground of polite civility in public and almost complete silence to each other in private. Yet he did watch me, as I watched him. I would glance up from my tea after dinner to find him gazing, softly, imploringly. The look was enough to send a warm tremor through me. Would I ever forget our moments of closeness, the gentle touch of his hands, his soft words of love? He still had a power over me. The love I'd known lingered on as a deep affection. Have I done the right thing? I couldn't help asking myself. Would the outcome have been different if I hadn't been a traveler in time? I didn't think so. It had been the deep differences in our basic attitudes and needs that had finally caused the change in my feelings.

He came out with Caroline and me on only the most important occasions now, and when he did, it must have been obvious from our behavior that there had been a change in our relationship. Still, the gossipmongers were unready to let such a juicy affair die a natural death.

I tried not to think of the slowly passing hours. Here, Caroline was of unintended help. She didn't like being alone, so she always asked me to come along on her trips to her dressmaker, the lending library, the jewelers to have one of her necklaces cleaned; busy tasks all carried out under a very false front of friendship.

Since our verbal run-in at the ball, I hadn't seen Radford anywhere, though I did hear a great deal about him. He was still in town, causing a stir by unceremoniously dumping his latest mistress and, for the first time in recent memory, making use of his seat in the House of Lords. I was sorry for our argument and missed our spicy conversations, especially now when there was so much I was trying to put from my mind; when more than anything else I needed a good friend to talk to.

Then one afternoon I ran into him accidentally in Grosvenor Square. Since the square was only a few hundred yards from the steps of Warringwood House, I'd gone there alone for a short walk. As I was entering the square through one of the wrought iron gates, a curricle passed by. I heard the vehicle suddenly pause in the road. When I turned, he was staring straight at me.

"I thought it was you," he said in a quiet yet carrying voice.

"Hello, Radford."

"Well, I am delighted at least to know that I am not to be snubbed." Suddenly he called back over his shoulder to his tiger, a slim boy perched precariously at the back of the curricle. "Come hold these hellions, Jeremy. Take them for a turn or two about the square. I wish to speak to this lady."

As the lad was still scampering forward, Radford entrusted the ribbons to him and jumped lightly to the ground.

As he strode across the pavement toward me, my heart began a very uncharacteristic banging. Was he going to carry on with the conversation we'd ended so tersely at the ball? But when he reached my side, there was no anger in his expression. He studied me for a few moments, his face markedly serious. Then he smiled.

"As a matter of fact, Marlena, I have been hoping we would run into one another. There is an apology I have been wishing to make. I was quite out of line at the ball."

"I am not one to hold a grudge."

He held the gate open for me, motioning me in. "Let us walk a bit. You do not mind if I interrupt you for a few minutes?"

"Not at all. I was only looking for some fresh air and a time away from the house."

"Oh? There is something you wish to escape? Ah, but disregard that question. I do not wish to tread those treacherous waters a second time."

"You have nothing to fear, my lord, for I shall ignore anything I prefer not to hear."

"Admirable. So all is well with you?"

"As well as can be expected. But I understand there is news in your corner. Quite a phenomenon, your taking your seat in the House of Lords! Is the Crown of England about to fall in ashes? Or has it been discovered that Napoleon himself is heir to the throne and the House has come to you to save the day?"

"I admit to having neglected my duties thus far—a fact that never disturbed me greatly. It is only that of late my other entertainments have been so thin, I thought I would try to discover if there was anything I had been missing."

"Are you Tory or Whig?"

"A cross between the two, I am afraid, much like a mongrel dog. Each has its worthy points. I thought perhaps a third party might be a successful idea." He glanced at me from the corner of his eye. "Have I not heard you involved in a similar discussion with Percivel, and what fears you both had for the future of England were a compromise not yet reached?"

"I am only a novice at politics."

"There appear to be a few of our noble lords who share your thoughts, however, on the future of England."

"Are you one of them?"

"As I have said, I am only dabbling at the moment. It passes the time."

"Yes, your hours must be empty since you dropped your last mistress like a hot coal." I grinned.

"This event is of some interest to you?"

"Only as a curiosity. It is so out of character for you."

"I seem to recall a similar discussion between us some weeks back," he said. "Apparently you had no faith in the sincerity of my words when I said I might give up the others."

"But if it has, as I have heard, been only a few days since you dropped Ravona, I would give you two weeks of living like a monk before you find someone else."

"Ha! Oh, woman of little faith! Shall I prove to you I can do it?"

"It would make an interesting wager on the book at White's. Unfortunately, I cannot enter that establishment to place it."

He smiled, and took my elbow to lead me around a small puddle in the path. "Yes, I have missed your whiplash tongue. I will make a concerted effort never again to allow an argument to come between us." He was looking down at me as we walked. Now his fingers tightened a little on my arm. "In fact I have missed you, in every way, very much."

I looked down at the stones of the path, not sure

how to react to this admission. He seemed sincere. "I was thinking of you the other day," I said after a pause. "I wanted a friend to talk to."

"Oh? I am honored that you should consider me, but is there not someone in your household who better fits the bill?"

"Caroline and I do not do much talking anymore."

"I was not referring to Caroline." Suddenly he scowled. "What is it you are not telling me? Something is wrong."

"No, of course not."

"Warringwood—what has he done? Has he hurt you?"

I laughed to put him off course. "Radford, you let your imagination carry you away." Although it would have felt good to unburden myself, I did not want to involve him in my problems. Hadn't I already learned the consequences of a too deep involvement with others?

Our steps had taken us in a circle, and we were back at the gate where we'd entered the square. I knew Radford wasn't satisfied with my answer, but before he could say more, we looked out to the road to see Radford's curricle flying toward us, his tiger perched on the seat with the broadest of grins on his face.

"It would appear Jeremy has been having quite a time of it. I think perhaps I shall have to bring him back down to earth. We shall talk again soon, Marlena. But I suppose it would not yet be the thing for me to call at Warringwood House."

"No . . . I am afraid Justin—"

"Say no more. We will run into each other soon enough around town." He took my hand. For an instant I felt his lips hot on my fingers. "I will be thinking of you, and you know that if you need me in any way, you have only to send a message."

Then he was smiling crookedly, and waving his hand as he dashed off to stop his curricle before it made another run around the block.

One last great fete was scheduled for the fall season—quite a surprise affair, especially at so late a date, when most of the ton had left for their country estates. But a singer of some merit was visiting London, and Lord and Lady Jersey had decided to sponsor a reception in her honor. Their London house would be open; invitations to the ton were sent out by the score. There would be a recital by the talented lady, one Angelina del Sorno, noted for both her soaring soprano voice and her equally arousing Latin beauty. There would be cards, dancing later, food and drink in bounty. Anyone who was anyone was agog with talk of it.

On the evening of the affair, as Caroline and I came down for an early dinner, Justin met us in the hallway.

Something was wrong. Before he'd said a word, the tenseness was evident in his face. He came straight to the point, looking at us both through troubled eyes. "I have just received a message from the overseer at Pemberton."

"Now?" Caroline frowned. "Whatever can he bothering you about at this hour?"

"There is trouble at the estate. I am afraid I am going to have to beg your excuses for this evening. I realize it is an important affair for you both, but from what Watkins's missive tells me, smugglers have been caught on our lands, their catch stowed up in the old barn on the south field. It is serious. I must go down immediately. I have contacted one of the king's men in London. He will escort me, and together we shall get to the head of it, we hope. I will be in touch; I should be away no more than three days."

At that moment the butler entered the hallway.

Justin saw him. "Is my horse ready, Williams? I will be down directly."

"Yes, my lord."

Justin took Caro's hand for the briefest of kisses. To me he gave a deep, enigmatic look that tore at my heart. "I shall see you in a few days' time." And he was off, bounding down the staircase.

Caroline and I buzzed together over dinner, but neither of us could make sense of the happening. It did seem strange that Justin would be plagued with smugglers now, with Napoleon out of the way at least temporarily.

Caro and I dressed and left for the Jerseys' at eight. Already, as our carriage drew up to the curb, there was a squeeze at the door. We waited on the steps as the crowd ahead of us slowly proceeded in. Langely would no doubt be there; I saw Caroline searching the crowd for his head.

We went up the staircase and waited to enter the ballroom, where the butler was announcing each guest in booming tones. Once we were in the room, a huge, high-ceilinged expanse whose proportions were more appropriate to the ballroom of a country estate than to a London town house, my eyes scanned the crowd. Our progress through the room was slow, hindered by the many people we passed who stopped us to talk. As we passed near the refreshment table and Caroline turned to chat with Lady Pomeroy, I heard someone come up behind me; felt a gentle tap on my shoulder. I looked up to see Radford, all twinkling eyes and cynical smile.

"We meet again socially at last. I was beginning to wonder if you had been hurried off to the country once more." He led me slightly apart from the crowd near the tables. "I see you and Caroline are alone. I understand from Sally that Warringwood was to attend."

"He had to go down to Pemberton. There were reports of smugglers caught on the estate."

"My, that is unfortunate. But how propitious for me." The smile was now one of delight. "We must toast the occasion. Allow me to procure some champagne." He bowed his tall, beautifully clad form, moved off, and in a moment returned with two glasses. "To us, Baroness, and our continued friendship. Drink up," he laughed. "There can be nothing so wrong in that proposal."

The champagne tickled my nose and bubbled into my veins, and suddenly I felt immeasurably more lighthearted than I had on entering the room.

Radford leaned slightly toward me. "Have I told you how ravishing you are this evening?"

I smiled. "No, but since I knew you would get around to it eventually, I decided not to let it bother me. You are looking rather well yourself."

He nodded, knowing that the hunter-green jacket he wore was magnificent across his broad shoulders.

"But I hardly know why you waste your time with me, Radford, when there is a beautiful guest of honor to whom you might be paying court."

"I presume you are referring to our illustrious soprano."

At that moment the lady in question came in our direction. She had been circulating the room on the arm of Lord Jersey, surrounded by such a crowd of eager admirers that I hadn't caught more than a glimpse of her until now. Raven haired, dark eyed, voluptuous of figure, she was everything her admirers said of her.

"Ah, the marquis." She spied Radford and came

immediately forward. "Such a delight to see you again."

"And you, signorina."

She pressed her small hands forward into his. Her eyes danced. "I see you have a lovely lady with you already. I will become jealous, my lord."

"With such beauty as you both possess, what place is there for jealousy? Signorina, may I present to you the baroness von Mantz. Baroness, the signorina Angelina del Sorno."

We nodded to each other, smiling, and I told the signorina I was eager to hear her much-praised voice.

"Signorina," Lord Jersey interrupted, "excuse me, but I believe it is time for your program."

"Ah, yes, and I must change my gown." Her eyes rested on Radford. "Marquis, I trust you will enjoy this performance as much as you have enjoyed those in the past."

His lids dropped over his dark eyes. "I know I shall."

She gave him a glorious smile, then departed with her entourage toward the back of the room, where a velvet-draped stage had been set up for her performance.

When she was gone, I turned an eye toward Radford. "Well. It would appear you and the lovely signorina are well acquainted. Let me guess. . . . You met on a moonlit canal in Venice."

"Much more mundane than that. It was in Vienna at a very dull political reception. I was there for my business interests; she was there to sing and was the only bright light in an otherwise intolerably insipid gathering."

"I'm sure you were yawning."

"My boredom was much alleviated when she appeared."

"Yes."

"Don't tell me you are jealous, Baroness."

"Me? Over you? Do not be absurd."

"True, we are only friends. I tend to forget myself. But your glass is empty. Allow me to get you another."

While he was gone, the curtains on the improvised stage parted, and the signorina stepped forward. Her voice was indeed superb. The fluid, high tones echoed through the room, sending vibrations down my spine. She sang three pieces, to resounding applause, then bowed, leaving the room in a strange, moved silence.

Radford had come up while she was singing and handed me my glass. I didn't acknowledge him until the end of the performance. "She is exquisite, and puts such feeling into her singing."

"Yes. Excellent."

"Did you have an affair with her?" I'd never have asked such a personal question if the champagne hadn't been loosening my tongue.

"No. Though perhaps the lady desired it. And perhaps that is my appeal to her now. Ah, but such intimate revelations do not set well in our relationship. I understand there is a card game begun in the other room. Will you join me while I try my hand?"

"I do not play."

"No? Then you can bear me company and bring me a bit of luck."

Surprisingly enough, I didn't feel the least bit silly standing beside him as he played out two hands. There were other women in the room, and such an air of good humor that no one noticed me. His pockets fuller after winning both hands, Radford rose.

"I don't wish to press my luck. Come."

As we left the card room, he paused for a moment in the deserted hallway, and took my arm. "You are *very* delicious tonight," he said in my ear. "Do you know that?"

"Yes, I do—because you told me so earlier, and are now repeating yourself. Radford, you have had too much champagne."

"Far from it," he laughed. "I know my limits; but is there no way to get through to you?"

"I always try to remind myself that you are an unredeemable rake."

"Then it is time to change your opinion," he almost whispered. "Or is that opinion just an excuse to keep me at arm's length. Do you really think me such a consummate scoundrel, Marlena?"

"Of course I do not, I've seen your deeper colors long before now."

"Yet you seem to be oblivious to them."

"I tend to see our relationship for what it is," I answered carefully, "and in any case do not want to become involved with anyone here—at least not until I assume control of my inheritance and learn all I must of the responsibilities it imposes. It may be that Germany or America will be my home."

"And what of Warringwood?"

"I do not want to talk about him."

"Avoiding an issue does not make it go away."

"You and I are friends now. Let us not ruin it with another argument."

"Very well." His hold on my arm loosened. "Let me take you back to the ballroom."

He left me once we were back in the main reception room, and went off to circulate among the other guests. His place was taken by others. From time to time as the evening progressed, he'd show up at my side, stay for a few minutes to talk, then disappear again. I didn't understand his behavior. I saw him with the signorina and two other beauties. From the look on their faces, I concluded his charm was having a positive effect on them and they were enchanted. Of course, the signorina had already been enchanted with him; and that thought somehow bothered me.

It was about eleven o'clock when I began to feel terribly strange. Radford had just brought me a glass of champagne, which, because of the increasing heat of the room, I'd drunk quickly. I didn't think that alone was enough to make me feel so lightheaded, but then again, it had been a long night. And maybe I'd had more champagne than I thought.

All I was sure of now was that my mind was floating, my eyes not focusing as they should. When I took a few tentative steps to a nearby chair, the room seemed to sway. I knew I had to get out of the ballroom to some quiet place where I could get some fresh air and compose myself.

Taking slow, measured steps, I made my way down the room toward one of the less-used exits. I made it to the doorway and from there into a candlelit hall. I walked past one door, and another, and finally spotted one that was partially open, soft candlelight streaming from within. It was a small anteroom, and fortunately was vacant. Slipping in, I closed the door and immediately made my way, stumbling, to the windows to unlatch them and throw them wide to the night air. I leaned against the casement and breathed deeply. The cool, bracing air felt good against my flushed cheeks—but didn't do much to clear my head, which was fuzzier than ever. Behind me was a chair facing the window. I almost fell into it, and with elbows on knees and hands bracing my head, I tried desperately to force myself into a more sober state. I had no sensation of nausea, but my head whirled. I couldn't concentrate on anything, even the disgrace that would follow if I was found in this state. Oh, for a cup of coffee, and a basin of icy water to splash over my face! Neither was immediately available, and I didn't have the courage to try maneuvering down any more corridors to find them.

Maybe if I walked around and around the room, I could work off the alcoholic effects. I was trying to rise, forcing myself upright by pressing the palms of my hands against the arms of the chair, when I heard the door open behind me.

I froze, afraid to turn around to see who it was.

"So here you are." A pleasant female voice spoke in my ear. Its owner came to stand before me, and I moaned in chagrin.

"Lady Jersey. Forgive me . . . I came in here to rest . . . I'm afraid I had too much champagne . . ." My tongue felt thick as I tried to articulate the words.

"I have told you to call me Sally, and there is nothing to be embarrassed about." Surprisingly, she was all sympathy. "Just sit. Why did you not beckon to me in the ballroom? I would have seen to it that you received a discreet escort home."

"I felt all right . . . until that last glass Radford brought me . . ."

"Champagne does have a way of catching up with one when one is least awares. It could have happened to any of us. You do not seem well enough to go back to the party."

I shook my head. The motion was enough to bring on increased dizziness.

"Stay here for a moment. I shall get your wrap and see if Radford will escort you home. You have no objection to that?"

"No, Radford is a friend."

"Good."

"But Caroline . . ."

"I shall speak to her—explain that you had a sick headache and that rather than cut her evening short, Radford took you back to Warringwood House."

"How can I ever thank you?" I was too befuddled to think of the impropriety of a lone man taking me home; I was only relieved to be getting away unscathed.

"It is nothing," Sally Jersey replied consolingly. "I liked you from the start. Now just stay put until I am back. Do not budge from that chair."

"No, no," I said, shaking my head more gingerly this time, wondering how I could ever face the woman again. She had every reason to condemn my behavior and feel exasperated with me, especially after berating me for my behavior with Justin at the Warringwood ball, yet she was going out of her way to make me comfortable. My confused mind couldn't digest it. The morning would be a better time to think.

It was only minutes later that she returned with Radford, his face set in serious and concerned lines. He came immediately to my side and bent over me. "Marlena. Sally has told me what happened. Come, let me help you. Here is your wrap. Wait . . . let me put it about you. We shall go out the back stairs. The carriage will be waiting."

I could only lean on his shoulder and let his strong arms support me as we left the room.

With no time wasted we were down the long back hall, Radford guiding my stumbling footsteps, then down the stairs and out into the rear courtyard. His coachman held the carriage door as Radford helped me up the step and into the plush seat. I fell back against it exhaustedly with a sigh of relief, and thought how fortunate I was to have such good friends. Sally Jersey had gone immediately back to her guests in order that no questions be raised at her absence.

The carriage started off. I tried to appear alert and keep my eyes open, but they refused to obey my commands. Radford gently tucked my head against his shoulder and drew the lap rug up over my knees. "No need to fret now, Marlena. You will soon be home."

I must have dozed. I was wakened by the sudden jogging of the carriage over a bumpy road. I opened my eyes and lifted my head to look around, but the window curtains had been lowered.

"Where are we, Radford? Shouldn't we be there by now?"

"A few more minutes."

"But I don't remember these bumps . . ."

"My coachman has taken a detour to escape the late traffic. Do not worry." He tightened his arm reassuringly about my shoulders.

"Oh," I muttered groggily. "I feel so tired."

"Then rest. I will waken you when we reach the door and I can escort you in."

Satisfied, I closed my eyes and once more let the sleepy whirlwind overtake me. I heard the clopping of the hooves, the turning of the wheels; felt the gentle sway of the rocking carriage, and soon was lost to everything. It seemed only seconds later that Radford was gently shaking me, prodding me awake.

"We have arrived. Here, let me help you up. Are you well enough, or shall I carry you?"

Shaking my head to force away the vestiges of lingering dizziness, I slid across the seat. "I'll be all right. Just give me your arm."

He moved through the open door, extended his hand, and helped me down the step. On the pavement, he held me a moment as I steadied myself. The night air assaulted my lungs, pricked my cheeks. I still felt terribly strange, but at least I was home.

"Radford, how can I thank you?"

"We will save that for another time. Let me get you up to your room. Come now . . . there are four steps."

But these proved my downfall; I stumbled and nearly fell. Then his strong arms lifted me up and carried me into the front hall, at this hour dimly lit. I let my head fall against the steadiness of his chest as he climbed the main staircase and turned down the hall. I heard the door to my room click open. He carried me to the bed and laid me on it.

"The maid will be in to help you in a moment."

I closed my eyes, and immediately the world receded from my consciousness. I didn't even remember the maid's coming to help me into a nightgown and tuck me between the clean-smelling sheets.

It was much later that I woke, craving a drink of water. I lit the candle on the bedside table, and looked for the carafe of drinking water that was always there. Except for the candlestick and matches, the table was bare. My thirst was horrible; my mouth like cotton; my lips dry and tight. Perhaps there was some fresh water in the pitcher on the washstand. I lifted myself to a sitting position against the pillows. Aside from my thirst, I felt all right; my head was clear, and there was no banging in my temples.

As I began sliding toward the edge of the bed, I realized something was very wrong. I glanced about the room in the dim candlelight. The wardrobe was not against the wall beside the bed. Instead, there was a desk in that spot, looking nothing like the one I remembered. For that matter, the bed had changed position too, and was facing in the opposite direction; and across the room from the foot of it, where the fireplace should have been, stood the wardrobe. The fireplace itself had moved to the corner, where the last embers of a fire were glowing warmly in the grate.

I thought for a moment I was going mad: could the champagne still be playing such games with my mind? Perhaps Radford, in his eagerness to see me settled, had brought me to the wrong chamber; but no, the servants would have told him.

In amazement I continued my surveillance. There were long windows to my left, now closed by velvet draperies that appeared almost blood red in the half-light. Next to them was a couch, and lastly a low tea table, a china service on its mellowly gleaming surface. Every color in the room was a shade of red or gold . . . warm, passionate.

The door to the hall opened. I started, swung toward it.

The blood slowly drained from my face. There, in a long, satin dressing gown, candle in hand, stood Radford.

He shut the door silently behind him. His eyes danced as he saw me sitting on the bed. Then he smiled, slowly, confidently; he was in full control of the situation.

"So, my love, you save me the trouble of waking you."

"Where am I and what are you doing in this room?"

"The explanation is quite simple. You are at my estate, Setly Manor, in Buckinghamshire. Since you are awake, I should think you might have surmised as much by now. Do you not like the room? I had it done especially for you."

"But why? Why bring me here?"

"Come, now, you are an intelligent woman. Is the reason not obvious?"

"If you are out to destroy every shred of my reputation, yes. But I cannot believe it! Why should you want to do this to me? I thought we were friends."

"Ah, we are . . . and I have cherished that friendship. But as I have tried many times to tell you, my sentiments for you have been growing much warmer." He walked toward the bed. "You would not believe me."

His dressing gown was tied loosely at his waist, the upper portion in a wide V to expose his chest, which was covered by a mat of softly curling dark hair. The flickering light danced along the planes of his face, carving hollows under his high cheekbones, reflecting from his thick raven hair; giving a satanic cast to the whole. His long legs carried him forward with the natural grace of a stalking cat, his slim hips and broad shoulders swinging easily with each step. "I have planned this for some time," he continued, "though in truth I would never have resorted to these measures had things not become so desperate. I had hoped to come in here to break it to you more gently, but that cannot be helped. What wakened you?"

"I wanted water. I was thirsty."

"Easily remedied." He swung across to the dressing table and returned with a jug and a glass, which he placed on the night table. "Here, drink. I should have remembered that thirst is often an aftereffect of the drug you have been imbibing tonight."

I had the glass to my lips and had swallowed half its contents before his words stopped me. The goblet nearly fell from my suddenly shaking hand. "What did you say? You drugged me? Do you mean to say *that* was what was wrong with me? Then I was not drunk at all! How *could* you? How could you do such a despicable thing?" In shock and fury I threw the goblet at his head. It missed its target, but crashed in a shower of shattering glass against the opposite wall. "And I trusted you!"

His soft laugh interrupted me. "No need for such violence, my love. As I said, I was desperate. I could think of no other means of getting you here."

"But surely you have enough ladies eager to satisfy your physical needs!"

"You should know I want more from you than that." He advanced again, taking a seat on the edge of the bed. He leaned toward me.

My breath was coming quickly as I tried to slide away from him.

"I fail to understand, Radford. Do you intend to keep me prisoner here as your chattel? Have you bored with the more conventional liaisons?"

He leaned closer still, one hand, resting on my bare arm, pulling me toward him. His flashing eyes glued themselves to me with dark fire, moving with slow deliberation from my face down my body. I was suddenly aware of the sheerness of the silk that covered me, the low and revealing lines of the bodice as it dipped between my breasts. A warm flush crept up my cheekbones as I stared at the powerful man before me.

His eyes met mine again; a slow smile moved his lips. "I want you for my wife. I love you, Marlena, with a passion that drives me toward insanity."

"Radford!"

"Had you, truly, no idea where our relationship was leading? Had you no intuition of the depth of my feelings? I find that impossible to believe. Or were your thoughts so wrapped with Warringwood you closed your mind to all else? In my own eyes I behaved as a rash and jealous schoolboy, unable to pass a day without thoughts of you coloring my whole existence. Watching Warringwood tighten his hooks upon you, forbidding you to see me! And when I heard the gossip in town that he had finally suceeded in securing you as his mistress, I knew even the urge to kill the man. I saw that unless I did something drastic, you would be lost to me beyond hope. Soon you would be leaving for the country, and it is no longer summer, when I could slip into Sussex to meet you riding across the Downs. I had to make you see the utter folly of your ways, even if it meant forcing that revelation upon you."

"If you had been so observant, my lord, you would have realized I ended it between Justin and me several weeks ago."

"For how long? You live beneath his roof, and it is obvious he yet desires you. If you could not hold out against him the first time, did you think you would succeed the second?"

"All you would have had to do, Radford, was to tell me how you felt . . . make your desires known honorably to me."

"And you would have given me your hand in marriage?" He grinned and shook his head. "I think not. Recall, Marlena, that I endeavored to do just that, and you could only laugh and remind me of my profligate past. You would not believe me capable of a permanent commitment. Recall, also, your guardian's sentiments. Not likely, is it, he would have given his consent! Now that you have been compromised, he will have no other choice."

"But *I* still have a choice. I will leave this house and return to London."

"As you wish. You are not a prisoner here. You *may* leave—any time it suits your fancy. However, I feel you have little to return to. The damage has already been done."

"I have been abducted and carried here against my will, but I have not slept with you and have no intention of doing so."

"Yes, pure as the driven snow. Can you prove that I have not touched you, my love?"

I stared at him.

"A physician, upon examining you, which I am afraid is what would have to be done, could not be expected to realize that it was not I but another man who took your virginity."

He had me trapped. I couldn't tell the world the truth; neither could Justin, even though he knew he wasn't the first. "Well," I brazened, "my reputation is already a shambles. It could not be made much worse."

"Do not deceive yourself. Though the rumors may be rampant, no one has ever had proof of the relationship between you and your guardian. Would you care to give them that proof?" He cocked a brow. "Face the facts, my dear. After spending the night with a man of my reputation, there is no other solution for you but to marry me. You do not hold me in aversion. As a matter of fact, I am of the opinion you care a great deal more for me than you will admit."

"I shall call Sally Jersey as my witness. She will testify to my character and confirm that I was taken advantage of in a most heinous way."

"Not if she wishes her role as my accomplice to remain a secret."

"She *knew*?"

"She helped me lay my plans . . . and enjoyed every moment of it. When she told you she considered me a particular friend, you should have believed her, Marlena. Even the party was specially scheduled . . . did you not think it odd that she threw a soirée so late in the season? And, of course, once our strategy was set, it was an easy matter to send Warringwood off on a false errand into Sussex—quite in the opposite direction of our present location—to prevent any attempt he might make at pursuit."

"That was your doing too! My God . . ."

"Actually, my own lackey delivered the message, beating a hasty retreat before he could be questioned. Warringwood will arrive to a scene of pastoral peace, and since the news of your disappearance cannot be gotten to him that quickly, he should be out of our hair for at least twenty-four hours."

The soft smile still on his lips, he made no further move toward me; just studied me as the full meaning of his words sank in.

I turned away from his probing eyes. I had to think clearly; but his hand reached out and took my chin, inched my head around. His face dropped toward me.

"No!"

He held me closer. "Yes! I could give you a thousand days for consideration, but there is only one way to take the fog from your eyes."

"*This* is not the way!"

"It is the only way. When we leave this bed in the morning, I promise you, you will want me as much as I want you."

"If you think you will sway me, you are wrong."

"No, I am right. You need a man, Marlena, who knows how to make you happy. I can sense that passion in you just under the surface. And the rapport we share in other matters too is not a meaningless thing." The burning desire in his eyes was almost palpable. "I do not think you will run away."

"What a conceited ass you are!"

"Conceited, yes. An ass, never!"

I wanted to laugh at him, scoff; but the unbidden thoughts his words were putting into my mind made my pulse rush. I'd often wondered what kind of lover he'd be, having had a taste of his lips, and experiencing as I was now the power that had kept so many of his mistresses so firmly under his control. But I'd never expected that I too would be absorbed by that power. Like a mouse transfixed by a cobra's stare, I felt unable to move or resist. But again I told myself I had to fight him . . . stand up against him. I couldn't let him win so easily.

Radford's breath was coming in soft gusts against my cheek, his nearness filling my senses. His lips were parted invitingly, and the sight of that dark, provocative face, his broad, hairy chest; the soft scent that emanated from his body—all were steadily weakening me. His hands moved longingly over my shoulders and neck, then in slow, gentle circles over my breasts. His brilliant eyes grew dusky as his mouth dropped in anticipation.

Fire leapt through my veins as his lips met mine; desire gripped my body, reminding me of my earlier responses to his kisses. He didn't just kiss me; he devoured me, his lips tasting, teasing, draining and drowning me so that nothing but the need for him remained.

In sheer fear of my own reaction, I roughly broke away, and rolled across the bed. With the bed between us, I faced him, not clearly understanding what I was doing. We stood like statues, our eyes locked together. Then I turned and rushed for the door.

With a quick thrust of his body, he was up and across the floor, blocking my way. His arms reached out, catching me, cushioning the impact as I collided with him. Holding me at arm's length, he spoke quietly. "Do not run, Marlena. Your emotions have caught you by surprise and you do not want to admit your need . . . that I was right and you would love me by night's end."

"That's not so! Let go of me!" I struggled against his hands.

"I will not give up that easily."

He pulled me against him. Again his warm mouth parted my lips; again I experienced a reeling of the senses, a loss of will as I tried to hold myself detached. It was no use. I knew it as the length of his body surged against me, his hands pressing against my buttocks through the nothingness that was my sheer gown. Oh, God, how I enjoyed the feel of him.

His right hand moved from my back to the front of his robe, loosening the belt.

"Radford . . . please, no! I haven't the strength to fight you . . ."

"Do not fight me anymore, my love. Come to me. Let happen what you know in your heart you want to happen. Let me love you . . . cherish you."

The belt came free. The front of his robe fell open to reveal his nakedness. Then his hands were on my gown, easing it up over my thighs, above my waist, gripping me, urging me forward so our bare skin touched. His manhood was a hard, throbbing staff against my flesh. My knees nearly buckled as the unexpected pure desire swept through my body.

Then I was returning his kisses, clutching him with an ardor equal to his own. His fingers went to the fastenings of my gown, loosened them, slid the lace-trimmed silk from my shoulders; the gown floated like a feather to the carpet. He lifted me in his arms and carried me gently to the bed. Shrugging his arms from the robe and casting it to the floor, he stood there for a moment, gazing at me. Then he lay down on his side, facing me on the bed. My fingers reached out to tangle in the curling dark hairs of his chest, rub over his firm muscles; I thrilled to the gentle strength of him as his fingertip tenderly traced the hollow of my cheek, the outline of my lips, the arch of my brow. He smiled and pulled

me nearer so my arm went around to his back. I ex-
plored the smooth expanse, from the thick waves of
hair at the back of his neck, to his broad shoulders, to
his hard, slender hips. I studied his face—the sharp
planes, the sensuous mouth, the tiny lines creasing
his tanned cheeks. His eyes still gazing into mine, he
too let his hands drift with the lightest of
touches—playing with the silkiness of my hair, then
smoothing it off my face, lingering at the nape of my
neck, massaging, swirling over my shoulder blades
with the same gentle touch, finding the small of my
back, reaching to the back of my thighs, slipping between them. His soft voice urging me to return his
caresses was full of caring, consideration . . . love.

"Give me your hand," he whispered, and gently he
placed it between his thighs at the core of his manhood. "Touch me," he sighed. "Get to know me as I
want to know you." He released my fingers to let me
explore on my own; his moans coaxing my fingertips
to linger on his hard length; his obvious delight in
my touch bringing delight to me.

"Ah, my love, you amaze me. Yes, I knew there
was untapped passion within you . . . but to such a
delightful extent . . ."

He slowly pressed me back onto the sheets. His lips
claimed mine once more, but this time they were
soft, sweet, persuading; sliding from mine only when
I was weak and languorous, to nibble down my neck
over the soft and sensitive skin, bringing tingling
thrills as he found my breasts and paid homage to
each, then moving lower, over my navel, my abdomen, deeper still. I clutched his forearms and let my
fingers play over the taut skin, as his tongue licked
and teased me until every nerve in my body was
alive with desire. I felt myself being swept up in a
warm wave of steadily increasing pleasure. He let it

grow until I cried out for him. All inhibition I had felt in mind and body was forgotten. I wanted Radford—all of him. Now.

And now he was sliding over me. I felt the heavy pressure of his warm weight. The hot staff of his manhood burned against my inner thighs. I reached to pull him closer, my arms sliding down his back, my hands gripping his waist. My hips lifted of their own accord to meet him, to increase the contact; I knew my being could not be fulfilled until he became a part of me.

"Wait, my love." His voice was again in my ear. "Savor it. There is no need for haste."

He gently moved closer, just touching me, exciting me further. He entered in slow degrees, an inch at a time until I could stand the tantalizing promise no longer and, in hunger, grasped and pressed him deep. We shivered in joy at the contact of our loins, his full penetration. Then he began to move slowly, deliberately, so that our ecstasy grew in a single, consuming flame, burning brighter, more and more intensely, carrying us to the peak of satisfaction together. Never before had a man pleased me so overwhelmingly; never before had I felt so completely and fully loved.

I listened to his deep voice speaking quietly in my ear that all would be good now; a new door opening. I wanted to think, assess, analyze what I felt, but the warmth and the coziness of his body next to mine under the cocoon of the bedclothes lulled my mind. Soon after I heard his slowed and deepening breaths, mine slowed as well, and we both slept.

EIGHTEEN

I OPENED MY EYES the next morning to find Radford already awake. He was at the windows, drawing the curtains wide to let in the morning sun. It spread across the room as a thousand golden fingers, glinting on and warming everything it touched. He felt no embarrassment as he stood before me naked . . . but then, of what had he to be embarrassed? His form was perfect; even the morning light itself could find no fault in him. I had never seen such suppleness, such grace in a man, and yet such strength too.

When he returned to the bed, he drew only the sheet over him against the morning chill. His hand reached out and touched me; he smiled, a full smile of brilliant teeth and happiness.

I didn't want the bubble of happiness to break. How often do such moments of complete joy enter anyone's life? They pass as fleeting shadows, never to be recaptured, except in old age when memories become more real than the present, to be relived with almost the fullness of the original event. Soon the rest of life would take over: the intrusions, the hard realities that would bring pain. If I was to take pleasure in what Radford had given me, I had to take it now.

"Did I not promise you," he questioned softly, "that with the morning's light you would love me?"

"Those were your words."

"And do you deny it?"

"I am confused."

He frowned for a moment, then chuckled. "Your body has already told me the truth."

"Reactions of the flesh and of the heart are two separate things."

He took my hand and squeezed it, "Ah, Marlena, you will evade me no matter how I endeavor to trap you. But it was good . . . that at least you can admit."

"Yes."

"We have plans to make. We will remain here for another day, then I shall bring you back to London to confront Warringwood. A date for the wedding can be set as soon as possible—"

"You go too fast."

"What is this? Have I overlooked something?"

"Nothing except for the fact that I have not agreed to marry you."

"But you must marry me. What other choice do you have?"

"I'm not ready to make that commitment, Radford."

His dark face studied me, his lips pursed. "I am willing, once our marriage intentions are announced, to give you time . . . not a great deal, since I am a very impatient man."

"Any marriage I make before the end of the year will forfeit my inheritance," I prevaricated, unable to tell him the real reason.

"I have more than sufficient wealth for both of us."

"But there is my duty."

His eyes narrowed. "So, you are still in love with that scoundrel!"

"No—"

"I will arrange a secret ceremony. We will be wed. I will have the security of knowing you to be my wife, and we will announce nothing to the rest of the world until your year is up."

"No, Radford. I'm leaving here for London now . . . will somehow try to explain away my night's absence. Perhaps I can say we were set upon by thugs—or that on waking to find myself in a strange carriage, I bolted and became lost in the London streets."

"Neither of which explanation would gain you much belief. And what if you are with child?"

"I doubt it. I just finished my cycle."

"I could keep you here and lay with you every night."

"If you are willing to stoop to that, then you have fallen in my esteem."

"You know I only jest. It might prove an enjoyable solution to my quandary, but I have no desire for a hateful bride. I want you to come to me on your own. I thought you would, after this past night."

There was pain in his eyes—out of character for him—and the sight of it touched a chord within me.

"Radford, it is not that I'm unfeeling. You have made me see that I could care . . . a great deal, perhaps. But there is more to it; so much more than that."

I hesitated, and he watched me silently, waiting. I didn't understand the impulse, but in that instant I knew I had to tell this man I trusted the whole truth about myself . . . the secret I'd hidden so well from the rest of the world . . . the truth I'd not dared divulge even to Justin.

I licked my lips nervously. The pressure of his fingers tightened. "Radford, there's something I must tell you. You are probably going to find it quite unbelievable, but it's the absolute truth, and for some reason, I feel you should know. I've told no one else; I never dared. I've lived from day to day rather carelessly, involving myself with people and events, but the life I lead here really is not my own to do with as I choose. I am not Marlena von Mantz. My name is Monica Wagner, and I am not a German baroness but an American of common ancestry." I had his full attention; his eyes never left my face as I outlined the events that occurred from the time of my arrival in London until my discovery of the baroness's diary.

"Things moved quickly. There was the will, and the guardianship, then my introduction into society, and I existed from day to day wondering where each would lead—and without realizing it, becoming more and more entangled in the web of life in this century, to the point that sometimes I almost forget this isn't my own world—that I will have to go back to the other someday.

"I don't know when it will end—but surely it will. One day I will return to where I belong, and all that I have experienced here will seem a mad, gay adventure . . . a dream that had all the characteristics of reality.

"I don't know, either, what became of the real baroness. I think perhaps she changed places with me in time, but there is no way of being sure. If she is in my world, I can only hope she's been able to fit into another world as easily as I have here.

"I only tell you this now, Radford, because I care for you. I want you to know the real reason why a relationship between us can go no further. I cannot marry you. I may have no more than a few days, a few weeks . . . how can I know? Then I'll be gone, and there'll be nothing in the universe that can bring me back. It's not like crossing land or an ocean—there can be no way to cross time at will. And I have to leave the real baroness's future secure for her when she returns, as I'm sure she will."

Despite my concerted effort, tears suddenly filled my eyes and overflowed down my cheeks. Perhaps they came with the relief of finally having shared my secret, or a hidden fear that he wouldn't accept my story. But he said nothing as his arms closed around me; his hand pressed my head against his shoulder.

He held me until I was in control of myself again. Then he lifted my face and spoke to me in a voice filled with awe and tightly held emotion. "Marlena, my sweet Marlena, I cannot believe the burden you have carried! Never in my life did I think to encounter anything like this! Yet much though it defies all my understanding, I believe you. No lie you could fabricate could be quite so outrageous."

"You believe me?" I was amazed.

"I always knew there was something very different about you . . . your outspokenness, your intelligence beyond that of the average woman, the way you carry yourself with such inner assurance, a number of subtle things about your conversation. Perhaps that is what has attracted me to you when others have made no impression—but to think of you not of this century; to think of losing you when we have come so far! That is the truly difficult part! You have no idea how this journey occurred?"

"None. In the beginning I considered the possibility I'd gone mad. There seems to be no explanation, but I am here—one night four and a half months ago I traveled the distance of over one hundred years with all the ease of a transatlantic flight."

"I wish to know more about this flying, this air ve-

hicle you speak of. Do you mean that man has actually conquered the mystery of flight . . . can take to
the air as a bird?"

"He's mastered the technology, the science of it,
has designed a special craft that, when in the air,
does look very much like a bird, though it's constructed of thin sheets of metal, with stationary
wings. The one on which I traveled to England would
seem of huge proportions to your eyes."

"Fantastic! Utterly fantastic. The cargoes I could
carry! And what did you say was the length of your
journey? It struck me as an inconceivably short period of time."

"Six and a half hours."

"My God in heaven . . . three thousand miles in
six and a half hours . . . that is over four hundred
miles an hour! Men can travel at that speed and have
no ill effects? What is the sensation? The body must
seem torn apart!"

"On land, perhaps, but in the air you're enclosed
in a pressurized cabin. You don't feel the speed at all.
Does that seem possible?"

"Hardly . . . but I have no facts by which to judge
such things. This is all far beyond my learning."
Radford was accepting my story all rather well . . .
far better than I would have imagined. I watched his
face as he digested the truth. The fingers on my arm
grew lax as he concentrated and pondered my words.
"What other marvels can you tell me about?"

"Oh, many, many." I didn't know where to begin. I
told him about cars and skyscrapers, television . . .
the marvels of twentieth century technology. "Oh,
Radford!" I exclaimed at last. "I could go on and on,
about modern medicine and dental care, agricultural
methods, the high standard of living. It will take
days for me to cover everything even superficially."

He rocked me excitedly, with the enthusiasm of a

small boy. "And I will *let* you go on and on. This is marvelous—more than I ever conceived! And all this time, under the surface, you have carried this knowledge of a world so advanced. We here must seem a gathering of the dumb and the foolish. You can talk to me for hours, for days. I will never tire! I want to know. I want to learn."

"We'll have to think of some explanation for my absence last night that won't cause a stir in London."

"What are you saying?" He grasped my shoulders and held me away from him. "After all we have just discussed, you still intend to return to London?"

"I thought you understood my reasons."

"We appear to be talking at cross purposes, madam. It is more imperative to me than ever that we be wed soon, knowing you might be snatched from my hands at any moment."

"Radford, we can't throw away logic, and I'm not even sure if what I feel for you is love. I like lying beside you and making love to you. Your touch makes me feel alive and passionate—but those are physical things."

"And what do you propose to do that is *logical?* Return to London, wait for the end of the year to protect this elusive baroness?"

"If I marry before that time I'll forfeit everything that belongs rightfully to her."

"I care nothing for that. You cannot be sure that she will return, or that you will leave, and in the meantime Warringwood will have you under his thumb."

"You don't have to be afraid I'll run back into his arms."

"But he will be *there,* just the same, and I will not. Would that I could wrap my fingers about your brain and force some sense into it."

"Please, Radford. I have to do what I think is best." It took all my willpower to say those words.

"You are being a fool!" he exclaimed. "I am not a man from the future, knowing all, but even I can see your foolishness. Your own future is so uncertain; how can you think of the baroness's? For that matter, how can you be so positive that you are going back?"

"It's a feeling I have. There's no sound reason behind it, except that I think nature corrects its mistakes. As for the baroness, she is my mirror image even though we're a century and a half apart. I feel a kinship with her."

"And has *she* been so busy protecting the life *you* may go back to?"

"I have no idea, obviously, but if we exchanged places, I was in England, not in the States."

"You had something awaiting you in England?"

"Only a vacation and an old friend."

"Who may be an old enemy by now."

"It doesn't matter. The baroness has much more to lose than I do."

"Don't be so unselfish! If you do not take care of yourself in this world, no one else is going to."

I couldn't help laughing. "That's a very modern opinion, Radford."

"But a truth nonetheless." He scowled, and turned his head brusquely away.

"Will you take me to London, Radford? Or shall I find some other means of getting there?"

"And what fine tale do you plan to fabricate to pacify our friends and explain away this past night?"

"I suppose to say we were attacked by robbers would be too much for them to swallow?"

"Neither would it say much for my prowess at being able to defend us. Think again." He was studying me with a cocked brow, though the disgruntled expression was still on his face.

"Well, I was sick—quite sick when we left the Jerseys'. A sick headache, I think, is what Sally would have told Caroline. We could tell them it became much worse. That I was nauseous and in a great deal of pain. Since we were near your London house at the time, you brought me there so your housekeeper could take a look at me and try to make me more comfortable. Your London house *is* somewhere in that vicinity, I hope?"

"To stretch 'vicinity' by several miles . . . although I suppose we could say we came upon a carriage accident blocking the roadway, and skirting around it, came by my door." A small grin was pulling at the corner of his mouth. "And your housekeeper," I continued, "would vouch for you if questioned?"

"Mrs. Morely has been in my household since I was a child."

"Well, there, then. We have it. We'll start out immediately for London. I'll wear a pained expression as though I'm still not well, explain to Caroline—"

"You are forgetting one rather important detail. How do I account for the fact I did not send a message to Warringwood House last night advising them of your situation?"

"It was quite late when we arrived at your house in London, and it took you and your housekeeper some time to make me comfortable. You were too busy to think of sending a note. When I finally began to feel more myself and you realized your omission, it was already the wee hours of the morning. I persuaded you that a messenger at that hour would only distress Caroline, who probably assumed I was up in my room asleep, and that you should wait until morning to deliver it. Simple."

"Not if one looks for flaws. However, it seems the best we can come up with. I see I must compose and dispatch a missive immediately if it is to reach London sometime before us."

Without further ado, he slipped from the bed and walked naked to the desk. Finding a piece of paper and a quill, he sat and began to scratch quickly. After rereading what he had written, he sanded the ink, sealed the note, and addressed it. Then he turned around in the seat toward me.

"This is not at all the way I intended this evening to end."

"I know."

"I must love you a great deal to allow myself to be so manipulated and set off my chosen course. I can yet force you into marrying me."

My voice seemed frozen in my throat. "I appreciate what you're doing, Radford."

He rose then, suddenly, strode over to the bed, and pulled me unceremoniously out of it. "You damn well better! Myself, I think I am a demented fool." His lips once more burned their impression on mine. "I shall dispatch this note now, but I will be back! We have one further item of business to conclude before we leave. Do not think you can run away, because I am locking the door—and if you dare to get dressed, I will tear every shred off your back and you shall go naked to London!" Grabbing his robe and hurriedly thrusting his arms into the sleeves, he slammed out the door. I distinctly heard the turning of the lock.

I sank down on the edge of the bed, more distraught than ever. I'd thought when I had told him the truth, he would reject me; instead, he'd accepted my story, understood my predicament, and looked for a means of tying us together despite it all. His reaction made it ever so difficult for me to stick to my decision. Perhaps he was right—perhaps I was being a blind fool to throw away even a brief interlude of happiness. But I'd jumped head first into an affair with Justin, and what had it gotten me but pain? No, it was better this way. Then, when I left, no hearts would be broken . . . except my own.

He entered a moment later, his eyes blazing with passion. "So I see you *can* listen to orders on occasion." He flung his robe away and stood before me, throbbing and tense. He extended his hands. "Come."

I went toward him. He drew me close, enfolded me, his hot breath in my ears. Then his lips began nibbling at my throat, then down to my breasts, where he lingered, building my desire to a level with his own. Then he loosened his arms, held me a few inches away, and stared piercingly into my eyes. I was totally aware of the power he had over me, of the rapid beating of my heart, of the persistent voice inside me telling me to give him all—everything he wanted. I forced myself not to listen to the voice.

As if reading my mind, his fingers suddenly squeezed my shoulders.

"I want you to know, my dear lady from the future, I care little for your reasons and procrastinations. We *will* love . . . and in the end, you *shall* be mine!"

NINETEEN

BEFORE ANOTHER HOUR had passed we'd dressed, had a light breakfast and tea in the bedroom, and were in Radford's carriage streaking off toward London. The sky was overcast, but fortunately the rain held off as we traveled the hour's journey to town. It wouldn't help to be bogged down and delayed by muddied roads.

As we neared the city, the traffic on the roadways increased, giving me pangs of anxiety at the slowing of our progress. Suppose Caroline had already read Radford's note and immediately sent a messenger to his London house to find it vacant, with no hint of our having been there for the last twelve hours? And suppose she had sent a message to Justin and he was already on his way to town? I hadn't considered these potential pitfalls when I'd so blithely manufactured my tale while at Setly Hall; but then everything had still had a dreamlike quality to it. Now, seeing the bustle of carriages and dray wagons, people hurrying to and from London on their daily, routine business, knowing we were only within a few minutes of it ourselves, the grimmer reality sank in.

I hid my apprehension as well as I could from Radford, who was determined to sit scowling on the opposite side of the seat, pressing his shoulder to his window as I was pressing to mine; telling me in every way except through words just what he thought of my running back to London and thwarting his plans. I wouldn't have called his posture a sulk, but a definite reprove, and a warning that though he was letting me have my way this once, it wasn't likely to happen again. I knew, of course, that all I had to do to soften his mood was to send him a warming smile, slide my body across the seat in his direction, and intimate that I was ready to admit I might have been mistaken in my haphazard dash from his loving arms. But this I couldn't do. Once I admitted doubt about the soundness of my present action, he wouldn't have allowed me to be separated from his side.

I knew now that I cared a great deal more for him than I'd ever allowed myself to believe. Yet I didn't want to contemplate that now. The more I allowed my emotions the liberty of following their own course, the more shattering it would be for me to return to my own world.

He spoke only once at length, when we were on Park Lane nearing Upper Brook Street. He looked at me, though he didn't alter the stiff repose of his frame.

"You are determined on this, Marlena? It is not yet too late to change your mind. We can reverse our course and find another spot for hiding until our marriage can take place."

Afraid to see the appeal in his eyes and afraid of the weakening effect it might have on me, I continued to gaze out the window. "I haven't changed my mind. There is no way I can, under the circumstances."

"Well, I refuse to make a damn fool of myself by pursuing the matter to an unprofitable end. I will just say that you are making a grave mistake. The only consolation I can gain from this madness is to know what your decision might have been had your life been your own to lead."

"Cocksure, aren't we?"

"Do not press. I can still turn this carriage about and head it in the direction whence it came—with you in it!"

"All right. But don't make this any more difficult for me than it already is."

He softened a bit. "I apologize. Of late my passions seem to carry me away with them. But I want no more of this cat-and-mouse nonsense, either. You will make it clear to Warringwood that you intend to see me; and see me you shall . . . each and every day."

We were now before Warringwood House. The carriage stopped. The coachman dropped from his perch to open the door. Radford exited first, holding up a hand for me. He followed me up the steps and waited as I knocked. The butler was immediately at the door, followed close on the heels by Caroline.

She pushed past the butler, across the threshold. "Marlena! Whatever happened! We waited all night. Langely was with me . . . escorted me home." And at my lifted brows: "Well, it would not have been seemly for me to have traveled across London at night without escort. He waited after your maid informed us you were not in your room, and left only when he received an urgent missive from his valet. His uncle has died. He is the heir, you know, and had to leave immediately for the estate."

"Did you send a message to your husband?" I inquired.

"Justin? Oh, no! That is, I . . . I wanted to wait until morning. What he would have said had he learned you were missing, I daren't think!"

"I am sorry, Caro. We would not have deliberately worried you, but I became so ill that Radford had no choice but to stop and allow his housekeeper to minister to me. When I did feel more myself, it was so late, I persuaded him to wait until morning to return me here, afraid you were already asleep and I would disturb you more."

"If you wish to lay the blame at anyone's feet," Radford interrupted firmly, "lay it at mine. I should have had some sense in my head and sent a message to the house last night anyway. For now I think the wisest course would be for both you ladies to get into the house and out of this damp air." Taking Caroline's arm and mine, he escorted us into the hall and then to the small drawing room, where a fire burned in the grate.

"Sit, both of you, before that fire. I shall see that the maid brings some tea." And with that he left the room, behaving as though he was issuing orders in his own home, not another's.

Caroline was the first to speak, only waiting for the door to close behind Radford before beginning, "So tell me what happened! All I received from Sally Jersey was the information that you had suddenly taken ill with a headache and had to be taken home. Radford obliged. But what an *on dit* that will make," she purred snidely, "should it get about town . . . you going off with Radford, then remaining away for the entire night."

"I trust the story will not get around, the only ones knowing of this overnight visit being the three of us—and Langely, of course, though I imagine he will be discreet; his own visit to this house would not bear public knowledge."

"He was behaving purely out of gentlemanly concern."

"I'm sure."

"But why did you not call me at the ball when you began to feel unwell?"

"I should have, I suppose, but it came upon me so suddenly, and I did not want to ruin your evening. I thought once I was home and in my own bed, everything would be all right. On the way here, there was a carriage accident. We had to bypass it, taking us on a longer route, and it was then my head began to throb unbearably. When I became nauseated, Radford decided I needed some immediate attention and, since we were near his own house, stopped there to have his housekeeper take a look at me."

"And she was in attendance with you all evening?"

"Yes. Radford, after assuring himself that I was in good hands, went off to his own chambers."

We heard the opening of the doors admitting Radford, which swiftly put an end to any further comments or questions Caroline might have offered.

He strode across the room on his long legs to pause before her chair. "Since you ladies have had a very trying last few hours, I will take myself off and leave you in peace. Again, my apologies to you, Lady Caroline, for causing you so much needless distress." He held our hands briefly. "I would suggest the two of you take yourselves off to bed." A secret wink was cast in my direction, and then he was off.

As I watched him walk out the door, I wondered again if I had done the right thing, but I wasn't going to allow impulse to rule me as it had before.

TWENTY

JUSTIN RETURNED from Sussex the following day, bewildered and cursing at having been sent on a wild goose chase. Fortunately, with the uproar of his arrival and all that he had to tell us of his frustrated investigation, the events of the evening of the Jerseys' party were completely forgotten, and he never learned of my night with Radford.

Radford came to see me every day, as he'd promised. With Justin out of the house so often during the day on business, the men's paths didn't cross, and I was able to postpone confronting Justin with the news that I'd be seeing quite a bit of his adversary.

The hours Radford and I spent together might have been delightful if I hadn't been so afraid of letting my guard slip, revealing to Radford that my determination to restore and maintain our relationship on a purely friendly basis wasn't as firm as I claimed. He was trying his damnedest to break down my resolve with a steady stream of light conversation, a courtly and unfailingly considerate manner toward me, a barrage of witty remarks that brought laughter to my throat. The coolness of my responses didn't deceive him at all.

He and I shared an enormous secret now, and it drew us closer together. We talked of my life in the twentieth century, the good and bad of it: my job, my family, my upbringing, my loves, my heartbreaks. Then he asked questions, never-ending questions, about the wonders of technology. All the things I had learned to take for granted were new to him and merited long explanations, even diagrams.

There was no filling him up, yet there could be no satisfying his dearest wishes, either. The servants became so accustomed to seeing him in the house, they no longer escorted him to the drawing room, but let him find his way there on his own. Caroline took a good deal of notice, but she said little to me. Langely was still in the country, and she carried about her a listless air, her enthusiasm for the social life having lost most of its sparkle.

But the wind came up, as I knew eventually it would. Justin came across me alone in the morning room one afternoon, and peremptorily took my arm and led me in the direction of the garden. "We must talk. In the garden—this house is overrun by servants."

Realizing he wasn't going to be put off, I followed. The air was chilly, and I hugged my arms, yet the sun skitting in and out from behind the clouds gave some warmth. He didn't pause, but led me to the back of the garden, behind the arbor and out of view of prying eyes.

"There are two matters I wish to discuss with you. First, that we will be leaving in a fortnight for Sussex. It will be an extended visit through the winter months, so have your woman pack accordingly. Secondly, and this is of far more concern to me, I understand you are seeing Radford frequently and openly, that he is often found waiting upon you in this very house."

"That is true."

"And what explanation have you for this behavior?"

"None. I want to see Radford, and I will. I would have told you sooner, except that we hardly ever see each other to talk."

"Which is no fault of mine! Obviously my opinions hold little sway over you outside these doors, but I do not want that man in my house!"

"You are behaving foolishly, Justin."

"Foolishly? Not I, madam. You are the one who acts with little sense. Must you rub salt into wounds that are still sore?"

"My intention is far from that—"

"There is no longer any need for this game. I love you. I will do anything to marry you, press divorce proceedings on to a speedy end."

"We have talked of this before, and I thought I made all my feelings and reasons clear to you. I will not change my mind, and I will not allow you to destroy yourself by getting a divorce. Your situation may seem intolerable, but mine is as well!"

For a moment I thought he was going to shake me, so livid was the fury in his eyes. Instead he thrust me aside. "Damn you, damn you, woman!"

When he'd gone, the French doors slamming behind him, I went to the bench and sat down, my knees weak and trembling. I buried my head in my hands.

I knew Justin was going to be home for dinner that night and, as was the ritual, we were all to meet in the drawing room beforehand for sherry. When I entered the room at precisely eight o'clock, Justin was already there, pacing restlessly. We endured several long minutes of silence as he threw covert scowls alternately at me and at the china clock ticking on the mantel. It was ten after eight and Caroline still wasn't down. I'd heard there'd been a terrible fight between her and Justin that afternoon. When Justin had gone to her to tell her to begin preparing for the trip to Sussex, she'd flown into a tantrum, screaming her usual complaints at him. But this time, instead of maintaining his usual front of indifference to the barrage, his temper had snapped. He knew perfectly well that her reluctance to make the trip really stemmed from the fact that Langely wasn't back in town yet and might not return until after our departure.

Finally, as I was thinking the oppressive atmosphere in the drawing room would surely smother me, there was a knock on the door and the butler entered.

"Your Lordship. Lady Caroline sends her excuses, but she is ill and will not be joining you for dinner."

The scowl on Justin's brow deepened. "Will she not! And what, pray tell, is the nature of her illness?"

"I do not know, my lord. Her maid only sent a message down with one of the footmen."

"Send her maid to me!"

"Very well, my lord."

Justin paced angrily around the room, until a few minutes later when Caroline's maid entered.

"You wished to see me, my lord."

"I did. I understand my wife is indisposed. She seemed quite full of energy this afternoon. What is her complaint?"

"The usual . . . the pains, my lord."

"We shall see about that!" He headed with determined intent toward the door.

"But, my lord! She's very poorly. Excuse me, sir, but she asked particular not to be disturbed."

He confronted the now shaking woman. "And her husband is included in that dictate?"

Obviously there was nothing the quaking woman could say, and knowing the answer perfectly well himself, he relented. He paused a moment, then said, with a motion of his arm toward the door, "Very well, go to your mistress. Tell her I will speak to her on the morrow! Come, Marlena, our dinner has been delayed long enough."

The silence that reigned over our meal destroyed what little appetite I had, and as soon as was politely permissible, I excused myself for my own room.

I slept badly, and came down rather late for breakfast the next morning. But as I paused outside the morning room door, I heard raised voices on the other side. Stunned by the tone of the conversation, I stood frozen, an unwilling eavesdropper.

"So, Caroline"—I heard Justin's voice cut—"I see I find you much improved this morning. I went to your room expecting to find an invalid."

"I came down for but a moment." Her voice was wavery. "I was on the point of returning to my room."

"We are having dinner guests this evening. I trust you have not forgotten—guests of some importance to me whom I would like to see leave this house with favorable impressions. You will be your usual charming self by that hour, I hope."

"As you can see with your own eyes, I am in no way fit for entertaining. You will have to excuse me."

"When you know what importance I have placed on this dinner? No, I am afraid I will make apologies to no one for this imagined illness of yours."

"You are insufferable . . . unfeeling!"

"What do you expect? The compassion of a doting husband? I know the only cause of your indisposition is a fear that you will miss seeing your captain. Are you laboring under the hope that I will postpone our departure for Sussex?" And at her sharply indrawn breath: "I am not as blind as you might have thought. Not that it disturbs me overmuch, since in this poor excuse for a marriage we have, I am sure he is not the first."

"And what of you and our dear baroness? Am I to sit back while my husband flaunts his affair in my face?"

"If I believed it was love prompting your concern, Caro, I might be moved, but any feeling you had for me died long before the baroness touched these shores."

"You are an intolerable tyrant! You make that clearer to me with each day that passes!"

"Take the balance of the day for your rest and sulks, but be downstairs promptly at eight this evening to receive our guests."

I fled and hid myself in a shadowed alcove as he stormed out of the room and down the hall.

Caroline made her appearance that night, elegantly gowned, but white and shaken. Her pallor could have been due as much to anger as anything else; there was certainly an icy shaft of hatred in her eyes each time she looked in her husband's direction.

Radford came to take me for a carriage ride the next afternoon. I told him of our imminent departure for the country. I didn't think he'd be pleased, and wasn't wrong in my assumption.

A stormy mask slipped down over his features. "How do you propose we see each other?" he inquired. "Or do you think Warringwood will permit me to come down to spend some time with you as his houseguest?"

"Don't you know anyone in the neighborhood you could visit? There's always Brighton, out of season though it is."

"Yes."

"I don't know what else I can do, Radford. It isn't as though I can stay behind in London when they go."

"Have you broached the subject with your guardian?"

"What a waste of breath that would be! As it is, it was awkward when he discovered we were seeing each other again."

"Why do you not forsake all of this nonsense and marry me as I wish!"

At my silence his frown grew darker. We were traveling up Piccadilly, and suddenly he pulled on the reins, turned the team of gray high-steppers to the right onto a narrower, cobbled roadway that I judged led toward St. James's Square. "Duke Street, my dear, since I know your natural curiosity prompts wondering." He flicked the whip over the horses' backs and set them to a trot again. We rolled over the cobbles for another minute or two; then he drew back on the reins and halted before a three-story brick town house whose architecture indicated it had been built in the previous century.

"My humble abode. You have no objections if we stop for a moment? There are some papers I neglected to bring with me this afternoon. Come in and I will show you the rooms where you supposedly passed the evening after the Jerseys' reception. Jeremy," he called back to his tiger, "Come hold their heads. Walk them back to the stables. We may be a few minutes."

The tiny groom bounded down from his perch on the rear of the carriage to grab the horses' bridles. Radford jumped to the pavement, dropped the steps for me, and reached up a hand to help me descend.

The butler was already opening the door of the house as Radford and I climbed the white front steps.

"A bachelor's residence, I am afraid, Marlena, much in need of a woman's beautifying touch."

"If that was meant as a jab, Radford, you've missed your mark."

The butler reached for our wraps, and Radford nodded to his greeting. "Good afternoon, Chalmers. I am returning sooner than I expected, but I left behind some papers that I am in need of this afternoon. May I present to you the baroness von Mantz."

Chalmers bowed deeply. "Honored, Baroness. Would you care for some refreshments, my lord?"

"Not at the moment. We will only be staying for a short time, but if we should change our minds, I will call on you."

"Very well, my lord." He retreated with our wraps, and Radford motioned to me.

"Come, Marlena." He took my arm and started across the black and white tiles of the front hallway. "The grand tour. This, as you have surmised, is the hall, and through here"—he opened a set of double doors—"the drawing room. Not so large a place as Warringwood House, though I have always found it rather comfortable."

I walked beside him into a long room running from the front of the house to the back, tastefully furnished but giving the appearance of not getting much use. An elegant black marble fireplace was centered on the outside wall, with a graceful grouping of furniture placed before it. To either side of the fireplace and to the front and rear of the room were tall windows framed by gold and green patterned draperies, a color scheme that was repeated in the thick oriental rug and on the chair and couch covers.

He drew me toward the end of the room. We passed smaller groupings of furniture, a lady's drop-leaf desk, and a curio cabinet, then proceeded through another set of doors, matching those at the head of the room, into a smaller, airy room, full of sunshine, with French doors leading out to the garden. I liked the placement of the round cherry table, the bright landscapes on the walls.

"The morning breakfast room," he explained. "And beyond here is the formal dining room." He continued the tour, leading me out into a hallway. The doors he threw wide revealed a room three quarters the size of the drawing room on the opposite side of the house, its aura especially appealing. The heavily carved furnishings spoke of great age—heirlooms perhaps handed down through Radford's family. Red drapes were at the windows, and a huge wall tapestry depicted a family gathered on a stream bank, the children frolicking, the eldest boy training a fly rod over the water with his father's assistance.

"How unusual."

"I am glad you noticed. Sewn by my grandmother—a replica of her own family. My father is the boy with the pole."

I tried to get a closer look at the nine- or ten-year-old holding the pole, but Radford was moving on.

"To the front of this room is the library. We will stop there last, when I retrieve my papers." He motioned me along the hallway toward the front of the house, then around and up the gracefully curved main staircase.

"There is something in particular I would like to show you up here, Marlena. You have an appreciation of art, I know. There is a painting that might especially interest you." We reached the top of the stairs. Radford walked forward down the long corridor, and stopped before a door at the end of the hall. "In here." He ushered me in and closed the mahogany door behind us.

It was a large room facing the back, the row of long windows giving a lovely view of the rear garden; a

masculine room of deep colors, a massive bed to the
left, fireplace, reading chair, and desk to the right, a
large armoire along the wall behind. I liked it. I
liked the feel, the lived-in warmth of the room. I
could almost see the shirt dropped negligently over
the back of the chair, the crumpled white neckcloths,
not tied to the dresser's satisfaction and discarded on
the bed in his morning haste; could smell the after-
scent of a wood-burning fire, of a man's spicy cologne
recently applied.

"You once expressed a curiosity about my dark coloring. You will recall my mentioning it skipped generations. This is my mother." His hand lifted toward
the gilt-framed portrait over the mantelpiece.

I gazed up in disbelief at the golden-haired woman
whose azure eyes seemed to catch my own as she
looked out from the canvas. Not a traditionally beautiful woman—her aquiline nose a shade too long, her
cheekbones a bit higher and more prominent than
conventional standards of beauty warranted—but a
striking woman, one who would have all heads turning when she walked across a room.

"An attractive woman, my mother, don't you
think?"

"Extremely. But with that fair coloring, it's hard
to believe she *is* your mother. Still, I can see something of her in you . . ." As I continued to study the
woman's face, Radford's fingers tightened on my
arm.

"Can you? I wonder how our children will fare?"

"The question will never arise."

"Will it not?"

He was drawing me closer. In a moment he took
my shoulder, turned me to face him.

"What are you up to, Radford?" Used to his teasing persistence, I wasn't alarmed, and grinned up at
his satyrlike expression.

"A moment's privacy . . . the two of us alone."

"So you've brought me here as a ruse—to steal a few kisses."

"There is that." He too grinned.

"It won't work." Yet for all my resolutions, I didn't entirely trust myself alone with him. "We should be leaving." My words sounded meaningless even to me. Already I felt his magnetism pulling me into his sphere, voiding my will.

"Should we?" he whispered. His fingers touched my cheek and slid round to the back of my neck, exerting a gentle pressure.

The dark eyes locked on mine, held them. "You do not really want to leave, do you, my love? Any more than I would willingly give up this opportunity to have you to myself. Kiss me."

His eyes stared deeper; I obeyed, not understanding why I was acting on his will and not my own. He made no move as I lifted my chin, reached toward his warm, waiting lips.

Only when my mouth was touching his, our lips caressing in a silent language, did his arm suddenly tighten across my back. He pulled me forcefully against his body.

Our loins met, and through the fabric of my gown I felt the pulsing, hard bulge of his masculinity. My passion burst like floodwaters from a ruptured dam. With each sinuous movement of his hips against the silk of my gown, the throbbing between my legs increased, and became an unquenchable thirst only he could assuage. He knew my need; his hand was upon my lower back, pressing me forward, intensifying the contact. His fingers slipped down into the neckline of my gown, under the silk, and stroked the soft flesh; his fingertips finally brushing over the nipple, lightly . . . ever so lightly . . . coaxing, concentrating the feathery pressure on the sensitive peak until it rose, firm and aching. The tender touching continued until I moaned with longing, felt the moistness of desire between my legs.

"Come, Marlena, love me," he murmured. "Let yourself be free."

His hands were lifting my skirts, loosening my petticoats so they fell in a puddle of lace about my ankles, then caressing my naked skin. I needed this man . . . more than just physically. I was beyond turning away; couldn't deny my instincts.

He took my hands, but led me toward the upholstered chair instead of the bed. "In the event we are interrupted," he whispered, but I barely heard him.

Pausing, his back toward the chair, he took my chin and gazed deep into my eyes. "Undo my breeches, Marlena. Don't always force me to be the aggressor."

Trembling, my fingers went to the buttons, unsure, unsteady in their course, but excited, full of anticipation. As the last button gave way, his swollen manhood surged forth. I ran my fingers up and down the throbbing velvet length.

He moaned; then, turning me so my back was toward him, he lifted my skirts above my waist and eased himself into the chair.

"Now sit, slowly, my love. Drop your skirts around us."

As I lowered my weight onto his lap, I felt him enter, thrust deep; felt the rough texture of his trousers against my bare legs; heard the rustling of silk as he moved gently beneath me, lifting his hips, his hand slipping under my skirts, over my thigh, between my legs.

"Shhh, quietly." His lips were hot against the back of my neck; his movements growing more fevered, intense; his fingers gently probing me so that

I gripped the arms of the chair, wanting to cry out in pleasure.

With the afternoon sunlight slanting in golden shadows across the room, our enforced silence stilling the sighs rising in our throats, we were joined, bonded into one flesh.

As his fingers brought me closer to drowning in the warm, sweet waves, he pressed himself more deeply into the cavern of my womanhood, filling me so that I thought I would die, yet wanting to pull him deeper still. He gasped, then sucked in his breath just as his finger touched that precious nerve and my back arched, my muscles tensed in spasms of delight. It was all I could do to hold back my cry of joy.

Moments later, relaxing into soft bliss, the warmth of him still filling me, I felt his lips again on my neck, this time as a tender nibble.

"It does not have to be this way—hidden, stolen moments."

"I know, Radford, I know . . ."

"Marry me."

"I can't."

"Let us share whatever time there is."

"It would only bring more pain."

"Why?"

"Because we'll have that much more to lose if—*when* I go . . . that much more to forget."

"Nonsense. We would have that much more to remember."

"No . . . I can't . . ." After our closeness, our ecstasy, I was near to breaking my resolve.

"Then let me pray I have planted a seed in your belly. Perhaps that will bring you to me when nothing else will!"

"Don't be angry. I'm doing what I feel I have to do."

His hand caressed my thigh in a soothing motion.

"You are being foolish. Someday you are going to realize it."

"You're not a visitor from another time. You don't
understand what I'm going through. I've set my
course; I must follow it. Someday I *may* look back
with regret, but for now I don't know what else to
do."

"Love me!"

It was too much. My swimming emotions warred
with the logic that kept thrusting its dagger point
into my mind. Finally I rose, hurriedly, and strode
across the room to retrieve my petticoats from the
floor. I couldn't look at him; couldn't face the expression I knew would be written on his features. With
my back toward him, I refastened my undergarments; heard him rise and adjust his own clothing.

An uneventful week passed—and then something
happened to shake all our foundations to the foot-
ings. Since Radford was in the Midlands on business
that Tuesday evening, I'd joined Caroline and Justin
at a small card party. It was a staid, rather dull affair. I found my thoughts more often on my personal
dilemma than on the cards in my hand. Caroline,
too, was preoccupied. Her drawn paleness, which
had been evident the past weeks, was more pro-
nounced than ever, accompanied by an uncharacteristic listlessness. Langely remained in the country
settling his uncle's estate, and perhaps she perceived, as I already conjectured, that now that he'd
inherited a title and the role of guardian to his family's heritage, Langely had suddenly realized the foolhardiness of his affair with Caroline. He would need
an heir and a mantle of respectability, and neither
could be gotten through a dalliance with a married
woman. My heart softened at the thought of her rude

awakening. If she was sincerely in love with
Langely, I could understand the pain she must be
suffering.

There was a furrow on her brow, as though she was
in pain, by the time the carriage returned to
Warringwood House and we entered the candlelit
hall.

Suddenly she gave a cry and clutched her hand to
her side. Her face was white as a sheet, her eyes
brimming with tears. She seemed barely to have
the strength to stand. "The pain!" she cried. "The
pain . . ."

Justin rushed forward. There was real concern on
his face; shock and confusion.

"Caro! What is it?"

She was beyond responding; nearly doubled over,
her hands clutching her middle.

He reached her just as she collapsed and swept her
up in his arms. Rushing for the stairs, he called back
over his shoulder, "Marlena, send out one of the men
for the physician! Tell him we must have him here
urgently!"

The best physician in London arrived to attend
Caroline that night, but she didn't return to full consciousness, only lapsing in and out of a laudanum-
induced sleep. The doctor had ordered that the drug
be given in sufficient dosages to relieve the pain that
had been racking her abdomen without cease since
her attack in the downstairs hall.

A rider was sent north to Yorkshire to notify her
parents and bring them to town. Since it would be a
full day's journey for a rider and a two-day journey in
a coach, it was only hoped they would arrive in time
to give their daughter some comfort: the prognosis
was not good.

The mood in the house was somber and frightened.

She was so young and did not deserve such pain. I suddenly felt a terrible guilt for the additional anxiety I had caused her through my relationship with Justin. True, their marriage had been in a sorry state long before my arrival on the scene, and she'd been the first to look outside the marriage for comfort with Captain Langely, but her knowledge of Justin's and my affair couldn't have helped her physical well-being.

I could find all kinds of excuses now for her behavior, and so could Justin; he blamed himself and his lack of compassion for an illness that was bringing her to death's door.

He came to me one night in the music room, as I sat alone playing quietly for solace. Two days' unshaven stubble shadowed his cheeks, and the purple shadows under his eyes were evidence of his having gotten no rest; he had been pacing a constant vigil along the corridors of the house.

As he sat in the soft chair facing me, he buried his head in his hands, seeming almost too weary to speak.

Finally he lifted his head, his voice a worn thread. "You know I do not love her . . . not as I should or once might have . . . no more than she loved me. But, my God, I feel torn apart . . . so damned guilty, as though I were standing before a jury, all with accusing fingers pointed in my direction. If I had not been so callous about her attacks . . . if instead of putting it all to selfish tantrums, I had looked deeper into the causes, sent her to other physicians last spring instead of taking the word of the physicians who saw her and claimed it was only a nervous disorder. Just a few weeks ago I stormed at her, made her get out of bed to come down to our guests. I keep seeing her face when she told me I was unfeeling . . . and all that time, she *was* ill . . . so seriously ill. Everything she accused me of is the truth!"

"Justin . . . you cannot tear yourself to pieces," I answered quietly. "We all feel it—the shock, the unexpectedness—and all we can think of is her youth, her pain and what we could have done to prevent it. I have felt the guilt—chastised myself for my behavior in front of her. Neither of us, if we had known the seriousness of her illness would deliberately have brought her more pain. But we did *not* know—perhaps she did not realize herself; perhaps she too thought it was no more than a nervous disorder."

"You know the physicians hold out little hope. They say it is a tumor. She is going to die."

"Yes."

"Strange how quickly they can diagnose at this point! Why could not they have seen this months ago, when they were first called in? And the pain she is suffering! My heart turns just to walk into the room."

"As does mine."

"Only laudanum gives her peace. If I had had some idea!" His lids dropped briefly over his tormented eyes. "I should have given her more consideration—though to be honest, I do not know if I could have brought her happiness . . . if it would have made things better between us."

"You need some sleep and some food. Have you eaten?"

"I do not recall."

"Come with me, then. We shall go to the kitchens. It may be beneath your dignity, but there is sure to be a kettle on the fire, and the cook can find something to put on a plate for you."

Whether he was aware of what he was doing or too

dazed from remorse and lack of sleep to balk, he rose and went with me from the room, even managing to smile as I took his arm.

"I am not yet enfeebled, you know."

"No, just tired."

We received word of Caroline's death in the early hours of the morning. She'd slipped off quietly in her sleep. For her it was probably a blessing that death came so peacefully and speedily. For the rest of the household, the news settled with black finality.

Her maid took it the hardest. She had stood up staunchly throughout, tending Caroline without rest during the days of her illness. But at the end she collapsed in hysterics, requiring the aid of both the housekeeper and my own maid, Jane, to comfort her and escort her up to her own chamber.

Justin walked about in a daze. His face, white and drawn days before, was now dark-shadowed and gray. Asking sympathy from no one, he took hand of the arrangements for the funeral with his usual efficiency, but it didn't take eyes as knowing as mine to see that he was carrying himself forward by sheer iron will.

Caroline's parents arrived late that afternoon, to find their only child already gone. Since her marriage they'd seen little of their daughter, the last reunion having been over a year before. But their pride and love had never diminished, and, fortunately, they'd never guessed at her underlying unhappiness. Though they held up a strong front, their grief was terrible. Justin tried to console them, and perhaps it was the sight of the pain in his own eyes more than anything else that brought them a small comfort.

A shocked and silent entourage followed us to Pemberton Hall in Sussex and the family burial plot.

I saw Langely standing at the back of the crowd gathered at the grave, his expression as shocked and grieved as any lover's could have been. Obviously he couldn't go to Justin with his condolences, but before he slipped quietly from the graveyard, I found a moment to go to his side.

"I'm very sorry, Captain."

He looked at me, his face pained, and nodded. "It is just so hard to believe. It was wrong, perhaps, what we did, but I loved her, Baroness, with all my heart . . . from the time we were children together. I promised myself when I returned from the war I would come to claim her. By then I would have something to offer. When I came, she was gone, married to Warringwood. I never planned to find her again in London . . . to pursue her as a married woman. It just happened. . . . I do not want you to blame her."

"I know there was unhappiness in her life. It would be impossible to blame anyone."

He nodded again sadly. "I must go now."

Radford had come down, and he too was subdued, more introspective than I'd ever seen him. He took my hand during the services at the grave, and stayed at my side in the Great Hall, where the mourners distractedly nibbled at the cold collation that had been set out for their benefit. I had a feeling that this death brought home to him, as it did to me, the suddenness and finality with which we too could be separated.

He said almost nothing to me, and left early in the evening for London. But perhaps he had been right, and I was a fool not to take advantage of a short-lived joy when it was offered.

TWENTY-ONE

THE REST OF NOVEMBER passed. Justin and I had returned to London after the funeral. There'd be no stay in the country for the holidays as had been planned. With the tragedy so fresh, Justin had no wish to participate in the traditional Christmas festivities at Pemberton.

Now that Caroline was gone, a cousin of Justin's moved in as my companion. A woman of some fifty-odd years, she was pleasant enough, although not especially bright or stimulating. Since she made up for this lack with a comprehensive knowledge of ton etiquette, a sharp eye for my behavior, and an absolute joy at the privilege of living in London for the first time in her heretofore unexciting life, I supposed she well fit the qualifications Justin had set for my social companion.

Though Justin ate with us, talked to me, there was no hint of the impassioned lover in his actions. He turned to me for comfort to ease his sore feelings of guilt, yes; but that was all. It was as though he'd withdrawn from the living into a private hell of guilt-ridden reproach.

Radford was the only one who could be counted on

to relieve the tedium and tension of the days. Now that the house was in full mourning, there was no thought of social activities. I found myself looking forward eagerly to eleven each morning, when he usually called to take me out for an hour in his carriage. Our small excursions together were marred only by having Miss Barton so often with us. She took her duties too seriously: she'd been hired as companion, and companion she would be. Few of Radford's or my persuasions could sway her. Of course, it was a diversion to see her well-padded, satin-encased body trying to lift itself into his sporty light curricle, or to see her trotting determinedly on our heels in the dreariest of weather when we demanded a walk in the park for exercise.

Radford and I found a few intervals when we could get rid of her and were able to talk openly, but the main and persisting thread of his conversation seemed to revolve around Justin and his attitude. How was he treating me? Had his behavior changed? What had he said to me since his wife's death? No matter how I tried to convince him that Justin was a man so wrapped up in his personal trial, he was all but unaware of my presence in his house, Radford had no peace. He used all of his persuasive powers to get me from beneath Justin's roof, finally shouting at me one day as we rode through town.

"Has it escaped your notice that he is now a free man? Where some sense of honor held him back before, there is nothing to do so now."

"If you had eyes in your head, you would see that what he wants from me isn't a romp between the sheets, but companionship—someone to talk to, to fill the hours of his day and the emptiness of his house. He didn't love Caro, but he feels guilt now for so long ignoring her illness."

Radford looked at me as though I'd gone mad. "He

has also been in love with you for many months and can now make you a legitimate offer of marriage. How long will it be before he wakes up one morning clearheaded to realize that the woman he has loved and desired is still beneath his roof?"

"I wouldn't marry him, any more than I've agreed to marry you."

"You say that now, but he is constantly there to work his persuasions. I am not! Marlena, my patience is nearing an end. I need you; my body craves yours beside it. Can you not at least slip away for a few hours one evening to my house?"

"Please, Radford. Do I have to go through all the reasons again?"

More evenings than I cared to count, I ended up sharing the fireside of the drawing room with my fuddle-witted companion, she immensely stimulated by her onesided conversation. I, bored to tears, tried to pretend I could sew the poor excuse for embroidery in my hands. Thank heavens she never showed enough curiosity to ask to see it.

It was only late December, and although it seemed to me that months had passed since Caroline's funeral, it had actually been only slightly over one month since that sad day. Since I wasn't an immediate relative, my enforced mourning was over, and Miss Barton and I had made arrangements to go to the opera. I suppose it was good to think of getting out of the house for an evening for the first time in long weeks, but I wasn't excited. The gay London whirl no longer seemed such an adventure.

I dressed indifferently in a deep-green velvet I'd worn several times before, finding when I'd finished that the result was more entrancing than I had planned.

The production was surprisingly engaging for an

off-season production, and after hushing Miss Barton's annoying comments and questions about the onstage characters and the people seated in the opposite box, I was almost able to lose myself to the music and drama of the opera. It was such a pleasure to be able to escape into another set of problems and leave my own behind, even for the briefest period.

Too soon it was intermission. Miss Barton found it beyond her ability to sit still any longer and practically dragged me out of the box with her to the lobby, where she hoped to run into a few friends and have a nice chat. I followed after her, tried to smile during the introductions to her friends, listened politely to their conversations for several minutes—then, looking up, spotted Radford at the other side of the foyer. He was alone, Sir Robert Bradshaw just having left his side. Radford saw me, and began to come forward. Seeing Miss Barton, he halted; motioned me to come to him, out of range of her hearing. Once I reached his side, he led me off, away from the crowd. Finding an empty box, he drew its velvet curtains closed behind us and brought me to the back, where no peering eyes could observe us.

Almost before I had time to take a breath, he'd pulled me into his arms. His mouth came down hard and insistent. His arms pressed my body against his as though he wanted to sear our flesh together.

"I have missed you. Oh, how I have missed you," he whispered after a long moment. "It has been too long since we have had any privacy, and I have counted every hour."

My response was as fevered as his attack, and he felt it. I wished for a short time only that I could forget all reason and abandon myself to the warmth and power of his arms.

"We must do something to end this torture," he said softly. "You have had time enough to consider, to realize the foolhardiness of the course you are following. We have so much together. The way we see things with the same eye, understand and laugh at the same jokes, talk for hours, and it surely can be said we are compatible in bed!"

"Radford!"

"No one can hear us, and there is nothing to make you blush in that statement. Your memory is as good as mine. Dammit, Marlena, I cannot stand it anymore! I love you. Have I not proved it by now? I am sick to death of your excuses, of pretending to be the gentleman when I want to rape you on the spot. I want every inch of you. Not just for now, but forever."

I choked back a sob. "You know my reasons . . . I can't . . . I must *wait* . . ."

"This is not the normal progression of things, in which a man can be asked to wait for a few months and expect, aside from undue tragedy, to have his lover there and ready. You may be gone from me beyond any hope of retrieving . . . into a world where I would have no part. Cannot you see the agony I am living?"

"I can see it . . . I can feel it myself, but if we become any closer to each other than we are now, the pain will be that much worse."

I ran from him then; felt his arms reach out after me, but escaped and returned to my box and the sterile conversation of Miss Barton.

Somehow I lived through the rest of the opera, through the next few hours—unhappily, knowing I may have handed Radford the last straw and that even his seemingly endless patience had worn to an end. It hurt me, but my whole world at that point had become such confusion and wretchedness, I couldn't concentrate on even that terrible loss.

The next morning I stood at the morning room

French doors, watching snow fall on the dead and gray garden. Radford came up behind me so quietly that I barely heard him until he spoke without preamble.

"I have come to say good-bye, Marlena. I am leaving London this afternoon."

I swung to face him. "You're leaving? Leaving for where? What do you mean?"

He stood stiff and firm, not even reaching out a hand to touch me. "I am going to the Continent. There are some business matters I have put off for too long."

"I don't understand. The Continent? Why now?"

In response he gave me only an unflinching stare. "The business calling me is urgent. I should have gone before now, if not for you. I shall be gone until the first of March."

"But Radford, that's two months! I could be gone in that time!"

"I know, and it grieves me."

"Then why must you do this?"

"Marlena, if I thought there was some chance of your relenting and coming to me as I want . . . of your accepting and returning the love I so willingly offer, I wouldn't go. But I have decided to follow your logic. I cannot bear things the way they are, so, for my own sanity, perhaps it *is* best that we never know the extent of what we could be to each other—that we part now before the pain of separation is too great to endure. Do you remember, Marlena, my telling you of that thwarted love affair of mine years past? I swore then I would never love again or put myself in such a vulnerable position. For a long time I succeeded. Then you entered the picture. I love again . . . more than ever before. But I will not allow myself to be misused and hurt. I do not want a repetition of history!"

"You're the only thing that holds me together," I cried. "Just to know that I'll see your face each day and hear your voice keeps me going."

"Are you saying you are finally agreeing to come to me as I want you, as my wife?"

"You know I can't do that. If it were possible—"

"Then it must be good-bye. If you are here, I shall see you on my return in March—which should coincide with the anniversary of your father's death and the end of Warringwood's guardianship. If not . . . you know I love you; I always will."

His hands gently took my shoulders. His kiss when his lips dropped to mine spoke to me of a warmth, a tender love, a longing, a wish that it wasn't ending . . . a promise that there could be more.

As he drew away, a sob escaped my throat. He didn't seem to hear. With a determined set to his shoulders, he swung around and was gone.

I stood by those windows in a daze for at least half an hour after he'd left, hoping I'd dreamed it all; knowing I hadn't. At last I went up to my room, threw myself on the covers of the bed, and sobbed. Too late I realized I should have gone to him; knew it in every bone of my body.

I spent my nights tossing on cold and tangled sheets, ravaged and miserable, dreaming dreams that gave me no peace. And during my waking hours I was even more anguished, wondering what kind of fool I must be, wanting him more and more, knowing fulfillment could have come with him.

I thought that terrible winter would never end. Aside from the physical discomfort I suffered through lack of central heating, of always having a shawl wrapped around my shoulders to protect me from the damp chill, a deep depression descended on me, the likes of which I'd never known before. The feeling was different from the desolation and numbness I'd felt in New York after my father's death. Then, at least I'd cherished the hope that things would improve. Now I wondered if they ever would. All I saw was complete and utter helplessness. I had no control over my own destiny. Would I go back to my rightful world not knowing if I could replace what I'd found here? Or would I stay in a time where I might already have lost the love of the one man who meant everything to me?

I missed Radford more as each day passed, and there was nothing I could do to fill the void. Justin wasn't any help, distraught and off in his own world as he was, and I couldn't find any inner resources on which to draw. I knew then that if I were somehow fortunate enough to be around when Radford returned, I would hasten to make amends.

I received no letters from Radford. I had nothing—just memories in which I relived with a new appreciation everything we had shared.

Though I was only partially conscious of it as the days went by, there was a subtle change taking place in the atmosphere of the house—the awakening that Radford had predicted. Justin was coming out of his self-constructed shell. Now there were brief spells when the lines of guilt on his face seemed less sharp; when the old spark of good humor occasionally lit his eyes. I noticed an increase in his awareness of the things going on around him . . . and of me. When he was free from business appointments, he began driving Miss Barton and me out on our errands, even suffered through a few evenings at home taking part in the driveling conversation necessitated by Miss Barton's presence. He gave a wide berth to the topics of Caroline's death and our past relationship, though he did once broach the subject of Radford.

"I heard at one of my clubs that he has gone off to the Continent on business." We were seated together in the carriage while Miss Barton ran in to collect something at the milliner's. "It is not my intention to pry, but is this an indication that things are finished between the two of you?"

"As you said, it is a business trip."

"Of long duration?"

"Until early March."

"I see." He paused. "What are your plans, Marlena? Time grows short until the year's anniversary and the end of my guardianship."

"I've made no decisions. Much could happen before then."

Still no word from Radford, and London was as dismal as my mood; rainy, foggy, cold, with occasional flurries of snow. The household couldn't help but be aware of my state of mind, but there was little anyone could do to brighten my spirits. One morning, Jane did bring up the issue.

"Something has been troubling you fearful lately, my lady. Would it help to get it off your chest? I know how it has been . . . you alone here with Lady Caroline gone."

"Thank you, Jane, but this is something I have to settle on my own."

"It would be the two gentlemen, if my guess is right." She brushed a curl of my hair around her finger and looked me in the eye in the mirror. "Probably stickin' my nose in where it don't belong, but I know how it was with the marquis and you, and some months back I saw the look in His Lordship's eye."

Suddenly I buried my face in my hands. "I never knew life could be so complicated."

"Now, no need to go and cry about it. Most ladies

would be busting with joy to find two such handsome ones at their beck and call. Weren't so good for you when Lady Caroline was here, but now she's gone . . . bless her soul . . . he is a free man. Begging your pardon, my lady, but you are not in the family way!"

Miserable as I was, I laughed at her expression. "No. Not that, thankfully. It's only that sometimes I don't know which way to turn—not just with the gentlemen, but in everything."

"Well, as my ma always told me, things have a way of working out in the end."

After dinner that evening Justin approached me. "Marlena, I have a feeling the two of us have been moping about this house long enough. Of course it is unhealthy."

I waited, wondering what point he was trying to make.

His gaze was steady, questioning. "I'd like you and Miss Barton to come with me into the country."

"To Pemberton?"

"Yes. A change of scene. We could leave on the morrow . . . or later if you need more time to prepare."

I could only think of the possibility that Radford would return and find me gone off with Justin. What would he think?

If Justin read my thoughts, he gave no indication, only looked me straight in the eye. "The trip surely could not make either of us feel any worse. For a change, Marlena, trust my judgment."

TWENTY-TWO

WE ARRIVED at the gates of the estate just as the gloomy winter dusk was falling. We'd made remarkable time, considering the condition of the winter roads, but we'd been lucky and hadn't gotten mired in the ruts or detoured by a flooded roadbed. I was given the same room—normally a warm and inviting one, but the damp, chill fog that had settled in over the landscape sent its creeping fingers into even this sanctum. Jane immediately lit the fire, and I began to unpack and set out my belongings, then washed and changed into the gown I would wear for dinner. To this I added a wool shawl.

We dined alone, Justin and I. Pleading a headache, a tired Miss Barton had excused herself, to Justin's relief and mine; her constant chatter was wearing increasingly on my nerves. As we ate, Justin seemed loath to let silence descend upon us. He began discussing the estate, talking to me as a confidante about some of the problems he was having with his tenants—the sagging agricultural market and the farmers' resistance to trying new crops that might increase the profits of the estate and their own prosperity. It was not, he stressed, as though he didn't always have a sharp eye to their well-being. All the cottages and outbuildings were in excellent repair and the lease terms more than equitable. He demanded a far smaller share of the proceeds of the harvest than did most of his neighboring landowners, who were bleeding their estates to death in order to support their own frivolous pastimes.

When the last of the dishes were cleared, at his suggestion, instead of going to the drawing room, I stayed at the table to join him in a glass of port. One glass became several as our conversation continued unabated, and the hours slipped by. When much later I found myself stifling a yawn, he smiled understandingly.

"Marlena, do go on up. I have selfishly kept you talking."

"I enjoyed it." The sincerity in my voice was not feigned.

"If the weather clears tomorrow, perhaps we can take a ride. It should be a bit milder here than in London."

Without protest, I rose.

Rising too, he took my hand, held it for a moment, then bade me good night.

I lay back against my pillows, feeling mellow from the wine, listening to the rain, which had followed upon the heavy fog, spattering the windows. Reflections of the flames in the fireplace danced on the ceiling. Gradually I dozed off, drifting through a kaleidoscope of rapidly changing images. I thought it was a dream when I felt arms lift me and carry me away from the bed—a pleasant dream in which I was held against a strong body, moving as though airborne. Then I was being lowered onto a softly enveloping cloud. A warm presence slid against the length of me. In my dream it felt so good to entangle limbs and share embraces. I drifted on with it, deep in sleep.

It was not until the middle of the night that my mind penetrated the cloud and I awoke, darkness all about except for the reflected light of the dimly burning fire.

I perceived outlines of a large room and its furnishings; the canopy bed in which I lay. The soft crackle of a glowing log in the fireplace, a drip of water off the eaves, the comforting sound of slow, regular sleep-eased breaths came to my ears. My body was warm beneath the layer of soft quilts and silken sheets, with another warmth pressing against me.

Suddenly I sat up. The skin of my arms and shoulders prickled at the unexpected chill. Half-consciously I straightened my nightgown as I tried to determine if my conclusions were correct. The sleeping body beside me stirred, flung up an arm over his head on the pillow, shifted the weight of his back on the sheets, then once again settled.

I knew then I was in the master bedroom at the end of the hall—a room I'd only seen once before as I sneaked a glimpse into its interior—and I knew Justin was beside me in the bed.

Then I remembered the dream, which hadn't been a dream at all. Cautiously, so not to wake him, I slid from under the covers until my feet touched the cold floor, and moved silently across the room to the door.

Still half-asleep, I groped along the darkened hall until I found the door to my room. I didn't understand any of it. Why did he do it? Did he think by sneaking me into his bed, he could bring us back to the ground we'd left three months before? All the time when I'd thought him immersed in his grief, had his mind instead been planning a reunion?

I woke early, and had a tea tray on my lap by eight-thirty. The sun had followed the rainclouds after all, and it was now warming my room through the open draperies as I puzzled through the events of the previous night. Had it been a dream? Then I looked down at my nightgown and saw the loosened ties.

I jumped when there was a sudden burst of noise in the next room—a door being slammed harshly, heavy footsteps. Justin unceremoniously banged into the room, clutching his robe about him and scaring the wits out of Jane, who was at that moment removing my dress from the wardrobe.

He took one look at her and pointed toward the door, "Out!"

She scrambled out, then he confronted me.

"Why do I find you here? Is my bed not good enough for you?"

I tried to appear calm, though my heart was pounding. "Would it be too much even to ask that in the future you give me some warning when I might expect to find myself in it? What could you have been thinking of, abducting me in the middle of the night?"

"I was thinking of last evening. We were laughing together, conversing. I had the impression this was what you wished, only were too proud to admit it."

"I fail to see how any act or word of mine could have been construed as an invitation to come to bed with me."

"But you enjoyed it! Of that I am most sure. Why the prim role now?"

"I was asleep. I certainly do not remember anything I did."

"Well, I do . . . explicitly." He took a step forward. "Did you think me so caught up in Caroline's death I hadn't realized that now I could come to you honestly? My marriage was all that ever came between us before."

"Do you think so? I never said your marriage was

my only reason for ending our affair. In fact I told you quite clearly there was another reason."

"Yes—Radford. But now he has forsaken you as I predicted."

"You could not know what has gone on between Radford and me, and you have no right to jump to conclusions."

His voice became more imploring. "I need you. I always have . . . even when you held yourself apart from me and refused what I wanted to give. Caroline's death shattered me, yes, but it has freed me, too! We can be married now. There is nothing to stop us."

"But I'm not ready to pick up where we left off, Justin."

"Can your feelings have changed that drastically?"

"They have altered, yes, as I told you before. I will not lie."

"Could you love me again?"

"I simply do not know . . . perhaps . . ."

He was astounded. "Perhaps?"

"All right. If you want the facts, I love Radford. My inclination is to marry him at the end of the year."

"You would have him after he has deserted you?"

"He has never deserted me. He had reason for leaving. And how can you place yourself on a moral plane above Radford? You certainly did not hesitate to take me as your mistress even though you were a married man!"

"If I recall, you were not exactly an unwilling partner!"

"And last night?" I smiled innocently as I took a sip from my teacup and then placed it leisurely back on the tray.

Suddenly, with one movement of his arm, he took the tea tray and sent it crashing to the floor. He grabbed my shoulders. "Goddammit! Do not give me this, Marlena." His eyes flashed at me. "My intentions have never been to dishonor you, as well you know, but to one day make you my wife! I have perhaps acted rashly in my need, but never have I done anything to deserve your slashing tongue!"

"Please, Justin!" I reached up to his forearms to loosen the grip that was pressing my shoulders painfully. "I know you have never been dishonorable, and it was only in my anger that I suggested otherwise. But everything else I have said is the truth . . . about my feelings. We have another month of living together under the same roof. Can we not try to make it as pleasant for each other as possible?"

There was no peace in the look he gave me, only a forbidding frown. Then, almost angrily, he shrugged his shoulders. "This seems to be the pattern of our relationship."

"Yes, so it seems."

He stared at me a moment longer, sighed; then, as if making a decision, he turned and went to the windows. "The weather is breaking. We can ride later after all."

"If you like."

"I have a mind to take a look at the new tenant over by the east meadow." He sighed, flung the curtain closed, and strode from the room.

The late February landscape was bleak here, in this southern country where snow rarely fell—only a dismal rain that turned everything it touched into a shade of blackish brown or gray. There were no heavy frosts like the ones I'd been used to in New England, only light evening freezes that penetrated just the crust of the earth, the soil turning to mud by midday.

Yet to avoid Miss Barton, I was more often out of

the house than in it. Justin was away every morning
and part of each afternoon. Dressed in buckskins and
an old country top jacket, he tended to matters of
broken fences, a tenant's leaking roof, a head count
of the dairy herd. Later, after cleaning the worst of
the dirt from his hands and boots, he'd come into the
house for tea. He'd sit with his cup in his hands and
tell me about the events of his day, with Miss Barton
trying to edge in every other word. After tea he'd go
to the library to work on the accounts, while I made a
last-minute check with the housekeeper and the
cook over the dinner menu—a task that had somehow fallen to me. Strange how easily our lives had
slipped into a pattern.

Only once did we entertain, and that on an evening when old friends of his, on family business in
the neighborhood, unexpectedly called. Delighted,
Justin asked them to stay for the night. Beds were
made up and the cook set to creating one of his spe-
cialties for dinner; a happy day for him after the
dreariness of feeding only Justin and me and Miss
Barton.

Lord and Lady Mays were a sparkling and attractive couple of about Justin's age; both were uproari-
ously funny at the dinner table as they offered dry
comments and witticisms on the social scene and the
comings and goings of mutual friends.

The atmosphere in the house was so ex-
traordinarily relaxed that when Justin came to sit
next to me on the couch and took my hand absent-
mindedly, I was engrossed with what Laura Mays
was telling me of the Prince Regent's last reception,
and left my hand in his. Later I wondered what our
guests must have thought of our apparent living arrangements. If they'd heard the gossip that at one
time had been circulating London about Justin and
me, they were too polite to allude to it even ob-

liquely. Of course, there was the token Miss Barton in evidence that evening to make everything appear respectable.

It was late when we went upstairs, agreeing on a carriage ride down to the coast in the morning before they left for home.

In the partial sunshine the next morning, we strolled along the pebbled beach. With the hoods of our cloaks drawn over our heads to protect us from the mist blowing in off the sea, Laura Mays and I chatted as we walked. She was such an open, modern-thinking woman, I found we had much in common, and since Caroline's death, hers was the first real contact I'd had with a woman my own age.

Justin came up alongside me as we walked and put his hand in the crook of my arm. Lord Mays did likewise with his wife, and so we continued, four abreast, the misty wind blowing us all damp. Somewhere in the distance I heard a gull's cry and the crash of waves against rocks.

I hadn't expected when we came down to Sussex that the days would pass with anything but leaden slowness, yet in seven days it would be March and the baroness's year would be up. I'd waited so long for this day. Now that it was here, I dreaded it with deep foreboding.

Radford would be returning. Instinct told me to be in London where he could come to find me, yet given the silence on his part, I was wondering if he would ever come back to me. Because of our long talks, long rides, evenings together, the chasm between Justin and me had narrowed. The feeling wasn't of the same intensity as before, but it was warm, and I needed his companionship now perhaps more than I'd ever needed it.

Radford had said he'd be back the first of March,

but so many things could have happened. He was attractive, charming, in possession of every characteristic that would draw women to him—women of far greater beauty and brilliance than I possessed. I knew, too, he was ready to lay down some roots and could easily find someone he desired who would accept him without reservation.

Yet that tantalizing, irresistible cord still tied me to him; a tie that, despite all the new things going on about me, had the power to pull me from deep sleep and fill me with aching for him. It was that common spirit that had always vibrated between us. It had taken a journey to this century to make me realize my nature—that I was as much the adventurer as he; that stimulation and excitement were what fulfilled my soul, not the dulling security of house and home.

The end of the baroness's year was reminding me, too, that my sojourn might not go on much longer. I'd already faced the truth that I didn't want to go back to the twentieth century anymore. My life was here, and I wanted to finish what I'd started. It was here I belonged; there wasn't anything to call me back to my old life. If only I could have known what was going to happen, one way or the other.

TWENTY-THREE

JUSTIN MADE NO MENTION of returning to London to sign the papers that would at last turn over the inheritance to me, though the thought was foremost in my mind. When I tried to approach him about it, he quickly changed the subject.

The day before his guardianship was legally to cease, he asked me to ride into the village with him to see a few of the local merchants.

The vicar was in his front yard as we approached down the muddied lane. When Justin spied the vicar energetically waving his arm to us, there was nothing he could do but to stop and say a good morning.

The vicar's eyes strayed back and forth between us, speculating, as he mentioned to Justin how badly the front roof of the parsonage was leaking; how good it would be for the congregation to have two new pews at the back of the church for those left standing during the service.

"Oh?" Justin interjected. "I had not realized our population had so increased in size and devotion that the church was now full on Sunday morns."

"Of recent date, Your Lordship, I assure you; of recent date. There are the Norwins, recently taken up at the crossing, with seven children between them, and the Johnson family here in town, who have taken over the livery stable, and they number twelve. And the Esmonds at the Rising."

"Enough, dear sir, you have given me evidence. There shall be a few new pews forthcoming."

"Oh, my lord, I don't know how I can thank you sufficiently." The parson beamed, and seemed ready to go off into an encomium on his lord's excellences for providing such abundance.

"You have thanked me sufficiently already, Mr. Browen. For now I think the baroness and I would like to be off about our business."

The suffused redness in the parson's face darkened further, if that was possible. "Ah, but my lord, I did wish to speak to you of that too. We here in the village—and I trust we do not raise our anticipations too high—hope to be in the way of giving our felicitations on a certain marriage in the future."

"Really?" Justin remarked. "Could it be Farmer Goodwin's daughter and the blacksmith's son?"

"I think you take my meaning, my lord," the parson chuckled. "Of course in view of your recent bereavement, it is perhaps precipitous of us to speculate about such an event until the year's end."

"Yes, precipitous."

"Yet we were so forward as to hope that when the happy day occurs, you might grace our lowly church and village with the ceremony."

"When that happy day occurs, we might consider it."

The vicar's face brightened considerably. "Then I have not been beforehand." He was clasping his hands and nodding. "Good, good!"

I urged my horse up next to Justin's and spoke in his ear, "What kind of promises are you making? I, for one, know that I am the second party referred to, and will have no part of it."

The vicar couldn't be expected to know that the delighted laugh that burst from Justin's throat was a ruse for his benefit. He smiled accordingly. But at that point I was so ill at ease, I swatted the hindquarters of Justin's mount to get him moving. We were off down the lane before the vicar could utter another word.

"How dare you!" I fumed. "Putting ideas in his head! He will have us as well as married when he starts talking around the village. You know as well as I that I have not agreed to anything!"

"You will admit I was in an awkward position."

"All you had to do was politely set him straight—not agree with him as though the date was all but set."

Later that day, after we'd both changed, warmed ourselves, and had our separate lunches, he invited me into the library to see some plans he had for the estate. He unrolled the papers on his desk and anchored their corners. They were all drawn and detailed by his hand. None of the proposed changes were drastic; most were improvements on the existing buildings—modernization of the kitchens, the installation of several of the new bathing chambers with stationary tubs. Although the principle of flush toilets had been conceived by that year, their design and implementation were only in the most experimental stages.

Justin had drawn out, to scale, the areas where each of the improvements was projected, and I marveled at his ingenuity in accomplishing the changes without defacing the grand style of the house.

I went to my room in the late afternoon to take a bath and dress for dinner. It was a tedious meal, the sounds emanating from Miss Barton's ever flapping jaw buzzing in my ear as annoyingly as a persistent gnat. But I was amazed at Justin's sudden announcement to her when the last course had been cleared.

"My dear cousin Anabel, I am fully aware of your reason for being here, since I made the arrangements to bring you into this household, but for this evening I think it best if you retired to your room after we leave the table." His tone brooked no argument.

Flabbergasted, the woman didn't know what to say. Always in the past she'd taken it for granted that her company was welcome and required, never suspecting what an utter bore she was, nor stopping to consider what might be going on in other people's lives that might make her presence an intrusion.

She blanched, then reddened. Highly offended, she uttered an indignant "Well!," dropped her napkin upon her plate, and left the room in a huff.

Once she was out of earshot, Justin and I shared a look of mutual glee, then pushing his chair from the table, he lightly took my hand. "Shall we go to the drawing room? I am in the mood to hear you play this evening."

"Delighted, but since when are you a connoisseur?"

"Since I last heard you play. Shall we go?"

His fingers took my elbow as we crossed the front hall toward the candlelit room where the pianoforte stood. He must have thought to forewarn the staff that we were coming here, because the fire in this room was blazing and enough candles were lit to give off a mellow glow. I went immediately to the instrument, while he consulted for a moment with the butler and told him when to bring tea and brandy.

"What would you like to hear?" I asked when he had once again turned to me.

"I remember a tune you played once for Caroline and me, gentle and very beautiful. I'd never heard it before."

"The 'Pathétique.' "

Instead of taking a seat and listening, he continued to walk around the room, thoughtful, caught in a strange mood, seemingly unable to let the music tranquilize him as it was meant to.

At the end of the piece, I stopped, took my hands from the keys, and placed them in my lap. He was by the windows, and it seemed to take him a moment to realize the room was in silence. When he did, he turned and gazed at me. His expression was grave, urgent, slightly uncertain. His eyes caught mine. He moved forward.

At that moment a tremendous hammering started at the front door—the peal of the brass knocker brought down repeatedly and impatiently making a clamor heard even at this end of the hall.

Justin frowned as the pounding continued without interruption. "What the devil!" he exclaimed. "Where is that butler of mine? Wait here. I shall see to it."

Turning swiftly on his heel, he hurried from the room.

Through the thickness of the door, I could hear voices raised in the hall . . . bits of angry conversation. I was at the point of investigating myself when the door was flung open. There, framed by the massive woodwork surrounding the threshold, stood Radford. Riled, arrogant, his dark eyes flashing with hell fire. To see him again! . . . My knees barely supported me; my hands began to shake.

He towered there, saying nothing; drinking me in with his eyes. Justin stood behind him, his furious look relaying volumes as well.

Words wouldn't come to my lips. I waited in agonizing silence; then Radford smiled slowly. "I feared, my lady, when I did not find you in London, that I had come too late."

"No . . ." I took a step forward. There was a ringing in my ears that grew more intense. The weakness in my knees became water. I tried to reach out my hands, but they wouldn't move. I felt powerless as the two men came forward simultaneously.

My head felt light. The images before my eyes blurred, and suddenly I was afraid.

I heard Radford's voice. It seemed only an echo, coming from a long distance off. He extended his hands. "Thank God I am in time . . ."

But was he? The pounding in my temples was a cold omen. It was ending . . . at that very moment . . . my sojourn was drawing to a close. Already I had the sensation of being more out of his world than in it.

He saw the panic in my eyes; his own reflected it back. "No! No, Marlena, no!"

Hot tears gushed beneath my lids. It was all so futile . . . meaningless . . . such a waste. Just when it should have been beginning . . .

Both men stared. I could barely see their faces anymore. My body was swaying with an overwhelming faintness. As though in a single motion, both Radford and Justin rushed forward.

One set of arms reached out . . . connected. I could feel them around me only as a fluttering touch before darkness enveloped me.

I knew I was with them no more.

There was noise in the distance . . . brakes squealing, horns honking—city traffic. The smell of diesel fumes permeated the air. There was a brightness against my eyelids, yet I felt so cold, chilled to the core. I shivered. Something warm was wrapped tightly about me. I snuggled into it, my hands unconsciously gripping. Slowly, from the mists, my mind rose; one impulse connected with another to make a flow of thoughts.

I began to remember and felt the pain of loss. My sojourn . . . it was over. Radford . . . Justin . . . gone . . .

Slowly I opened my eyes—not wanting to view my own world again, though I knew it was there around me. It would seem horrid in comparison to all I had experienced, an empty void.

In the glaring brightness of a streetlight, a face leaned over mine, its eyes intent, familiar, warm. For a moment I thought I was dreaming. It couldn't be! Then the lips broke into a joyous smile. I felt comforting hands on my shoulders; gentle lips on my cheek.

He was looking down at me in sheer, glorious victory.

Radford!

His arms pulled me close; he lowered his head toward me. Amid the clamor of horns, engines, all the noise that was twentieth century London, we kissed.

He was with me! Everything was going to be all right. We had a new world to conquer.